The

ROAD to BABYLON

The
ROAD to BABYLON

Dana Lyons

Black Lyon Publishing, LLC

THE ROAD TO BABYLON
Copyright © 2014 by Dana McEndree

Our books may be ordered through your local
bookstore or by visiting the publisher:

BlackLyonPublishing.com

Black Lyon Publishing, LLC
PO Box 567
Baker City, OR 97814

This is a work of fiction. All of the characters, names,
events, organizations and conversations in this
novel are either the products of the author's vivid
imagination or are used in a fictitious way for the
purposes of this story.

ISBN-10:   1-934912-63-8
ISBN-13: 978-1-934912-63-8
Library of Congress Control Number: 2013954504

Published and printed in
the United States of America

Black Lyon Romantic Adventure

I would like to express my sincere gratitude and appreciation to Whitley Strieber for his fine work on Dreamland, and to William Henry for his Revelations Stargate Radio program, both at unknown country dot com. Listening to William and Whitley's intriguing interviews over the years has brought me a wealth of challenging and provocative ideas to explore in my writing. To you, gentlemen, I dedicate The Road to Babylon.

Ultimate Power
becomes
Ultimate Weakness

Long before mankind's written history, a great people lived on this earth. This civilization possessed the ability to command the forces of the planet, and more, with power and technology they attained by theft to satisfy their dark desires.

Abuse of power brought their inevitable destruction, incurring retribution so complete, all evidence of this society was erased, even as those responsible escaped.

The existence of these ancient events is a distant echo within the collective memory. These dark desires live on, as constant as the cosmos … waiting for dark hearts to rise again.

Eschatology: The study of the end days, including events that mark an end to ordinary reality and herald humanity's reunion with the Divine.

CHAPTER ONE

Boston, Massachusetts, 1985, Spring

"Tell me again, Momma, how I'm special."

Ellen Peterson hugged her son close, no longer intimidated by the magnitude of his future. She kissed the top of his head, inhaling his scent from the cloud of baby fine, static-charged hair that lifted toward her face. She would do her best to prepare him for his extraordinary life, just as any mother would for her son.

"You will grow to be like your father—your real father. Your future is carved in destiny."

His gray eyes were so calm, somehow seeming incapable of surprise. Even though they had discussed this many times, she wondered how a four-year-old could comprehend such things. She rubbed his little arms, more to dispel the rippling waves of anxiety racing along her arms than his.

"Will you help me?" he asked.

Another chill came across Ellen's heart, bringing a fresh wave of goose bumps to her flesh, for she knew she would not be there for him—the latest lab test result confirmed her diagnosis. She pushed the dark thoughts away and let bright hope fill her face. "No," she said, "but there will be others. You will not be alone."

His smooth brow puckered, telling her he was not fully convinced. "Did my father know about my ... destiny?"

She paused, remembering those few, magic days she spent with a man from another place in time—days that passed like a dream, except for the precious evidence she held in her arms. "Yes, he knew," she whispered. "That's why he came to me, to make you."

Tears blurred her vision as she thought of the miracles her son would witness and perform—events explained to her, along with the specific guidance she was told to give him. She picked up his right arm and rubbed the birthmark on the inside of his thin forearm with her thumb.

He asked again, clearly needing to hear the words and the conviction in her voice. "My father came to make me special, so I would do special things?"

"Yes, so that you would grow to be like him ... a man not of this world."

•

London, England, 2012, John Hanlon's Office

Peterson sat across from John Hanlon, Director of European Operations for the Illuminati.

"I need your talents for a job of particular importance," Hanlon said. "A special project, for which I feel you are uniquely qualified."

Is this what I've been waiting for? Peterson wondered. Hanlon's simple, unsuspecting message was worded perfectly, echoing the exact words he was told so often as a child. The realization of what this meant seeped into his mind.

At last, just as Mother said—

Was the door his mother had prepared him for throughout his childhood ready to open? While the details she gave him as a child were specific about certain points, they were also scant. If this were the beginning of his quest ...

My life will never be the same from this day forward.

A shot of adrenaline-fired excitement poured down his spine, shocking his body into reaction. His mouth went dry, even as his neck sweated and his pulse began to fly. He covered up these physiological responses by assuming a nonchalant expression, letting his eyes drift out the window. In the recesses of his memory, his ears came alive with his mother's words, spoken so long ago.

You will be chosen. When they need you beyond any others, know your quest has begun. Listen for these words—

He picked at a non-existent speck on his jacket, giving his heart time to ease down. His family's long association with the Illuminati gave him some degree of latitude with Hanlon. He probed. "What is so special about this assignment?"

The old man took his time, delivering a hard squint designed to make people squirm. But Peterson knew how to play the game, and in fact, he played it better than most.

He had to, for he was not what he seemed.

At last Hanlon answered. "One of our members is spending a great deal of money on a research program. I would like to know what that research involves."

Peterson pursed his lips. "And which member is

this?"

After a long scrutiny that fanned Peterson's excitement and trepidation, Hanlon's response came. "Solomon St. Germain."

The St. Germain name settled into Peterson's mind, bringing his mother's voice and an odd sense of comfort.

There will be others. An old friend—a saint—will help you.

Was this Solomon St. Germain the reference his mother spoke of? He wished he knew more.

Hanlon continued, his voice breaking into Peterson's memories. "You will participate in the research as a test subject at Cambridge University. Your name has been added to a list of past students—"

One of Peterson's eyebrows shot up. "Cambridge?"

Cambridge was never mentioned as a marker in his destiny. Suddenly not sure, he changed direction and interrupted Hanlon. Sitting forward, he prodded further. "When did I attend the University?"

Momentary agitation froze Hanlon's face, but he shifted smoothly and answered. "You were a student from 2006 to 2010."

Peterson sat back, letting the surprise from this Cambridge element settle in his mind. Unsure of the relevance of Cambridge to his destiny, he stowed the fact with a question mark before returning his focus to his Illuminati boss.

Hanlon's reputation showcased his career-long philosophy of "the end justified the means." However, Hanlon was the victim of a telling affliction: his eye twitched when he was agitated.

This physical manifestation of Hanlon's gave Peterson a never-ending opportunity to thumb his nose at the Illuminati. He thumbed with glee—but carefully.

Hanlon was gathering steam, preparing what would undoubtedly be a fine intimidation speech. His eyes bugged and he tapped one finger on the desk in time with his words.

"These trials are private, not publicly announced. The subjects are being pulled from exclusive, internal student lists. The selection process is rigid ... quite rigid. I had to pull considerable weight to get you in under cover."

And there it began, Hanlon's own personal stink-eye. A small tick bloomed beneath his right eye, its spasms matching the cadence of his claw-like finger tapping the desk. Peterson looked down, giving himself a moment to savor his satisfaction at provoking Hanlon. Not entirely a fool, Peterson recognized well the message in the twitching flesh: *Do not interrupt again.*

Suddenly, Hanlon sat back, his expression as obvious as a cat with a mouthful of bird. Peterson braced himself.

"The trials begin next week and are of critical interest to me," Hanlon said. His words landed without inflection, warning Peterson further. "You will treat this assignment with utmost secrecy." Next came a look known to curdle the intestines of many a hardened operative as Hanlon finished with a surprise. "I am handling this assignment personally. You will report directly to me."

Peterson accepted Hanlon's warning to behave with grace, but now he was more curious than ever. He gazed back with his best well-practiced, contrite expression.

Hanlon ignored Peterson for a few moments, settling into another long, brooding inspection. Finally, he scribbled a note and passed the paper across the desk. Having delivered a verbal spanking, he calmed down, and his eye relaxed.

A stiff silence settled around the desk. Peterson gave a mental grunt. In spite of Hanlon's appearance, the old man's skill and power had to be respected. And yet that power and the Illuminati could not stop Peterson from achieving his destiny.

As if sensing Peterson's thoughts, Hanlon added, "Your family, particularly your father, have served us well. We have hopes that as much will be said of you one day. With this assignment, you'll have the opportunity to continue your family's legacy." His eyes glittered with unsung expectation.

Or was it contempt?

Unbeknownst to Hanlon, Peterson knew the words were prophetic. He held back a burst of laughter. Even with Hanlon's vast resources, the Director could never know the secret of Peterson's true origins. Only Peterson and his mother knew his true biological father.

Being beyond Hanlon's reach inspired a fresh breath of recklessness in Peterson. He looked straight into the old man's eyes and lied. "You won't be disappointed, sir. My life's quest is to fulfill my father's legacy."

•

After Peterson left, Hanlon sat behind his massive desk, the winds of speculation whistling overtime through his cavernous mind.

"Young Peterson is a riddle in a plain brown wrapper," Hanlon groused. "I don't like it."

The boy's talent with subterfuge was all fine and good as part of his job, but Hanlon had paid for Peterson's training. He didn't like being on the receiving end of such techniques.

And that air of defiance is unsettling.

Hanlon didn't like mysteries. He had not attained his high position with the most powerful organization on the planet by letting mysteries lie unsolved. "I'd like to know what makes that boy so cocky."

His assistant, Fischer, entered the office and sat in the seat just vacated by Peterson. Responding silently to Hanlon's musings, Fischer simply nodded in agreement.

"In spite of Peterson's glib, assuring words and his family's long reputation of service, I believe we should keep a vigilant eye on him. A very vigilant eye." He scribbled a notation in Peterson's file and pushed it toward Fischer. "Don't forget—anything concerning Peterson, Solomon, and this research is for my eyes only. No one upstairs need be bothered."

Fisher reared back, his chin tucked with surprise. "Is that wise?"

"Solomon's research interests me," Hanlon replied. "I represent the Illuminati with that interest. Should the research prove to be of importance to those upstairs, there is always time to tell them when we have ... something to tell. Now, speaking of Solomon—"

From a desk drawer came another file, this one of fine leather bearing the name Solomon St. Germain. Imprinted on the leather was a gold all-seeing eye within a triangle—the symbol of the Illuminati.

"Dear Solomon, how you interest me these days," Hanlon intoned. "Why does your name come across my desk twice in one morning?" He opened the file and gazed at the official photograph of Solomon, patriarch of the extensive and wealthy St. Germain family, a man blessed with the commanding face of an Aegean king.

"Unlimited funds for speculative research," Hanlon murmured. "And not just unlimited funds, but very secretive funds. What are you trying to hide, Solomon?" He tapped the file and the busy winds inside his head blew faster. "Research into what? What have you found that is so interesting you feel the need to conceal it?"

Unaccustomed concern laced the sparse flesh of Hanlon's forehead as he looked up at Fischer. "Make sure I get Peterson's reports immediately. I want to know what interests Solomon."

With effort, Hanlon kept his face blank. He envied St. Germain's assets—a vast, international family extending to biblical times along with wealth that knew no bottom. He coughed to loosen his throat. "While we could never intimidate Solomon to extract information, there are other means of obtaining what we desire."

The St. Germain file was thick with numerous photographs of historical artifacts. Hanlon selected one photo and held it up. A slight tremor shook the sheet of paper.

"I am certain St. Germain has the answers we need." He dropped the photo. Light from the desk lamp flared across the gold in the picture, creating a searing flash that illuminated a stunning image of the Ark of the Covenant.

"Bring me St. Germain," Hanlon commanded. "It has been some time since we chatted."

•

London, One Week Later

Solomon St. Germain entered The Omni Club, public haunt of the Illuminati, precisely at five of three, as indicated on the invitation. He looked around the dark décor and suppressed a shiver. The place stank of lies and whispers, manipulation and abused power. He longed to turn around and leave, but even the vast St. Germain wealth did not give him room to snub an invitation from the Illuminati.

Let's make this quick and give Hanlon nothing.

St. Germain saw Fischer in the back, motioning, drawing Solomon to the electronic-sensitive meeting rooms.

"Good afternoon, Mr. St. Germain," Fischer said with a polite nod.

Solomon held his face in a smile and hoped his eyes didn't give away his revulsion at this bug-eyed little man. "Good afternoon, Fischer." Protocol did not require them to shake hands, so Solomon walked past Fischer and entered the meeting room. He closed the door behind him.

Hanlon stood waiting, his eyes as dark and flat as the buttons on a rag doll's face.

"John Hanlon," Solomon said, seeing the hand extended in welcome. This hand he had to shake. "An auspicious occasion must have generated this request. What do the Bilderberg—"

"Illuminati, if you will, Solomon. You're entitled to the word, seeing that you are one of us."

Solomon replied smoothly. "Wealth opens a ... potpourri of opportunities, wouldn't you agree?"

While Solomon maintained a congenial expression, he knew his unspoken reminder of who-could-buy-who would strike Hanlon in the gut perilously close to his wallet.

"Ha ha!" Hanlon barked aloud in laughter. "Well, Solomon, you haven't changed a bit, still a smooth talker carrying a big stick. Please have a seat. There is something I would share with you."

Solomon sat. Hanlon's uncustomary congeniality set his nerves on edge. He braced himself mentally while maintaining a cool façade. Hanlon retrieved a photograph and placed it on the table.

Despite Solomon's preparations, he was stunned.

The Ark?

Even though it was just a picture, Solomon's heart stuttered with this reminder of the Illuminati's long-held interest in the ancient artifact. He picked up the photograph and stalled for time, responding without saying anything Hanlon could use. "Just where did you get—?"

"This photograph surfaced last week in the Turkish antiquities black market," Hanlon answered.

From the quality of the photograph, Solomon knew Hanlon's story was a lie. Not willing to trust his hand to stay steady, he put the picture down and placed his hands in his lap. He studied the photo, allowing his brow to pucker in concentration. "What is this supposed to be?"

"Don't you know?" Hanlon challenged. He sat back, a "gotcha" smirk flickering across his thin lips.

Solomon stared at the photograph.

How do I answer? What is the old man after?

Solomon analyzed the difference between what he saw in the photo and the truth he knew from his family archives. This only served to increase his anxiety. "I'm not sure what you want from me, John."

Hanlon scowled and his right eye began to spasm. "Are you saying you don't recognize what the artifact is?"

Solomon shook his head slowly in negation and shrugged. "Anyone can see what the photo is supposed to be. And a photo," he added with emphasis, "that anyone could produce."

The razor's edge of conversational roulette made a bead of sweat skitter down the center of Solomon's back. He shifted in his seat, thankful his suit and tie obscured the pounding he felt at the base of his throat. He spied Hanlon preparing to deliver either his pitch—or his bait.

"Supposedly, this is the Ark," Hanlon offered. He threw this out with impatient and obvious emphasis, as though flabbergasted his star witness was suddenly witless. "The Ark of the Covenant," he added, speaking like Solomon had suffered a stroke.

"It is being offered to the highest bidder, which should cause you some alarm. Because your reputation with such artifacts is legend, I wanted your opinion about the authenticity of this piece. If the claim proved valid, we would have to … intercede."

Solomon remained composed, finally sensing what Hanlon was after. He touched the photo and pretended to study the artifact. "All we can go by is Biblical description and measurements. No one knows what the Ark looks like," he lied, keeping his eyes on the photo. "I am no more able to authenticate this photograph than any other man who has read the Bible." He pushed the picture across the table, praying his face passed Hanlon's fierce scrutiny.

Hanlon's face closed up. He deftly took the photo

as though they passed nothing more than a luncheon menu. But the telltale facial tick flailed his eyeball mercilessly. "I appreciate your attending the invitation. I realize this was short notice."

He stood abruptly, blinking in a poor attempt to quell the spasms of irritation in his eye.

Clearly dismissed and their business apparently concluded, Solomon rose, unsure how convincing he had been. Hanlon didn't extend a hand.

"I'm sorry I couldn't be of more help," Solomon offered, feeling as though something important had just slipped by him. He walked to the door and paused, hand on the doorknob. With escape so close, he couldn't resist a parting shot. "If you are so concerned about this artifact," he said, turning the knob. "The Illuminati has deep pockets—just buy it."

Solomon opened the door and drew a breath of relief, seeing the front door within sprinting distance. But Hanlon hadn't answered, and a prickle of foreboding danced across the back of Solomon's neck, demanding he look over his shoulder. He turned as naturally as he could.

Hanlon's normally dead black eyes were bright with a fanatical light Solomon couldn't identify, setting fire to his prickle of foreboding. When Hanlon spoke, the flat tone of his voice was even more disturbing. Just shy of sincere, he said, "Thank you, Solomon, for your time."

"Good day, John." Solomon nodded with his parting and walked on as if he hadn't seen Hanlon's face. He strode out the front door, his heart lodged in his throat.

Hanlon watched St. Germain leave. He squeezed his right eye tight and massaged his cheek.

"Yes, sir?" Fischer said.

"I want surveillance on him," Hanlon ordered. He pointed with agitation at Solomon's figure just exiting through the front door. Ignoring the shocked look on Fischer's face, Hanlon issued his command. "Watch him. Watch every move Solomon makes. He's going to find the Ark for us."

•

Solomon stood outside the Omni Club.

I will not panic, he thought as he waited for Henri and the Rolls-Royce. The limo pulled up to the curb and Solomon slipped into the rear seat.

"How did it go?" Henri asked through the open intercom before pulling out into traffic.

Solomon knew Henri's concerned blue eyes watched from the rear view mirror. The unassuming Frenchman's casual air was deceiving, for his intelligent eyes missed very little. Henri had been by Solomon's side since childhood and knew him well. Even though Henri's personal wealth would support any lifestyle, he chose to stay and work for the family. His keen expertise covering the history contained in the family archives was unparalleled.

Solomon rubbed his face. With so many thoughts and questions rushing about in his mind, he was unable to voice anything. He stared out the window, refusing to let his last vision of Hanlon taint his thinking.

I thought I was through with secrets.

"He has a photograph of the Ark," Solomon blurted.

Henri's face twisted with perplexed wonder. *"Non ...* how is such possible?" he croaked. His eyes jerked back to the traffic.

"He has a photograph of a reproduction based on standard biblical descriptions," Solomon said.

"Ah," Henri gasped with relief, "so he doesn't have a

photograph of the real Ark, *oui*?" He grabbed his throat. "Whew, you frightened me. So what does he want?"

"I can only assume he wants the Ark." Solomon shifted in the luxurious leather seat, hesitant to put his burgeoning doubt into words. Before fear could paralyze him, he asked softly, "We do know where the Ark is, don't we?"

Henri silently maneuvered the big car through the tight city streets. Anticipation crept into Solomon's muscles as he waited. He searched the mirror for Henri's expression, leaning forward as though by doing so he could hear better, could thus guarantee the right answer, could then make the vision of Hanlon's face go away.

At last Henri answered. "Not exactly."

Solomon sat back with a whoosh.

Now we can panic.

•

Same Day, Cambridge University

Peterson, wearing headphones, occupied a tiny soundproof cubicle in his third session as part of the Cambridge University research trials. If any other test subjects were participating, he was unaware. He knew nothing beyond the micro-cosmos extending from the edges of his cubicle to his mind and his deepest thoughts.

Why am I here, he wondered? Cambridge was not a specific clue given him by his mother. *Is being a test subject,* he thought, *part of my destiny?*

Although he was in uncertain territory, a little voice inside him kept urging him on, to do his best. He adjusted the full-cover ear pads and settled into his comfortable but solid, upright chair, careful not to dislodge any of the leads attached to the complex bio-monitoring equipment.

The laboratory literature described the testing as a guided meditation in the form of specific tones designed to lead the test subject to a deeper level of mind, the delta state, and beyond.

Peterson wondered, *What is beyond the mind—the ultimate consciousness? Do they expect to find God?*

In spite of certain events in his life that created what he perceived as his destiny, he was not an overtly religious man. While he knew for certain there was a higher power, to which he tossed an occasional prayer, the particular name of this power and how it should be worshiped was not something he spent time thinking about.

A series of tones began in the headphones, pleasant and faint at first, slowly becoming clear, ringing with vigor, claiming his full attention. The tone changed to a deep bass, smooth and lulling, then sinking, going deeper, switching from one ear to the other, drawing him down into the lower levels of consciousness.

He was comfortable with the hemi-sync manipulation of mind levels, as biofeedback was part of his field training. Externally, he felt his body gently rocking back and forth. Inside, he felt apart from his body, separated, yet with a curious capacity to be both "here" and "there." With a strange sense of remoteness, he observed himself as the participant.

The tones in his headphones rose in pitch, going back to the low and slow pace, drawing him deeper into the stillness of—what? Unlimited potential?

Chill bumps raced along Peterson's back, as though he teetered on the edge of something vast, something far beyond his comprehension. The tones drew him deeper and deeper. Floating as though he was little more than vapor, he felt his substance ease through a portal, oddly feeling the pressure of a grasping tug as if he had burst through some sort of barrier.

He floated free, unrestrained. Beyond his physical body, he pulsed, as pure as infinite energy.

Picking up the pace, the tones darted from ear to ear in playful concert, delivering a melody that evaporated as soon as it emerged. A second layer of tones melted into the first, producing a fine line of ecstatic harmony. Like the initial melody, the harmony disappeared as soon as it became identifiable.

Bring me the harmony, he commanded.

In response, the tones became a fine tuned synchronization, a song of absolute perfect pitch and frequency so beautiful his mind strained, seeking—

—to join.

Simple desire, as energy from his heart, took him into the melody. An all-encompassing sensation of immense compassion instantly overwhelmed him until all he knew was wave upon wave of bliss. Passion and power electrified him.

Comprehension of oneness with the super consciousness pealed through his vibrating energy fields like the song from a star's birth. As one, he merged with the song, his energy accelerating. The sudden boost of vibrations generated by these unique sound waves ricocheted through his DNA, penetrating his molecular structure.

Back in the tiny cubicle, medical equipment registered immediate changes in respiration, heart rate, and brainwaves. In another room, abrupt fluctuations in the electromagnetic field of both the heart and the brain sent a graph into chaotic swings. Sensitive measurement of the heart's electromagnetic field recorded results soaring off the scale.

Multiple cameras filmed the body rocking in the chair.

Peterson was unaware. He existed purely as a cascading field of coherent energy platforms—and in this condition he became one with the sea of conscious energy, the quantum field of infinite potential.

Conscious awareness brought forth—ignition.

In the softly rocking chair, the prefrontal cortex in Peterson's brain began producing chemicals unknown to the modern human body. Brain wave measurement from other areas considered inactive showed sudden and intense electro-magnetic activity.

Unique and completely new combinations of nucleotides washed through his body, restructuring his DNA and stirring dormant receptors to life. Atoms mysteriously disappeared and reappeared throughout his pineal gland, suddenly bearing new bonds in unknown combinations.

Every particle of energy in Peterson's body reacted, cloaking him in a burst of light.

•

Peterson walked out of the Cambridge testing facility on wobbly knees, grateful he could even stand. When he reached his car, he collapsed behind the wheel, his thoughts scattered in a wild wind. Amidst a rising field of questions and chaos, one horrifying fear rose clear in the back of his mind.

The Illuminati will want this.

He rubbed his forehead, remembering.

After the test, when the tones stopped coming from the headphones, all the sensations stopped. His awareness of infinity, his being absorbed by the song, his vision of the quantum field of infinity—

All stopped cold.

When he opened his eyes, the cubicle light was on. The room was busy with technicians who moved about the cramped space without a word as they efficiently removed the equipment leads from his body.

He watched them carefully, but none passed a guarded glance, or coughed out of place. No eyebrows were lifted surreptitiously. No questioning glances came his way.

"Don't forget to sign out," the last technician said before the door closed.

Peterson was alone in the tiny cubicle. He sat quietly, unwilling yet to try and stand. Somehow and on some level, he knew he was changed from when he first sat in this chair. Oddly, he thought of the story of the princess with a pea under her mattress.

What ... what is that? What do I feel?

He spied a pen and the sign out sheet left by the technicians. He reached for the pen, and when his seeking fingers were six inches away, the pen rolled across the desk and jumped into his hand.

•

Hanlon's Office, Two Days Later

"Test results from Cambridge," Fischer said. "You'll

want to read the notes at the end of the summary. Also, Peterson's personal test data is on top."

Hanlon took his time. As he went through the extensive report, he felt his thin eyebrows march up his forehead by degrees. "What does this mean?" he demanded.

Fischer shook his head. He asked, "To the Illuminati, or to Peterson?"

Something in Fischer's tone caught Hanlon's attention. He glanced up. Fischer's face, normally calm and placid, bore an intense expression Hanlon had never seen.

"What would it feel like to command such a power—" Fischer whispered.

Hanlon felt his hackles rise, and thought of a picture he had once seen of a cobra nestled in a stack of clean folded towels. Fischer blinked and the intense expression on his face evaporated—the placid visage returned. Hanlon filed the moment under "oddities" and brought his focus back to Peterson's report.

"He lit up?" Hanlon barked. "Did he actually produce photons? This is not possible—" He sat back in his chair, one hand instinctively covering his throat as he struggled to comprehend what would cause a human to light up like Peterson had.

He swung his chair back around and scattered the papers, looking at the other test results. "None of the others registered this anomaly? Only Peterson ... made light?"

"Correct."

"And this energy, what is its source?" He scattered the papers haphazardly, unable to find the report he wanted.

"The term is *heart wave*," Fischer answered. "It refers

to the electromagnetic field produced by the heart." He reached through the mess Hanlon made and extracted the right pages, pushing them toward Hanlon.

"All humans produce this heart wave," Fischer went on. "Some generate a stronger wave than others. But the power Peterson generated shattered the scale. The other test subjects were all within normal levels, meaning, they generated a modest and unremarkable response."

"So Peterson is the only one generating this energy to such degree," Hanlon concluded.

"And he was the only one with the light expression, however that happened," Fischer said. "The scientists cannot explain it." He leaned forward and spoke quietly. "Shouldn't we—?" He gave a short nod and looked up.

Hanlon ignored Fisher's comment. Instead, he studied the graph and re-read the notes until a small ripple of excitement stirred from the bottom of his heart. He stacked his fingers and thumbs together and fixed his gaze on his immaculate manicure. Long seconds passed before he could decide what to say.

Finally he formed the question necessary. "Do the researchers feel this ability of Peterson's will develop in the others?"

"The consensus is that while all the other test subjects' results remain within normal ranges, a small percentage of participants are beginning to exhibit an increase in power."

Hanlon nodded and returned to his manicure.

Such power, he thought, *will unseat what the Illuminati have planned.*

Global governance was built on the corporate-government marriage that would at last crush the specter of an individual with a voice and rights. The final stage was developing nicely as humanity teetered on the edge of contrived collapse, with imminent imprisonment and totalitarian control around the corner.

The question was, could the Illuminati contain and control a population able to wield such a power?

Silence moved into the room like circling vultures, spiraling to a foregone conclusion. "Make sure no one upstairs sees this," he hissed. "Schedule Peterson for a personal report. I want to see him ... since he has done the impossible."

•

Same Day, St. Germain Townhouse, London

"You have found the Ark?" Solomon asked. He sat with Henri by the fireplace in *la petite librairie*. Rare summer sunshine streamed through the windows, matching St. Germain's expectation for good news.

Henri shook his head. "I would not say so just yet."

Solomon frowned. "You said you found—"

"I said I found out what happened to the Ark," Henri clarified. "I have scoured the family archives, following the trail from continent to continent. We know the Templars brought the Ark to France from the Holy Land, along with the *Book of Love*. These items were entrusted with the Cathars. History liberally recounts the genocide levied on the Cathars at the hands of the Church, but few know the truth about why.

"Into this picture comes Count LeBlanc, a St. Germain from France who witnessed and recorded the desperate last days of the Cathars in his personal accounts. LeBlanc swore in his personal writings to possess documents that survived the destruction of the great Library of Alexandria. Within these documents was discovered the means by which the Cathars concealed the Ark in a place of ultimate safe-keeping."

Solomon was perched on the edge of the sofa, engrossed in the story. He leaned forward, expecting Henri to say where the Ark was. When no location for the Ark followed, he grunted. "Eh?"

"Here the clues come to a halt," Henri said. "LeBlanc writes in his next entry only that the Ark and Book are now safe, not to be seen again 'until anchors fly."

"Until anchors fly?" Solomon asked. The corners of his mouth drooped with doubt while his eyebrows lifted in inquiry. He waved one hand palm up, seeking. "And this reference to flying anchors is supposed to mean—"

Henri shook his head. "This is unclear, but I did find a symbol that could be called an anchor having wings. This was buried within an obscure collection of scrolls from Babylon. In this collection, there is a Scroll of Destiny, along with other documents presenting the story of this symbol. But I could find nothing else that links the Destiny Scroll and this flying anchor to the Ark."

"So you believe the Ark is safe, even though we don't know where it is?" Solomon asked.

"Yeeess," Henri said, drawing out the word with faltering conviction. "I believe we can consider the Ark safe as long as Hanlon doesn't have access to this 'flying anchor."

Solomon groaned, unsatisfied, and squelched the fear he felt hovering at his shoulder. He stared out the suddenly dark windows that had been so bright only moments ago. "Dare we hope this is enough to keep the Ark from the Illuminati?"

•

The Following Day, St. Germain Townhouse

Madelyn Fox, archaeologist and a woman of many talents, stood beside Nick Carter in the lift to Solomon St. Germain's townhouse. She argued, "The curse of King Tut is absurd."

"Besides," she protested further, "you didn't open the tomb. The tomb was opened by your great, great uncle." She waited patiently for the lift door to open, refusing to be drawn any deeper into the argument.

"I'm just trying to say—" Carter protested. He drew a breath to elaborate, but let his words fade. Instead, he stuck his hands in his Seville Row jacket and delivered an aristocratic, "Humph."

Mady snorted and blew a wisp of blond hair from her eyes. She hated to look at him, knowing a defeated expression would mar his classically handsome face. "You just wish it were true," she blurted. "Then you'd have the perfect excuse—" She clapped her lips tight, realizing she'd just slipped into the argument.

The lift door opened and Carter tossed her a sharp glance, asking for her silence. She rolled her eyes and passed him a look that said, "Don't push."

Before they could step out, Henri appeared. "*Mes amis,*" he cried, his arms open in greeting, his French élan in full force. "Come to *la petite librairie.* He is waiting for you."

They followed Henri down the long hallway filled with paintings by Monet, Renoir and other masters, before entering the smaller library. Nothing seemed to have changed since their first visit, the night they battled Maelstrom over the alien artifacts. She saw St. Germain staring out the bank of windows, so deep in thought he did not hear them enter.

"Solomon?" Mady said. He turned quickly and smiled, but not before she noticed the lines of concern across his brow.

"Forgive me for not hearing you, my friends. My thoughts run deep these days. Please come in. I have news." He motioned to seats arranged before a television. "I have a video I wish to share."

Carter and Mady sat next to each other. He took her hand before speaking, and asked, "What stirs your deep thoughts, Solomon?"

Mady shot Carter a glance. Of late he'd been so moody she wanted to ask him the very same question. In spite of their angry words in the lift, he sat close and gripped her hand like a man with vertigo.

Solomon shrugged and poorly laughed off Carter's question. "Oh, it's nothing—just the old Chinese curse of living in interesting times, that's all."

Mady held her breath at the word curse. A quick glance at Carter showed a stiff smile on his face. She turned to Solomon, asking, "Do you have a problem?" before looking at Henri. He waved his finger at her. "*Non, non,*" he mouthed.

"*Cherie,*" Solomon said with a smile that lacked full conviction. "What problems could we have? We have much to be grateful for, no?"

Mady knew he referred to the creature Maelstrom, who they bested with the help of a very brave man named Jack Greer. She shivered with a rush of memory from that long night—the excitement of opening artifacts left by an ancient Master race, the thrill of translating the alien symbols, the terror of Maelstrom dragging her by the hair. On that fate-filled night, from out of horror and death, something wonderful had been discovered.

The birth of disclosure, hope for power and freedom—

"The new paradigm?" she asked. Excitement for the future dispelled the clouds of concern that hovered over her relationship with Carter. She squeezed his hand and glanced at him, wanting to see hope come alive for him as it did for her, wanting to see the haunted, desperate look gone from his eye, wanting the chill gone from between them.

Carter evaded her gaze and looked down.

Solomon picked up a remote for the television and sat with them. "Yes, the new paradigm, exactly. We have a video and a report from the first trials on the ancients' protocols for developing the Divinity power. This is the beginning of that new world we hoped for when we discovered the truth about humanity's true destiny."

He clicked the television on.

The door chime rang.

Solomon's eyebrows jumped in question. Henri shrugged in response and got up to see to the door. "Don't wait for me," he said, and left the room.

Solomon turned on the video and paused it without sound. "The research I am funding is dispersed among several top international universities. Cambridge was the first to begin. What we have here is the culmination of the first two weeks of testing. The subjects were drawn at random from lists of prior students—"

"Someone here to see you, Solomon," Henri announced. "A Mr. Peterson, who is rather insistent."

Solomon stood up. "Henri, is there not—"

"I tried. He would not be dissuaded ... politely."

A man stepped into the room behind Henri. He looked American. Tall and casually dressed, he was handsome, with eyes the color of storm clouds. His voice was smooth. "I'm sorry to interrupt, Mr. St. Germain—"

Mady elbowed Carter in the ribs, pointing to the face on the TV screen and then at the man in the doorway. They were the same man. She saw conflict on the stranger's brow as he scanned the room. Desperation crinkled the corners of his gray eyes. "Please," he said, "I need your help."

CHAPTER TWO

Peterson studied the occupants in the room. His career field training screamed for him to "wait and evaluate" before he spoke, but a deep pull within his heart told him to give these people his trust.

"Follow your heart in times of conflict," Ellen always told him, so he shook off the troubling disparity between his superficial training and his deeper intuition. He looked at Solomon and said, "Please, I need your help."

"Well, how can I help you?" Solomon answered. He paused, seeming perplexed. His focus drifted and he cocked his head, as if suddenly hearing music in the next room. When his attention returned, he gave Peterson a startled look. "We are having a private meeting, as you can see." Solomon motioned toward his other guests.

"Solomon," Mady whispered. She tugged on his sleeve as his arm passed by her. "Solomon."

"What—"

"He's your test subject. Look at the video."

Solomon looked at the face on the TV screen and back at the visitor. "Your name again is—"

"I'm Peterson, and yes, I'm one of the subjects in the program you are funding." A vision of the animated pen responding to his desires danced through Peterson's mind, but he pushed that memory aside. He did not believe the odd incident at Cambridge was connected to his destiny. His goal today was to follow his mother's directives. "I'm here on another matter."

Solomon stared at Peterson intently for long moments, but then seemed to let his concern pass. "Come in, Mr. Peterson," he invited. "If you are not here about the research, tell us how we may be of assistance."

Moving into the room, Peterson looked over the others more closely. Since his last day in the laboratory at Cambridge, he had been seeing people's auras. He quickly learned to determine the state of each person's mind and body by the colors he detected in their energy field.

Right now, he sensed a man suffering from great fear, and saw a woman of great power. If this couple holding hands were meant to accompany him on his journey, he hoped the road would be kind to them.

"I am Madelyn Fox," the woman said.

Peterson shook her hand. Her touch was warm and dry. In her eyes, he saw blue lights openly filled with challenge. He felt compelled to give her a subtle nod of respect.

"Nick Carter," said the man surrounded by the darkness of fear.

Aside from the wealth and social stature obvious from this man's clothing and bearing, Peterson noted Carter's hesitant gestures, the haunted look in his eyes followed by a quick glance away. When they shook hands, Peterson experienced a rush of compassion. On the heels of this, a prescient flash roared through his mind, too fast to decipher. He frowned and released Carter's hand.

Solomon drew Peterson into the room. "You've met Henri. Now, we were about to view your testing video—"

Peterson answered quickly. "I was told to enter these trials because they would lead me to you."

The small crowd of faces was washed with confusion and bewilderment before turning blank. Peterson looked down and shuffled his feet. He was not accustomed to speaking honestly, much less sharing his secrets with strangers.

How much do I tell?

He removed his jacket and rolled up his right sleeve.

Everyone stepped closer, inexorably drawn, expressions shifting into curiosity. Anticipation and expectation crowded Peterson's throat, constricting his vocal chords. He let his exhalation whistle out and swallowed to loosen his voice. When he could speak, he said, "Do you know this mark?"

Mady extended her hand to him, asking, "May I?"

At his nod, she grasped his arm and studied the mark while the men looked over her shoulder.

Peterson waited.

"This is unique," she said, "but I'm sorry, I don't recognize this exact symbol as having any special meaning."

Peterson refused to consider defeat. He watched Solomon peer at the mark, but he, too, shook his head.

Carter moved in to join the examination. "This looks natural," he said.

"Yes, it's a birthmark."

Henri slipped into the front of the group and bent over Peterson's arm.

Solomon asked, "Why do you believe your birthmark is significant, and in what way?"

The question hung in the air, drawing all eyes to Peterson's face. He opened his mouth to answer—

"Ooohh!" Henri gasped. His face was startled, his eyes huge. He slammed his lips together and pressed a hand to his mouth.

Everyone pulled back and stared at him.

The obvious recognition in Henri's eyes fired a thrill through Peterson. The strength of this man's reaction continued to reinforce everything his mother had told him years ago.

Her words have never failed me.

His thoughts took off in an explosion. Along with a strong sense of rightness came the release of a lifetime of questions. The anticipation he had lived with all his life, the unrelenting need to know, the drive to discover the full truth about his quest all became unbearable. He whispered, "Tell me."

While the sound came from Peterson's mouth, the words were not in his voice. What Peterson heard was scraped from another's vocal chords, sounding massive and ancient, the words thick and barely distinguishable, as though they were a foreign language to the speaker.

Peterson clapped his mouth shut, stunned.

Solomon, Mady, and Carter halted in mid-syllable, mouths hanging open. Even Henri, who had not moved since his exclamation, looked up with alarm.

Mady was the first to shake herself from her shocked stupor. She studied Peterson with a frown, asking Henri, "How do you know this symbol?"

Henri didn't answer.

"This is—" Carter mumbled. A brief intensity rang in his voice, but the words died off. Silence finished his sentence, drawing the air in the room as taut as trapeze wire.

Solomon peered over Henri's shoulder. "Is there some … concern?" he whispered in French.

Henri grunted. "Look, it is the flying anchor—" he responded in French.

Mady blurted, "No fair speaking French—"

Carter started. "Listen, I—"

Peterson demanded again, "Tell me," this time speaking in his own voice.

They all spoke at once.

Solomon held out his hand for silence. He and Henri communicated in a silent display of dancing eyebrows until Solomon's mouth slowly sagged open. At last he asked, again in French. "Are you sure?"

At Henri's confirmation, Solomon raised his eyes to Peterson's face. "Please, tell us, what can we do for you?"

Grey eyes met brown. Peterson dared to speak, praying the other voice didn't return. He didn't know what caused the bizarre voice—and he didn't want to know. Too many doors were opening, some he hadn't anticipated. "If you know anything, you must tell me," he said with rising urgency. He had waited thirty years for this moment. He would not wait another second.

"Certainly," Solomon spoke, answering cautiously, as if evaluating the word as it rolled from his tongue. Another quick glance passed between him and Henri.

"If you will share what you know," Solomon invited. "Then Henri can answer your questions in more detail."

Peterson rubbed his eyes and pinched the bridge

of his nose. Abruptly, he lowered his hand. "I have the birthmark, and I have stories from my mother about ... my father and—my destiny.

"I've been told enough to get me here, enough to know I have something important to do, enough to believe you are supposed to help me." He finished softly and drew his shoulders back. Once again, he waited. And prayed.

Solomon gave the floor to Henri. "In this matter, you're the expert," he said.

Peterson felt his heart gain speed. He was never given a choice, had been thrust into this destiny, forced to confront events he couldn't even comprehend. His breath slowed as Henri spoke.

"Several ... very ancient scrolls," Henri said, "were found near the holy city of Babylonia—"

A scowl sprouted on Mady's face, announcing an impending complaint.

"Wait, let me finish," Henri rushed on. "These scrolls were found about fifteen hundred years ago."

At this announcement, Mady pushed back in her seat, the scowl replaced by a ready barrage of questions.

Henri continued, choosing his words with obvious care. "The scrolls are a collection containing, among other things, instructions ... to assist a special son ... of unique origins ... to fulfill certain tasks ... his destiny."

Henri's words so closely echoed Peterson's that a silence swallowed the room.

Mady coughed and squirmed in her seat, glancing from Henri to Peterson. "Can either of you fill in the gaps a little more? For instance, how do you come by these scrolls, Henri? Can you verify their authenticity?"

"As you know, the St. Germain family has been dedicated collectors of … mementos of history for centuries." He shrugged, seeming to ask humble forgiveness for events beyond his control.

"When the scrolls were discovered around 500 AD they were purchased by a branch of the St. Germain family in Persia. The original materials were quite fragile. They were immediately copied onto another medium and saved in the family archives, along with the remains of the original. I would consider the documents, their translation and transcription to be absolutely impeccable."

Peterson felt as if his heart and lungs had stopped working. The room telescoped from sight, dragging out Henri's words until each syllable stretched like something from a cartoon.

"I have studied these documents," Henri continued slowly. "And quite recently."

Another quick glance passed between him and Solomon. "So I recognize Mr. Peterson's birthmark from those scrolls," Henri finished. "Give me a few minutes and I will see what I can access from the archives." He hurried from the room.

Peterson stood and watched Henri leave. Without thinking, he followed for a few steps, making his way to the door before he realized he was meant to stay behind.

Solomon came to stand with him.

Peterson sighed, the sound heart breaking even to his ears. He glanced up at Solomon and, strangely, felt the consoling presence of an old friend. "I have waited a long time—" he struggled. He couldn't finish. He knew so much, and yet knew so little. His life had never given him any choices. Every step he made into the unknown demanded another.

Solomon placed a hand on his shoulder. "Relax, Mr. Peterson. You look a little tense."

From across the room, Carter watched Peterson and Solomon talking by the door. Henri's story about secret scrolls had loosened several tumblers in Carter's memory, but he couldn't put his finger on anything exact.

"What do you think of Mr. Peterson?" he asked Mady. "He is quite the enigma."

Mady leaned forward and folded her arms on her knees, taking her time to answer. "I'm interested in these documents Henri mentions. As for Peterson, my intuition raises no alarms. You are right. He is definitely a mystery." She looked back at Carter and lifted her eyebrows as if to say, "Speaking of mysteries."

Carter looked away, unable to bear that unspoken question he saw ready in her eyes, the question he dreaded to hear her ask. He coughed and looked past her, feigning a search for Henri.

Mady sighed at his rebuttal and returned to watching Peterson and Solomon, leaving Carter with a view of her back.

As always, he admired the steel in her posture, her attitude, her convictions. Strength and certainty were so easy for her. He was reminded of the night he carved a tracking chip from her back. She had trusted him then. Would she feel the same if she knew the truth? Would she still love him?

If only I were so brave.

She looked back at him again, the blue in her eyes troubled, as if reading his thoughts. "Carter—?"

"Henri is back," he said. He rose, cutting her off.

Henri returned with a handful of pages and proceeded to a round table near the windows. Everyone was gravitating that direction. Peterson remained standing, needing to be on two feet when he heard what these people knew about his destiny. Mady, Carter and Solomon took seats at the table. Henri set his papers down. Peterson saw the top page was his birthmark.

All eyes turned to him.

He wasn't sure he could walk. Excitement and dread shot through his limbs, making his legs feel stiff and unresponsive.

"So, what ... what do these scrolls say? About my birthmark?" he stuttered with a tongue suddenly as paralyzed as his legs. Adrenaline continued to pour through him, and he walked toward them on legs that felt like stilts. He reached the table and eased into a chair.

Henri picked up the top page. "This is the symbol as copied by hand from the original scrolls over fifteen hundred years ago."

He passed a copy of the page to everyone at the table.

"The original text was translated from cuneiform to Hebrew, then Latin, and later into modern language. The St. Germain scholars who did the translations were dedicated to accurate record keeping—there is no dispute of the accuracy.

"The collection starts with an introduction. Read this," he said to Peterson, "and see if the words mean anything to you." Henri passed copies around.

Peterson took his copy with a shaking hand. He closed his eyes, intending a prayer, but he couldn't decide what to say. He snapped his eyes open and read the words. "This mark proclaims the one who brings the song of creation. Know your seed is of another place, another time. Such sets you apart. Only you may pass."

The ancient words were smooth in Peterson's mouth. He couldn't say how, but he knew instantly the document was written for him. He glanced at the others.

Henri stared as if he expected Peterson to perform a miracle on the spot. Carter withheld something behind a shuttered expression, while Mady looked ready to spring. Solomon sat with his head tilted, as if mesmerized again by some distraction.

Peterson suddenly felt his mouth lined with felt, making him desperate for a drink. With difficulty, he repeated a line from the page, "The one who brings the song of creation."

A hum, like a small bee fired up in the center of Peterson's skull, filling his head with a vibration that spread down his spine and into his nerves. He stretched his fingers out and saw a wave of distortion ripple off the tip of his fingers then dissipate after the vibration sped through his hand. He rubbed the tingling hand against his pants and looked down, certain his chair was sinking right through the floor.

Henri leaned toward him. "Are you all right?"

"What did you ... see?" Peterson asked.

Henri absently shuffled the stack of papers. "Nothing. Exactly ..."

Peterson looked at Mady. She frowned. "I saw—" Abruptly, she clamped her mouth shut, changing her mind. She blurted, "Nothing. What do you—?"

Peterson shook his head, covering his lack of answer with a shift in his seat. After a lifetime of waiting, now things were happening very fast. He took a deep breath, and asked Henri, "What else do you have?"

The small crowd continued to stare from Henri to Peterson. Peterson sensed their need for an explanation he ultimately couldn't provide. He ignored their questioning looks. "Please, let's hear it."

Solomon cleared his throat. "Yes, Henri, show us what is next."

Henri selected another page and passed copies around. "This is all we have of the prophecy."

Peterson hesitated before he took his copy.

Prophecy?

Suddenly his sinking chair was connected to a Tilt-a-Whirl. He wondered what rabbit hole his life had fallen through. He gulped and cleared his throat, but his voice still quivered as he read. "When dark hearts command the day, beware, for the song follows." He swore the room shifted and he grabbed his chair. His Tilt-a-Whirl seat didn't come with a seat belt.

"Mr. Peterson?" Mady asked.

Compassion filled her eyes, reminding him that his journey had just begun. He ignored his waffling equilibrium and placed the prophecy page carefully with the other page. "What else do you have?" His somber voice lumbered heavily around the table.

"These are … your instructions," Henri stated. All eyes watched the new page settle around the table. No one moved.

Peterson picked up his copy, praying he survived this trip to Solomon St. Germain's house. A thin chuckle struggled for life, but evaporated.

Of course I survive. I have a destiny—and now a prophecy—with instructions.

He read.

"Seek those who know the way." He looked around

the table and the message needed no further explanation. "Shatter the jasper. Gain the eyes and ears. Use your heart to open the door. Come before the Keeper of Balance bearing the anchor and wings of your destiny."

Peterson turned the page over and looked at the back. There must be more. He didn't know what these instructions meant. Nothing Ellen had ever told him made sense out of this. He closed his eyes, wanting to shake his fist at the unseen forces that had plotted his life long before his conception. He needed someone to help him understand—

"Jasper," Carter cried, slapping the tabletop. He pointed to Peterson. "And balance." He slapped the table again. "I knew your birthmark looked familiar."

Carter looked around the table at their surprised faces. Mady was pressed against the table, her mouth open mid-syllable. Henri's eyes were big as saucers. Peterson stared, looking near ready to fly around the room like an escaped balloon.

Solomon rose and walked to a side table. He returned with a tray bearing a crystal decanter and five glasses. "Thank heaven we have missed tea," he said dryly. He poured himself a healthy portion and took a deep swallow while the glasses and decanter went around the table.

Carter took a quick sip from his glass, too excited to savor Solomon's fine brandy. The remnants in his memory were screaming for attention. "The wings and anchor are part of Hammurabi's lost text—"

Mady released a breath of disbelief. "Hammurabi's lost text is a myth, there's no such thing—"

"Oh, yes there is," he countered. "You must trust me when I say this story comes directly from Howard Carter, my great-uncle."

He coughed and let the thrill of knowing this answer sparkle in his blood. "In King Tut's tomb there was a journal from a high priest. This priest, Kheti Kadash, was a royal family favorite, a holdover from the old days of Akhenaten and Nefertiti. Kadash documented the return to power of a radical arm of the Amun-ra priesthood, along with their secret program of oppression by creating imbalance. Kadash refers to these lost Hammurabi texts in his journal as supplying the ultimate argument for the necessity of balance."

Mady sat back, crunching this new information. "And how is this connected to Mr. Peterson?"

Carter asked, "What do you know of the lost text of Hammurabi?" He enjoyed giving her a challenge, for she never let him down. He glanced at Solomon, Henri, and Peterson. Their relaxed expressions showed the brandy was a wise idea.

"The rumored lost text of Hammurabi," Mady said, her skepticism blatant, "is an alleged dissertation by the Babylonian King Hammurabi on the importance of balance, and the threat posed to humanity by those who cultivate imbalance for profit. Hence, he wrote *The Code of Hammurabi,* ensuring balance within the world." She tipped her glass at Carter.

"You said my birthmark was familiar," Peterson said.

Carter answered. "Kadash's journal was packaged with an artifact—a piece of jasper carved with your mark—the wings and anchor."

Solomon gave Carter a startled look. His voice was suddenly serious and commanding. "You have seen this jasper stone?"

"Yes," Carter answered. "And more important, I

know where the jasper is." He watched raised eyebrows race around the room. "If we hurry," he added, looking at his watch, "we might be able to see—"

Peterson shot to his feet. "May I keep these papers?" he asked Henri. "Mr. Carter, do you have transportation? If not, I have a car." He collected his papers and pushed his chair back before either Henri or Carter could answer.

Mady rose with Carter. "Where are we going to see this jasper stone?" she asked.

Carter shrugged and tossed a believe-it-or-not grin. "It's at the museum." He turned to Peterson and the two walked off in deep conversation.

Mady watched their retreating backs for a moment before turning to Solomon. "Are you coming?"

"Yes," Solomon answered quickly.

She noted his eagerness. "What do you make of Peterson?"

Before Solomon answered her, he shot a look at Henri.

"*Oui*, we will take the limo," Henri said.

Mady knew they kept something between them. She shrugged mentally. The day was ripe with secrets.

Solomon was slow to answer her question. He studied Peterson. "Something about him, *cherie*. When he first appeared, I was both startled and delighted, as if an old friend had suddenly shown up. And I thought I heard—"

"Music?" she asked.

"Yes. I mean no—not music, but … harmony?"

"Perhaps," she said slowly, nodding. "And when he read the introduction, there was a vibration. Yes, as you say, harmony."

"*Oui, harmonie,*" Henri added. He looked at the stack of papers remaining on the table. "But there is more. We must call them back." He pointed to Peterson and Carter. "*Mes ami,*" he called, "Please, come back."

Peterson and Carter returned to the table, their faces flushed with excitement like a pair of boys planning trouble. Mady spied the twitch in Carter's fingers, a sure sign of his exhilaration.

He misses tumbling his gold coin.

Carter stepped aside and pulled out his cell phone. Mady heard him ask for Sir John Winter Jones, Director of the London Museum. She kept one ear cast Carter's way.

Solomon announced, "With so many of us traveling to the same destination, we should go together. Henri will drive."

"Can we hurry?" Peterson asked.

"There is something else you should know," Henri announced. He handed pages to each of them. *The Warning* glared from the page.

Peterson said, "The Warning. Where is this from?"

Carter turned toward them with the cell phone at his ear and eyed the new sheet on the table. He held his hand out and Mady gave him the page. He mouthed, "The Warning?"

Mady noticed the high color in his cheeks and the fire in his eye—fire she had not seen in some time.

Henri waited with keys in hand. His usually open face was closed, but Mady could see the wheels turning inside. He passed a look to Solomon, who turned and made a hurry-up sign to Carter.

"We are leaving right now, Sir John," Carter said, and he put the phone away. "I have scheduled a private viewing of their out-of-place-artifacts collection, but we must get going."

"See the last page," Henri said, "from the collection. This is The Scroll of Destiny."

They picked up the page and silently read the brief lines as they walked toward the door. Mady looked up. Peterson waited for them calmly, as if he already knew the words. She saw the pulse pounding at his temple and recalled the sensation of harmonic resonance she felt earlier when he spoke.

Mady watched Carter read *The Warning* and saw him frown, not with fear but with the excitement of a challenge. He looked up, transformed into the old Carter she fell in love with, filled with daring and conviction, eager for an adventure.

They bunched at the doorway, held in a silent limbo.

Solomon's face was uncharacteristically tight and opaque as he watched Peterson.

Henri shifted from foot to foot before clearing his throat, collecting everyone's attention. "The Scroll of Destiny is a brief document, as you can see. Perhaps Mr. Peterson should do the reading."

Peterson didn't read from the page, instead he spoke the lines, and his voice came from those earlier, strange, ancient and frightening vocal chords. Mady would have jumped at the bizarre voice had she not been so disturbed by the words.

"Companions old and new will mourn your death. Beware when carrion birds fly."

CHAPTER THREE

Shortly After, John Hanlon's Office

Sitting at his desk, Hanlon stared at the surveillance photo. "When was this taken?" he asked. The photograph clearly showed Peterson entering Solomon St. Germain's building. Hanlon shook his head and tisk'ed, sucking air through his teeth.

Fischer said, "The cameras directed onto Solomon's residence are cleared every hour. The Peterson photo is from one hour back."

Hanlon placed his fingertips against his right cheek below his eye, massaging the flesh before the onslaught began. "Did Peterson get the notice to come in?"

"He has not responded," Fischer answered.

The first spasm of angst jerked below Hanlon's eye, feeling like the rap of a tiny ball peen hammer. He peered at the second photo, straining to see past the darkened windows of St. Germain's Rolls-Royce. "When did the limo leave the garage?"

"We caught their exit just before the hourly collection—figure fifteen minutes ago."

Hanlon tossed the photo on the desk. What was Peterson doing, other than creating light? Why was he at Solomon St. Germain's when he should be here?

What brings those two together? Could this have anything to do with the Ark?

The facial tick tortured Hanlon while his mind pondered his options in the wake of this irregular behavior by Peterson. He spun his chair around to gaze out the window.

London, a city built on tyranny.

When would the masses accept that others would rule them? How many had died in the last ten thousand years as those in power repeatedly assaulted the ideal of individual autonomy?

Apparently not enough had died, he feared, for humanity not only refused to heel, they continually sought paths to empowerment in spite of the oppression and ignorance levied upon them.

The problem persisted, Hanlon knew, because humanity held the power—they just hadn't figured it out—yet.

God help the Illuminati the day they do.

A shiver rolled across Hanlon's shoulders. Each morning he asked if their reckoning was upon them, feeling the tide of opportunity turning.

Now this.

His throat released a sound of deep remorse. Why did the Illuminati not remember their catastrophic failures from the past? Their ancestors, the rulers of Atlantis, and later the Amun-ra priesthood had both succumbed to the same weakness: underestimating the will of the human spirit to be free. He shook his head with despair. Humanity could only be suppressed so far before they rebelled against their masters.

"Well, such is not my job," he announced to the fog. He spun his chair around, facing Fischer, who waited for orders. The faithful assistant simply raised one eyebrow in question, as words were often not needed between them.

"My job," Hanlon elaborated, "is not to make them understand what they are up against."

"Make who understand?"

"The Illuminati."

Hanlon picked up the photo of Solomon St. Germain's Rolls-Royce. "I assume Peterson is with Solomon, which makes our job a little easier. Find them. With all the cameras in London, they cannot hide Solomon's limousine."

He placed the photo on the desk. "Find them ... now."

•

The London Museum

Everyone piled into the ancient elevator and held their breath as it creaked and rolled in its descent to the third floor basement.

Peterson listened to Carter and Sir John's chatter, their words nonsense, as if they spoke a foreign language. His mind was filled with a flood of familiar thoughts, all ranging from the past to the future, leaving little room for thoughts of the present. To him the present had always been a transition phase between the other two more important time frames. Such thoughts had sustained him for thirty years.

Now suddenly, the present was the future, and beyond finding this piece of jasper, he wasn't sure what to think.

Ellen had drilled into him, "Your strength lies in knowing you were chosen for this destiny by those who love you." He closed his eyes and conjured her face, so bright with hope that even now a smile came to him in sweet memory. She had chased away his fears as a child, and continued to do so even now.

The elevator came to a stop. Sir John led the way. Peterson stuck close to Carter, and Mady followed with Henri and Solomon in tow.

"This is highly irregular," Sir John said. He paused to eye the crowd, and seemed somewhat mollified by their well-heeled appearance. He nodded to Mady in recognition. "Miss Fox."

"We need only see the one piece I told you about," Carter said. "If you could give us, say … ten minutes?"

They stopped in front of an unmarked door. Sir John inserted the key, but before turning it, he passed his eye over them once again. He was too polite to sniff with disdain, but he took a fleeting moment to express his disturbance with a deep, pain-filled sigh.

He turned the key and they entered a small, crowded room. From a wall filled with drawers he selected one, unlocked it and withdrew a heavy cardboard box. He placed the box on an examining table, removed the lid and visually checked the contents. "Very well, Mr. Carter. Please call when you are finished. I will wait in the hall." He left and closed the door securely behind him.

Peterson didn't know what to do. Events were moving faster. Each new pivot point presented more of a challenge than the last. Sweat sprouted at his temples. He looked sharply at Carter, who stood closest to the box.

"Of course," Carter said. He flipped on the table light. Peering inside the box, he said, "Yes, this is exactly as I remember." He pulled on a pair of gloves from a dispenser and picked up the artifact. After a cursory examination, he presented the jasper for all to see, carved-side-up.

At first sight of the jasper, Peterson felt the buzz kick on in his head, as when he read the words, "The one who brings the song of creation." He thrust his right hand out in time to feel the wave of energy shoot through his fingernails before jumping *from* his fingertips. He clenched his hand. The vibration centered in his palm like a tiny tuning fork.

He could feel the jasper's desire, realized the jasper wanted him as much as he wanted it. A siren's call came from the stone, piercing the depths of his brain, stirring atoms and molecules, neurons and nucleotides.

And memories.

He shut his eyes and staggered as images darted across his mind, images too fleeting to discern, and yet he knew their substance. His right palm burned and tickled and itched in a chaotic sensory scream until he pressed his palms together.

Four startled gasps drew his eyes open.

The jasper was emitting a soft gold light.

Peterson reached for the stone.

"You must put on gloves—" Carter blurted.

As Peterson's hand approached, the stone jumped out of Carter's hand into Peterson's palm.

Carter jerked his empty hand back. Mady was at his side immediately, while Henri and Solomon's faces stretched in surprise.

Peterson closed his eyes again. Within the entire universe, all that existed was this ancient piece of stone filled with gold light. His body flowed with tremors from the singing vibration. Deep in his chest the frequency merged with the sensory barrage streaming from his hand. An energy wave expanded from his heart in an overwhelming emotional surge. This nova of feelings blew through the center of his body, making tears squirt from his eyelids. Love, compassion, joy and excitement crippled him in a burst of euphoria.

He opened his eyes and released the jasper.

"No," Mady shouted. She jumped for the falling stone.

Carter's gloved hand snatched the jasper out of its free fall. The gold light blinked out as soon as he touched it.

Peterson wavered as a final bolt of energy rocketed through his limbs. A sizzling tingle shot down his spine, curling his toes.

Suddenly, the door opened a crack, bringing Sir John's concerned voice. "Mr. Carter, are you all right in there?" Before anyone could answer, the door opened wide and Sir John stepped in.

"Yes, we are through now," Carter said. Beneath the examining light, he displayed the stone in his gloved palm before carefully placing the jasper back in the box.

Sir John rushed over and snatched up the box and lid. He peered into the box with an odious mix of suspicion and relief. When he looked up, he encountered the elite stare of Nicholas Alexander Carter.

Carter sniffed and pinned Sir John with an imperious gaze while he removed the gloves. From six-foot plus, he towered over the museum director.

"Sir John," he said. The deep, crisp, articulate voice was riveting. "Your accommodation is most appreciated." He accentuated the word "appreciated" and tossed in an arched eyebrow.

Sir John clutched the box, now apologetic. "Of course, Mr. Carter. For your family's esteemed history, and contributions, we are pleased to be of service." He gave the artifact a final inspection before returning the box to its home under lock and key.

All eyes turned to Peterson. He stood with his right hand jammed into his pants pocket. A heat burned in his palm where the stone had touched him, and startling images from buried memories ran wild in his mind. He thought of the message the stone gave him, and asked, "Where is Liddington Castle?"

Mady shrugged. Solomon looked at Henri, who shook his head no. Carter opened his mouth just as Sir John said, "That's out in the country, past Swindon. There's nothing there but crop fields."

Peterson cocked his head. A thrilling hum had settled around his heart. He had no idea what was happening to him, but the exhilaration within his body was like a magnet, pulling him along. Whatever doubts he felt earlier were gone. He had no idea what was going to happen at this place in the country. Perhaps another clue would be revealed when he got there. After all, the jasper had told him—

See you there.

•

Hanlon's Office

"They are going west, into the country," Fischer said.

Events were playing out in a fashion that left Hanlon with no choice. He should have known better than to keep a secret from his superiors.

Too late now.

He continued to wonder what Peterson was up to. While there could be some logical reason for his contact with St. Germain, Hanlon's intuition told him there was much more here than met the eye.

Peterson was a highly trained operative and knew exactly what the rules were, along with the repercussions of violating those rules. Factor in Peterson's bizarre test results and his mysterious meeting with St. Germain, and the subsequent responses were preordained.

"Place a drone on them immediately," he said. "Make sure you appropriate for surveillance with the feed coming directly to my office."

Before Hanlon finished the sentence, Fischer was up and out of his seat. He shot through the office door, pulling his headset from his pocket as he angled toward his computer. His fingers danced across the keyboard before he sat, as he appropriated and ordered the launch of the radio-controlled air surveillance.

Hanlon watched Fischer through the open door and let his mind ponder the day's peculiar events. He did not believe in coincidences. All motion had its origins within other events. Trace any event far enough, and you will find the connecting factor and the driving force for subsequent action. Experience taught him that people and events collected because of a connection.

Solomon and Peterson, he thought, *might their con-*

nection and the source of this power include the Ark?

Fischer appeared in the doorway, a satisfied expression telling the tale. "A low-orbit satellite has located St. Germain's limousine; the drone is loading and preparing for launch. Once it is in the air, the satellite will transfer the vehicle's location. Expect live video within minutes."

Hanlon folded his hands together and propped them in front of his face. Two claw-like digits tapped one another in sync.

"Excellent," he murmured. "Excellent."

•

The Rolls-Royce Limousine

For the long ride through the English countryside, Peterson sat next to Solomon, across from Mady and Carter.

Conversation was sparse.

No one dared to ask, and Peterson was too shaken up to volunteer, at least not yet. He was still reeling from the experience of holding the golden jasper in his hand. The communication between him and the stone had been a transfer of pure energy and information. The light was the energy. The images and messages he saw, heard and felt were information.

Pure energy. Pure emotion. Euphoric. Ecstatic. Bliss.

The residual effects nestled in his mind and his body, now a part of him. He couldn't undo what he experienced. He couldn't forget what he saw, what he learned, what he felt.

He was forever changed.

So, what am I now?

He rubbed his right palm against his thigh. *I'll see you there*, the jasper said. Peterson looked out the window to see a recently harvested crop field. The hum fired in his head, and the nerves in his hand screamed. "Pull over," he called out. "We are here."

The limo slowed and pulled off the road. Gravel crunched beneath the tires sounding like exploding glass. Henri pulled away from the road and into the compacted dirt left by harvesting equipment.

Why am I here? Peterson wondered.

To gain the ears, for the jasper has given you the eyes.

He looked at the field and saw a great round stone, exactly as the jasper told him. "Shatter the jasper—" he said softly.

"Are you sure this is where we are supposed to be?" Solomon asked.

Peterson nodded. Carter opened the door and climbed out with Solomon. Peterson watched as Henri joined them. Their curious wonder was obvious, for the field lay barren. Peterson knew they could not see the great stone.

Mady asked, "Why are we here, Mr. Peterson?"

He wanted to tell her, but the vibration was spreading through him, making verbal communication difficult. A new siren call was filling his head, coming from the invisible stone in the field.

The itch in his right palm peaked, so insane he thought he might rip the flesh from his hand to make it stop. Suddenly, a cool heavy mass solidified in his palm. He pulled his hand out of his pocket carefully.

See you there.

He held the jasper. The burn and the itch had ceased,

his flesh content now with the stone in hand. The jasper was warm and impossibly smooth, the carving in raised relief. Energy rang from the stone wings and anchor like the peals of a bell, pulsing through Peterson's hand all the way to his shoulder.

Mady grabbed his left arm. "How did you—?" Her voice quivered. "We all saw the jasper go back into the locked drawer."

To put into words what he experienced invited failure. "Like this," Peterson said. He raised his left hand. She hesitated, but he nodded. "It's okay, I promise."

She matched her right palm to his left. A squeal from the jasper ricocheted through Peterson's head on some impossible frequency, causing him to wince, but he flattened his flesh into hers. He closed his eyes and recalled the sensations from the museum, envisioned he and the stone in their common goal.

He felt the jasper flare with light.

Mady screeched and jerked her hand away.

Peterson felt the light wink out. He opened his eyes. Mady massaged her right hand, and her vivid blue eyes filled her face. "Holy mac—" she blurted.

Peterson nodded. "Exactly," he said.

Carter and Solomon peered in the opened limo doors, exclaiming in unison. "What happened?" Solomon cried.

"Are you all right?" Carter asked Mady.

Mady climbed out, holding her right hand over her heart. Carter helped her, concern riddling his expression in spite of the blistering smile on her face. "Mr. Peterson has something to show you," she said.

Peterson stepped out of the limo and opened his hand, revealing the jasper.

Solomon and Carter inhaled in startled surprise. Henri joined the gathering. He gasped when he saw the jasper and looked at Solomon, who shook his head no. Solomon nodded toward Peterson. They watched, waiting.

Peterson turned the jasper over and over in his hand, caressing the stone. Its gold layers fired and glowed, casting a subtle warm light. Never had he felt such completion, such satisfaction. He was amazed he cared so much for the little carved stone. "We are entangled," he said softly. "Our destiny is one."

The jasper shone even brighter.

He smiled. "I can only say I need this stone to complete what I must do. And the stone needs me to complete its destiny, hence we are connected ... entangled."

"Shatter the jasper," Carter said.

"*Oui*," Henri chimed in. "Per your instructions."

As one, they turned toward the field.

Peterson asked Mady. "Can you hear the great stone calling?"

"Noooo," Mady said. "But I feel—?"

Henri and Solomon exchanged mystified glances. Carter stepped next to Mady and peered into her face. "What do you feel?"

She struggled for the words, saying finally, "Power—unstoppable power." She grabbed Carter and pulled him to her, keeping her eyes on Peterson.

Peterson stared out at the field. Love for this quest, his life, and for those who traveled with him bloomed in his heart. The hum kicked on and the power fired through his limbs. He didn't bother to watch the wave of distortion ripple from his fingers—he felt it, knew the power was there, was aware of its existence now hovering around them.

A sense of familiarity warmed him, and he realized this was akin to the sensation from Cambridge. A frequency of perfect pitch fired within him, ringing in exact synchronous harmony, tickling his bones and teasing a broader smile to his lips.

The light from the jasper was now a brilliant pure white. "Maybe you should stand behind the vehicle," Peterson said. "I can't say exactly what is going to happen."

Henri and Solomon looked askance at the armored and bulletproof Rolls-Royce. "Would it not be better to sit inside?" Solomon asked.

Peterson was walking out into the field. He called over his shoulder, "The jasper says you should stay behind the vehicle, Solomon."

Mady bounded to the far side of the limo with Carter in tow. Her face was flushed and her eyes bright. She giggled and Carter reared back to stare. Her smile was so infectious, he joined her, grinning ear-to-ear. They crouched down and peered over the big front fender. Solomon and Henri collected at their backs.

Solomon whispered, "What happened to you in the car, *cherie*?"

"Watch," she said.

Peterson went to the center of the field. He seemed to locate what he wanted and circled, but they could see nothing on the bare ground.

"What is he doing?" Carter asked.

"Can't you feel it?" Mady said. She put a hand to her ear and rubbed.

Henri swore quietly under his breath.

They watched.

Peterson felt their eyes on him. He stood in the center of the empty field and craned his head back, staring at the sky, his left hand shading his eyes. He turned about, finally finding what he sought. Pointing with the hand that held the jasper, he laughed and shouted to the sky, "I see you."

He turned back to the great invisible stone waiting for him. The stone's siren call swamped his body, exhilarating and frightening him at once, swelling his heart with waves of power.

Shatter me, commanded the pulsing, bright jasper.

Peterson drew his hand back and, as the little carving desired, brought it down on the stone with all his might.

•

Hanlon's Office

"What is he doing?" Hanlon asked.

"The feed is live and conditions are clear, visibility unlimited," Fischer said. He stepped back and crossed his arms.

They watched Peterson walk to the center of a field and briefly circle something they could not see. They saw him look up, searching, turning with uncanny precision toward the cameras so high in the sky on the bird.

Peterson's tiny form seemed to point right at them. The camera on the drone zoomed in and Hanlon could see Peterson's face as he laughed and clearly said, "I see you."

Peterson then drew his hand back and brought it down onto thin air.

A brilliant light exploded. Hanlon squeaked and

pushed back against his chair in reflex.

The computer screen went blank.

•

In the empty field, the jasper was pulverized instantly. A beacon of light shot vertically into the sky just as a pulse of energy burst horizontally at ground level. The energy lifted Peterson off the ground and tossed him thirty feet. He landed on his back with an *oomph*.

The frequency filled his ringing ears. He struggled to sit up and a wave of nausea lifted his stomach. He gulped and held his hand to his mouth until the sensation passed. "Oh," he groaned, mustering some saliva to spit, wiping his mouth on his sleeve.

He looked at the limo, and saw no sign of his friends.

"Solomon," he cried out. He worked himself up from the ground on stiff legs and limped to the front of the limo. The vehicle seemed to have seen no evil. He sagged onto the hood, and then rebounded off it as his fingertips registered hot metal. His flesh hissed. He stuck his fingertips in his mouth.

Beyond the car, bodies lay on the ground, flattened and strewn haphazardly. "No," he cried, looking from body to body. His sense of alarm expanded until he saw Mady's belly quivering.

She giggled. Quickly, her humor expanded. "Woo hoo," she gasped. "Now that was a blast."

Next to her, Solomon lay. "Eh," he grunted with a chuckle.

"Whooa," Carter cried. He sat up, blinking.

Peterson reached to pull Mady into a sitting position. She looked up at him, and choking laughter burst loose.

Peterson started to chuckle. He looked at the others,

and his chuckles expanded. He pointed to Solomon and threw his head back and roared.

Solomon looked confused.

Henri spotted Solomon and his eyes bulged. He howled. "Oh, hoo hoo," he chortled, pointing.

Solomon realized why and began chuckling. He looked over at Carter and said, "Oh my." He threw his head back and laughed.

Mady had tears running down her face as she gazed up and down the line. "Ho ... holy mac—" she stuttered. She got a full look at Carter's face and burst anew with laughter.

Carter pointed at her and lost his composure again.

Peterson sank to the ground and gave himself up to the hysterics. All their eyebrows and eyelashes were blasted white, leaving them with clownish faces. They laughed for some minutes until finally, there was no more.

Mady wiped the tears from her eyes and looked up at Peterson. New gales filled the air as they struggled to stand, helping one another. Solomon looked at Mady and asked, "What just happened?"

While they took hilarious inventory of their faces, Peterson walked to the far edge of the field. He picked up the mess of melted fiberglass and wires, and returned to the Rolls-Royce. He touched the hood gingerly; it had cooled rapidly.

Good, he thought, *because we need to go.*

Carter called to Peterson. "What's that?"

Peterson couldn't help but smile at their animated white-haired faces. However, the party was over. He said, "I hope the limo works."

Solomon winced, but otherwise ignored the comment. "What have you there?" he asked Peterson.

They gathered all around, still wiping away tears of humor, waiting to hear what he would say.

"This," Peterson said, "is Hanlon. He was watching us."

CHAPTER FOUR

Peterson dropped the mangled remains of the remote controlled surveillance craft. He looked up at his four companions with white-haired faces and knew his association with the Illuminati was a secret he could no longer keep.

How much should I tell?

"Hanlon?" Solomon asked.

Peterson swallowed his regret about keeping secrets from this man. While he did not believe the time was right to tell them about the power from the Cambridge research, their lives depended on his telling them about Hanlon. He watched Solomon and Henri pass a glance from matching rigid faces.

And what does Solomon know that he is not revealing?

"Who is Hanlon?" Solomon asked again. A quality in the tone of his voice stilled the last of the laughter. The circle of comical faces turned serious.

"Hanlon," Peterson said, "is a very powerful man with a large organization you may know of as the Illuminati."

The words landed like cinder blocks.

Solomon's expression closed so smoothly Peterson almost missed the transition. Henri looked down, inspecting the tops of his shoes. Carter rubbed his hand over his face, fluffing his newly whitened eyebrows and exposing deep creases of concern around his eyes.

Mady threw her hands on her hips and peered into the sky. She asked Peterson, "Why is this Hanlon person and the Illuminati interested in you?"

Peterson watched Solomon closely. "I'm not sure I'm the only one Hanlon is interested in." When Solomon gave no reaction, Peterson walked to the limo and opened the driver's door. Henri was there and the two nodded, suddenly sharing awareness of a new priority. "You are skilled in offensive driving?" Peterson asked.

"*Oui*," Henri answered. "I can take this vehicle through the eye of a needle … if needed."

"You may have to."

Henri slipped into the seat and turned the key; the big Rolls-Royce fired up.

"We must go—" Peterson started.

"And talk—" Solomon finished. He stepped to the car and opened the door. He motioned for Peterson to enter.

Peterson grasped Solomon's forearm in the ancient way of old friends. At contact, the hum fired in Peterson's skull and the awakened effervescent harmonic frequency spun outward from his mind to race through his limbs.

Solomon turned an ear, listening, his focus captured again. He shook his head and smiled, hesitant at first, then warming to a full display of white teeth. "Yes, I believe we have much to discuss, my friend."

Mady and Carter entered the limo on the other side.

The four settled in, with Solomon sitting in line with Henri's rear view mirror. Close to Solomon, Peterson caught the same view of Henri's blue eyes surrounded by white eyebrows and lashes. The Frenchman's eyebrows peaked in silent question, prompting Solomon to ask, "Who knows where we go next?"

Peterson was the front man again, but he looked at Carter, for he needed Carter's help. New respect for Carter and his abilities flowed from Peterson. "When the jasper shattered, I saw a beautiful woman holding a golden sphinx statue with sapphire eyes. She wore a tall, slender headdress, Egyptian, I think—"

Carter gasped and Mady grabbed his hand. She grinned, dollish with her stark white eyebrows and lashes. She nodded to Carter and said, "Go ahead. Tell him."

Carter gave her a long speculative look, prompting her smile to grow. Watching her closely, he answered Peterson.

"I believe you are describing the sphinx of Nefertiti, one of the most beloved artifacts of Egypt. My uncle, Howard Carter, discovered the sphinx in 1903. The statue is about eighteen inches high, the eyes are sapphires, and there is a breast collar of—"

"—emeralds," Peterson murmured. He rubbed his forehead. He had been leaning forward in his seat, but as he recalled the emeralds from his vision, the hum fired up in his skull and vertigo swept through his ears. "Oh," he gasped.

He sat back and clutched his abdomen, eyes scrunched. The hum in his head spread to his ears, chasing away the vertigo, leaving behind a tingling anticipation. An image and a voice moved through his mind.

Use your heart to open the door—go beneath the

paw.

Peterson pressed his fingers to his ears. "All right," he blurted. "I understand." The tingling ceased. He opened his eyes.

Mady was quietly grinning at some inner amusement while she massaged her right palm. Carter and Solomon had reared back and stared at Peterson as if witnessing a lunatic parade.

Peterson squirmed under their scrutiny, reluctant to try and explain his outburst. "What happened?" he asked. He glanced at Solomon and coughed. At the resulting incredulous look, he stammered, "Did, did you hear something?"

Solomon's expression turned dry, with a hint of amusement at the corners of his mouth. "Well, after Carter described the sphinx, I ah, I didn't hear anything." He shrugged with elegant nonchalance. "But, you apparently heard something."

Mady snorted and turned toward the window, some secret filling her with glee. Carter turned from Peterson to inspect Mady. "What happened? The two of you have been snickering," he protested, "like little girls at a pajama party."

Mady pointed to Peterson. "Entangled. Ask him."

Peterson felt all eyes upon him, but he kept his gaze on his hands.

How do I explain this?

"When the jasper jumped into my hand at the museum, I experienced memories, not just within my mind, but through my body," he said.

"These memories seemed to come, by the feel of it, from a very distant past." He heard what he was saying and fought the urge to cringe. But he continued, for the intensity and integrity of the experience could not be denied.

"These memories stirred an awareness in me ... of an ancient bond between myself and the jasper. The round stone upon which I shattered the jasper was invisible to you, but I saw it and knew what to do. I believe the jasper had its destiny, and I had mine. Because our paths were cast together, we were—unstoppable."

Mady whispered, "Yessss. That's what I felt, unstoppable power."

Carter frowned. "And how did this awareness come to Mady?"

Peterson gave Carter the full impact of his gaze, knowing he would not like what he was about to hear. "She believed. That is all."

Carter clamped his lips together and sat back, his curiosity suddenly expired.

"Tell us more of Hanlon," Mady said.

Peterson paused to allow Solomon to jump in, but there was only silence. He said, "I was sent by Hanlon to infiltrate Solomon's research and deliver reports to the Illuminati." He left it at that, and waited.

Solomon stared out the window long enough to attract everyone's attention. After some time, he said, "I am a member of the Illuminati. But I don't belong because I agree with them. Membership is hereditary and not something you can refuse. I remain in the association only to keep my eye on them."

"It appears they do the same with you," Peterson said. "I suspect they were watching your residence."

He paused again, hoping Solomon would elaborate. When nothing came, Peterson added, "Tracking the Rolls from your home was easy. We should consider less conspicuous transportation." The hum settled along his nerves, pushing and pulling, calling him. "Where is this sphinx?" he asked Carter.

"In Egypt," Carter said. "The sphinx is in a center display case in the ground floor of the Cairo Museum."

"Egypt," Peterson said. "We will need an airplane."

Solomon looked toward the field where the jasper satisfied its destiny. "Can you say what you intend to do with this sphinx?"

Peterson smiled. The vibration was rising, singing through his bones with the near-orgasmic tingle of harmony. "I was told to go beneath the paw."

"Oh," Henri exclaimed. "This is what Mr. Cayce said—" He stopped and let the end of his sentence evaporate.

"No. A different sphinx," Carter said. "But such a feat is ultimately impossible with Nefertiti's sphinx." He dismissed the topic and looked from Peterson to Solomon, concern making his white eyebrows rigid. "What do we do about Hanlon?"

"We can't escape Hanlon," Peterson said. "All we can do is try to stay one step ahead of him."

"And how do we know if we're one step ahead?" Carter asked.

"When Hanlon catches up," Peterson said, "we'll know."

"How do you propose to go beneath the paw of this statue?" Solomon inquired.

"I have no idea," Peterson said. He realized the truth was bare of details and big on the unknown. Perhaps the statue would tell him what to do when he got there.

"We'll be better off chartering an aircraft," Solomon

said. "If we take my private plane, Hanlon will know who we are and our destination."

"We have to return to town for our passports," Mady said.

"As do we," Solomon added.

"I have mine with me, so I'll go with Solomon," Peterson said. "Carter, once you have what you need, park in the public lot at Heathrow. You can catch a shuttle over to the Civil Aviation Terminal."

"We'll see you there—" Solomon said. His words faded as he looked at his watch and frowned.

Carter was also examining his watch. Mady glanced at hers and laughed.

"I expect the energy released by the jasper—" Solomon mumbled. He shook his wrist, but the Rolex hands refused to budge.

Henri called through the intercom. "So we go back to town?"

"Yes," Solomon answered. "And quickly."

◆

Hanlon's Office

Hanlon shrieked, "What the hell happened?"

Fischer was already up and running, the ubiquitous earpiece sticking out from his head.

Hanlon swiveled his chair toward the window, his startled heart floundering in his chest. Beyond the window, the early edge of dusk was not far off, and London's sparkle of lights would spread out like a huge flattened Christmas tree. Such a clear night was becoming more common, and this troubled him—without the fog, too much was shockingly clear.

They always knew technology would be the final blow to individual power. When you accumulate everyone's data, you acquire everyone's secrets—politicians in particular were vulnerable to coercion. But even climate change, a natural event, was an opportunity for the Illuminati.

By manipulating weather data, they hid the truth—that the sun drives the earth's weather—as it does all the planets in its solar system. This enabled the lie of man-driven climate change and fanned the flames of global warming hysteria. Every facet of modern life dovetailed with the Illuminati plan to control food, energy and money.

But Peterson's Cambridge test results would thwart everything. Disbelief still skittered down Hanlon's nerves at the thought of—

Individuals creating this incredible power, thus capable of neutralizing containment and control.

He had seen the video from Cambridge. Peterson's eyes were closed. Did the man even know he produced light? And what happened in that field in Liddington? Were there any survivors? Perhaps Peterson was dead, fried like a toad on a hot rock. If so, his death would be best for everyone.

If not, I want to see him.

Fischer appeared in the doorway shaking his head. "I have made inquiries to see what transpired, but it's too early for any information. The low-orbit satellite was also knocked out. We have nothing."

Hanlon rubbed his face, wondering how he was going to hide the destruction of a satellite.

First light, he thought, *now energy.*

Energy potent enough to disable a satellite six hundred miles up. Had they somehow discovered the power of the Ark?

Regardless of what, where, or how this power happened, Peterson and Solomon's involvement must be covered up. Hanlon picked up the Cambridge report.

"Get me answers from whoever knows what happened out there," he said. "I want to know the source of that energy."

He turned to stare out the window.

I can't hide the death of a satellite, he thought, *but maybe I can keep Peterson and St. Germain out of the picture.*

•

2:30 AM
Heathrow Airport,
Civil Aviation Terminal

Solomon and Henri waited in the chartered Gulfstream 450 jet. "Speak quickly while he is in the gift shop," Solomon said.

"I have an idea of where Peterson's quest may be headed," Henri answered. "There is more to the Sphinx of Nefertiti than Carter knows. Nefertiti was a priestess, reportedly accomplished in many esoteric arts. Ancient lore says she hid vast wealth in the Egyptian Hall of Records to keep it safe from the Amun-ra priests. This sphinx statue we go to see is rumored to be the true guardian of the Egyptian Hall. And if Peterson is seeking to go beneath the paw, as Mr. Cayce said—"

Henri paused and looked out the window for Peterson. "There are three Halls of Records, each supposedly holding a cache of artifacts, gold, and ancient technology from the time of Atlantis. I suspect this Hall of Records below the sphinx is where the Ark was deposited by the Cathars and Count LeBlanc."

While Solomon had a great understanding of humanity's past, it was Henri who possessed an extraordinary expertise gained from his years of study from the vast St. Germain family archives. "You believe this Hall of Records actually exists?" Solomon asked.

"Oh, *oui*," Henri stated with assurance. "The Egyptian Hall, in particular, was thoroughly documented in the Library of Alexandria. Ptolemy wrote at length of the Hall and its contents in his texts." He gave Solomon a look that clearly suggested this quest had taken on special importance for them.

Solomon watched Henri move to the middle section and stow his gear, leaving the rear of the plane open for Peterson. Henri's revelations troubled Solomon. A disturbing thought struggled in his mind. He closed his eyes and exhaled a deep breath, allowing the thought to break free.

With Hanlon so close behind, are we leading him to the Ark?

Solomon flinched at the thought.

Just then, Henri rapped on the tabletop and nodded toward the door before he ducked out. Solomon heard him greet Peterson out on the boarding ramp. Peterson entered the cabin and Solomon called to him. "You found what you needed in the gift shop?"

Peterson walked down the aisle and claimed the seat across from Solomon. He displayed his meager bag of purchases. "I have learned to travel light," he said. He placed his bag in a compartment and looked around, admiring the jet's cabin. "You travel in nice style."

"Wealth definitely has its privilege," Solomon said. He pointed to the galley. "Make free with what you find there. I understand we have about four hours in the air." When Peterson didn't move, Solomon ventured, "Ah, do we have a plan for Cairo and Hanlon?"

Peterson glanced over his shoulder at the empty cabin. Softly, he said, "I am not concerned for myself, but if there is something between you and the Illuminati, perhaps you should speak up, before someone gets hurt."

Solomon held back a smile. "I was just going to ask you this very question," he stated. He was astonished at the similarities between himself and this man. He asked, "If I answer your question, will you do the same for me?"

Peterson sat back as if to say no, then relented. "Fair enough."

Solomon pressed his lips together, pondering the intricacies of what to tell, what to give, what to keep. "I think Hanlon wants the Ark of the Covenant," he said. "And he thinks I know where it is."

Peterson sat back with a whoosh. He pulled his chin in, amazement filling his face. "Do you?" he asked. "Know where the Ark is?"

Solomon glanced past Peterson at the still empty cabin before leaning forward to answer softly. "Almost." Solomon sat back.

Peterson squinted and gripped the armrest, his face expressing alarm and confusion.

Solomon immediately understood.

He does not realize his connection to the Ark.

Solomon tapped the table. He prompted Peterson to reciprocate. "Now, what about you and Hanlon?"

"Cambridge," Peterson said, speaking as if he had not heard Solomon. "Maybe Cambridge wasn't just about me." He had thought the Cambridge power was part of his quest.

"You must continue with your research," Peterson blurted. "The results are … essential." He stopped and turned. Footsteps came up the boarding ramp, along with Mady's voice.

Peterson leaned across the table and whispered, "Do not let Hanlon get his hands on the Cambridge protocols." He turned abruptly in his seat and watched Mady and Carter come aboard, appearing thankful for the interruption.

Solomon couldn't piece together how his research into the ancient protocols connected to Peterson and the Ark. He waved Mady and Carter in, as glad as Peterson to have this odd conversation halted.

Mady entered the cabin and saw Peterson and Solomon well established in the back, so she selected the seat closest to the front. She placed her bags in the overhead compartment and took the window seat. Carter settled his bags and eased into the spacious seat next to her. He hadn't said more than three words since Peterson's comment about her believing and receiving the awareness of entanglement.

She glanced at his face. A baffled and cheated look was settled around his eyes.

Why does he have to make things so difficult? What is he hiding?

She knew something frightened him, and this talk

of the curse of King Tut was all a front. Her heart constricted with sympathy, knowing something deeper bothered him.

He stretched out in the plush leather seat and put his head back. With eyes closed, he appeared relaxed, but she saw tension lurking at the corners of his mouth.

Mady looked away and massaged her right palm. Even though the emotional euphoria she felt in the field in Liddington subsided as they drove away, her hand continued to tingle. And just as her hand couldn't forget, neither could her heart. The incomparable elation that reverberated through her at Liddington came from a connection she could not explain. She had never felt so electrified, so ... powerful.

She thought something happened beyond initial awareness—

Awareness and ... recognition?

The thought opened avenues of tremendous excitement.

Henri came on board and nodded to her and Carter. "*Mes ami*," he said. "There is food and drink in the galley. We will land around 7:00 AM Cairo time." He retreated to a seat mid-cabin.

His reserved demeanor was an instant red flag. Mady glanced at Peterson and Solomon in the back. Neither was talking.

The jet's engines had been running for some time. A crewman walked through to check seat belts just as the pilot's clean British accent announced, "Lady and gentlemen, please prepare for take-off."

Mady pulled off her shoes and stretched her legs out. No doubt sunrise would bring a long day. She spread out a cover and closed her eyes. As she relaxed into sleep with her tingling hand kept close to her body, one thought echoed loudly.

We all go to Cairo with secrets.

Whatever the secrets, she was not afraid. She felt herself drift into sleep with a smile.

Carter knew from Mady's breathing when she fell asleep. He peeked at her from one eye. She lay curled in her seat as much as her long-legged frame would allow. Her right hand lay on her chest. Her other hand was extended, reaching toward him.

He closed his eyes, unable to look at her beauty and rock-solid confidence without seeing his own deficiencies. The constant disappointment he felt in himself gnawed incessantly. Even now, he couldn't understand how she developed convictions of steel about things she couldn't see. He simply didn't have that spark of faith to enable him to believe.

At first, when they learned about the protocols left for humanity by the ancients, he was excited. But at some point, fear had overtaken his hope for himself and humanity. His faith withered, leaving him riddled with despair and doubt.

Solomon's research into the ancient protocols!

A shiver of dread slipped down his spine. Would the ancients' protocols provide the answer they wanted? Or would the research end up being the next opportunity for man to fail? He wanted so desperately to feel as Mady did, but he couldn't bring himself to believe God would actually put such a power in the hands of man.

Especially when men like the Illuminati existed.

He rubbed his sweaty palms together and blew into his hands. With the death of Maelstrom, he thought they had seen the ultimate evil put behind them. Instead, a greater fear had taken residence in his heart.

Mady sighed and moved closer to him. Her hand inched across his torso. He lifted it and kissed the back of her fingers. When she squeezed him in response, he looked into her sleepy eyes.

"Hey," she said softly.

"Did you sleep?" he asked. He hung onto her hand, comforted by the strength in her grasp.

"A little. Nicky, I dreamed about it—"

He lifted one brow in silent inquiry, not daring to trust his voice. He knew what she was going to say, and wasn't surprised her dreams were filled with visions of power.

"The jasper stone and the energy blast—" she said.

"What happened with you and Peterson in the car?" he asked. He licked his lips, wanting the fates to deliver him an answer he could believe in.

She shrugged. "We put our hands together and I felt a current flowing into me—"

"Like an ocean?"

"No ... more like something electric, but even that's not right. There are no words for it. Pure power is all I can say. Power that made me feel ... invincible."

Carter exhaled, cheated of any satisfaction. Her words could not help him. He did not have her experience, and so could not form a judgment or an opinion. All he had was this hollow feeling of having missed out again. He wanted so desperately to know how it felt—

—*to be invincible, and thus fearless.*

She squeezed his hand, and he swore the warmth of confidence flowed from her into him. She whispered, "Would you like to try—?"

He went very still, his lungs slowing while his mind

kicked into high gear. Did he want to soar as she did, beyond the grasp of mortal fear?

Could I?

"Do you think you can pass this power?" he whispered.

"I'm not sure, but we could try."

He looked into her eyes. They were so clear he could see from the bottom of her soul all the way to the love in her heart.

Do I deserve such love, such trust and faith?

Her eyes searched him deeply, challenging him so completely he had to look past her out the window. Far to the horizon the first light of dawn broke through the clouds, looking woefully overwhelmed by the surrounding darkness. Fear that he would let her down closed around his pounding heart.

Suddenly, he didn't want to know.

"Perhaps now is not a good time," he said. He let her offer go and reached to unbuckle his seat belt. She released his hand and he felt the strength and warmth slip away. He rose reluctantly, a change of heart struggling to attract his attention, but he didn't know how to go back.

"I'll see what's in the galley," he said, and ducked into the aisle.

Watching Carter walk away, Mady released a breath she'd been holding while she prayed for him to accept her offer. She didn't know what power she could pass to him, if any. But she thought he would jump at the opportunity.

I don't understand his hesitation—

Turning to look aft, she saw Solomon and Peterson looking like two prematurely aged boys with their white-haired faces. She leaned down to pick up her make-up bag. The plastic clasp on the bag's zipper gently lifted toward her hand.

"Cripes," she muttered, and snatched up the bag, unsure if it would jump like Peterson's jasper stone did in the museum. *Maybe Carter is smart not to want this power,* she thought, *for I don't know what is happening to me.* She just knew she wasn't afraid.

She walked back to Henri, who sipped steaming hot chocolate by the looks of it. A plate of pastries sat within reach. *"Mademoiselle,"* he said, some of his boisterous élan restored.

Mady smiled and pointed at him with mock reproach. "You and I need to talk history," she said. She rummaged in her bag and dropped an eyebrow and mascara wand on the table.

"Ah, *merci,*" he chuckled. He waved his eloquent white eyebrows.

"Can you do this yourself?" she asked.

He pulled a comic expression, drawing a burst of laughter from her. *"Oui,"* he declared. "I am French."

Mady left Henri to his good cheer and went to the rear of the plane. Solomon and Peterson both seemed somewhat refreshed. "Good morning, gentlemen," she said. "Did you get any sleep?"

Peterson responded, "I rested quite well, actually."

Solomon shot a surprised glance at Peterson and pulled a face of disbelief, reminding Mady of Scooby-Doo saying, "Uhh?" Contrary to Peterson's words, Solomon's expression told her he knew different. She peered at Peterson—a new depth in his eyes brought chills to her arms.

What does he know?

She sat and glanced at her watch, saying, "Since we are landing soon—" She stopped and shook her wrist, then snorted with humor. "Not again." She glared at Peterson with comic accusation. "You!"

"Don't blame me," he protested. He smiled with more mystery than humor and shook his head in innocence. Displaying his wrist, he said, "As you can see, I gave up wearing one."

Solomon laughed. "Ha! Just in case, I wore an old wind-up." He thrust his wrist out to display the handsome antique.

Peterson pointed to Solomon's watch. Very matter-of-fact, he said, "You know, linear measurement of time really is inaccurate."

Solomon's white eyebrows shot up, but he said nothing. Mady considered any number of obvious retorts, but she, too, clamped her lips together. Enough was happening as it was. At the crack of dawn, she wasn't prepared to enter a discussion about the different dimensions of time.

She opened her make-up bag and presented them each with a mascara and eyebrow wand. "Black for you," she said to Solomon, "and brown for you," to Peterson.

They accepted the make-up with identical skeptic expressions.

"Come on," she chided. "Henri managed." They glanced mid-cabin at Henri. The stout Frenchman displayed the results of his effective application to eyebrow and eyelash. He batted his enhanced eyes at them.

Solomon looked down.

Peterson crushed a burgeoning guffaw.

"One coat," Mady said, laughing, "is enough."

Solomon rose and picked up his mascara. "If you

will excuse me, I believe I'd like to do this in private." He left them, exiting with as much boardroom grace as the mascara wand in his hand would allow.

Mady watched Solomon leave, glad for the moment alone with Peterson. Eager, she began, "I slept and dreamed about the power in the field—"

Peterson took her hand. An expression of great relief came to his face, causing her to lean closer to hear him.

"Words cannot say how glad I am you are here with us. You have your own power, Madelyn, one I didn't give you. You are blessed by the goddess," he said.

Mady felt chills shoot down her back. His words held the sound of prophesy. "Carter told me the same thing the night we met," she said. She looked over her shoulder to watch Carter moving about in the galley.

"All he needs is a miracle to believe in," Peterson said.

Mady felt the same way. She sucked in a breath and rushed on. "I thought he might witness something in the course of your quest—"

"No, not witness," Peterson responded. "The miracle will come from him."

When he said *will*, Mady's heart slowed to a painful pause.

"Tell me. What do you know?" she asked. Her breath stalled, waiting with her heart. All sights and sounds of the jet disappeared into the background while she waited for his answer.

"I know you have nothing to fear," he said. "Carter's heart holds more faith and belief than you know, more than even he knows."

Mady's blood jumped to life and she exhaled with a rush. "I have nothing to fear—" she repeated. A flood of questions rushed through her mind, but in her heart, echoes of the field's frequency still reverberated. Feeling herself on a threshold, she released her need to analyze and let her faith in the outcome be her final thought. Wherever Peterson was taking them, she wasn't afraid.

"What about you?" she asked, suddenly concerned for Peterson. Somehow, in spite of Peterson's assurances about Carter's mysterious miracle, she felt her lover's answers were tied to Peterson and his quest.

"A woman in love is a powerful entity," Peterson said.

His out-of-context words startled her. She frowned, but before she could speak, Carter arrived at the mid-cabin table with a small feast on a platter. Her stomach rumbled and all thoughts of miracles and mysteries fled in the face of hunger.

She and Peterson rose together.

"I smell bacon," Peterson said.

"Look," Mady exclaimed. "Fruit, and lox and bagels."

Solomon joined them, appearing from the bathroom with his mascara expertly applied. A furtive glance was passed around the table and the resulting smirks were tightly reined in.

They sat to do justice to Carter's preparations.

The food slowly disappeared and camaraderie settled over them, Mady thought, as though they had known each other a lifetime. Each individual's veil of secrecy seemed to have slipped away for the moment.

Their plates sat empty and the second pot of coffee was gone. Mady cleared her throat, drawing all eyes. "So, what are we doing today?"

She looked to Peterson, giving him the floor, and caught a flash of emotion across his eyes. She recalled his earlier words about Carter: The miracle will come from him. His speaking in the future tense, along with his earlier reference to time made her wonder ... what was in his dreams?

Peterson looked around the table and slowly answered, "I'm not sure about ... everything."

Mady's chills turned into excitement. "What *are* you sure about?" she asked. She smiled and tried not to sound like an interrogator, even though her heart flip-flopped with a perverse mix of thrill and dread for the unknown.

"How far is this museum?" Peterson asked.

Henri answered. "It is near the river, about ten miles, maybe a little more, from the airport."

Peterson's eyes turned dark. The way he phrased his request sent more chills down Mady's arms. "I think it would be better if we rented a car," he said. "Can anyone drive here?" He glanced at Henri.

"*Oui*, I can drive here. I spent many years in Egypt. I know Cairo well," Henri said.

With no sign of surprise as though he knew Henri would answer this way, Peterson continued. "Good, then we will drive to the museum. I'll just go beneath the paw—"

Carter mumbled something inarticulate into his coffee cup.

Mady wrapped her right hand around his free hand, and his mumbling ceased. "You were saying?" she said to Peterson.

Peterson waited with calm patience. "We will see what happens at the museum. I believe the statue will show me what to do," he said. "My concern is not about what happens with the sphinx."

"Then what is your concern?" Solomon asked.

"We should be prepared for Hanlon to show himself in some fashion—"

"I thought we were one step ahead of him," Carter said. He set his cup down with a clunk on the table. The lines on his face were deep.

"We were," Peterson said. "But by now, I suspect our lead has evaporated."

At that moment the pilot announced, "Lady and gentlemen, prepare to land. We have reached Cairo, Egypt."

CHAPTER FIVE

Hanlon was exhausted. He was too old for such all-night shenanigans. His eyes felt like little sacks of grit, and what he ate for dinner was an unpleasant memory. Despite his discomfort, finding Peterson was his priority. He took the pages from Fischer with anxious fingers.

"A private charter left Heathrow for Cairo, filing a flight plan with five souls on board," Fischer said. "The purchase was executed through a buried account out of the Caymans. By the time we discover the account holder, these 'five souls' will disembark and be long gone."

Hanlon's face crinkled with a look of frustration. "You have no other trace of Solomon, either at home or with any other form of transportation?"

Fischer nodded. "That is correct."

"And the couple from the museum report, this—"

"Nicholas Carter and Madelyn Fox are not at Mr. Carter's residence," Fischer added.

Hanlon said, "Solomon, Peterson and the couple

make four. The video from the drone showed five people—that would be Solomon's man Henri as the fifth. We have no bodies from the field, so I assume all five survived. Now we have five souls in a hurry to Cairo."

He became silent for long seconds, his brows pulled together. Finally, he tapped the charter manifest. "I'm willing to bet this is Solomon," he announced. "Who do we have in Cairo?"

Fischer pulled out a dossier. "We have Butler, Richard Butler."

Hanlon took the file. "Has Peterson worked with Butler?"

"Yes, they know each other well," Fischer replied. He pulled out another sheet and passed it to Hanlon. "They trained together in Africa, and worked on several missions together."

Hanlon scoured Butler's psychological assessment.

Mission-oriented, creative under fire, experienced killer.

"I want to talk to him," he said.

Fischer disappeared into his outer office to arrange the call on a secure line.

Hanlon surveyed the documents on his desk lined up in chronological order—the Cambridge test results and video, Peterson's unanswered summons, and the photo of Peterson entering St. Germain's residence.

Next to the drone video of Peterson's escapades in the field was a report from a private Illuminati installation. The energy that knocked out the drone and the satellite bore a unique energy signature—the same signature as this heart wave Peterson produced at Cambridge.

With a great deal of manipulation Hanlon had kept

the details of the satellite destruction obscured—for now. The question was, did this tremendous surge of energy in the field come from Peterson?

If so, Peterson was a walking weapon of mass destruction.

A shiver shot up Hanlon's spine.

What the Illuminati could do with this power—

This thought was short-lived.

What this power could do to the Illuminati.

It was a lot to keep secret.

Fischer reappeared in the doorway, signaling the call was live. Hanlon picked up his phone. "Butler, whatever you're working on is canceled. I have something more important for you—something very hush-hush."

•

Peterson felt the plane touch down. Through the windows, the Cairo sunrise flitted by, promising a beautiful, hot day.

A day to remember.

He glanced up the aisle at Mady talking to Carter, and smiled with relief for her presence, her part in his quest. The complexity of forces in operation, as revealed to him last night, was beyond his comprehension. He couldn't take the time to ponder ... or fear what he knew was coming; all he could do was pursue his destiny.

"After we clear customs," Solomon said, "we'll go straight to the museum. We should be the first through the doors." His expression encouraged Peterson to fill in the blanks.

"I cannot thank you enough for your assistance," Peterson said. He grimaced, knowing his words sounded like a farewell.

Solomon gave him a sharp look. "Is there something

you should tell me? Last night—"

"No," Peterson said abruptly. "What I learned last night was for my ears only." Solomon let the inquiry go and Peterson rushed on. "I know I've asked for a great deal of trust—"

Solomon grasped Peterson's arm. "You need not explain yourself. Henri and I are privileged to assist you."

Peterson saw the sincerity in Solomon's eyes, yet he knew his friend also kept a secret. He could not take the time to wonder what Solomon withheld, for the siren song of the sphinx was rising, reaching for him with the exquisite harmony of her call.

"I'm ready," he whispered.

•

The drive to the museum was a straight shot from the airport to the Nile River, reminding Peterson of their ride out to Liddington Castle. Earlier, when they went through customs and the car rental, he had been so full of anticipation he could barely talk. Now that the museum and the sphinx were within reach, a calm certainty settled over him. The siren call of the sphinx was alive in his bones. He would know what to do when he got there.

Henri parked their Mercedes sedan. A brief walk to the front of the museum, and it turned out they were, indeed, the first to enter. Peterson climbed the first few steps and paused.

His companions collected around him. Peterson felt his heart accelerate, every molecule in his body electrified, on the edge of something enormous ... a metamorphosis?

A shiver ran down his back; he needed someone to pinch him. His sense of power was expanding, making his connection to the perfect harmonic frequency so intense he felt like he walked in a reality beyond what he perceived with his senses.

As further proof of his continuing metamorphosis, he had advanced in the last thirty-six hours from seeing auras to experiencing invincibility in the field at Liddington. Last night he had witnessed the future and conversed with an ageless being from another dimension.

He stared at the museum door, several steps above him.

Use your heart to open the door. Go beneath the paw.

He glanced at his companions. Solomon and Henri stood ready at his back, and Mady joined them, her face alive with expectation and hope. He felt the energy surge when she approached.

Carter stepped to Peterson's side. "The statue is in the center of the first floor, displayed beneath a four-sided pyramid of glass atop a granite pedestal." He licked his lips and glanced up at the building, clearly anxious. "There are 120,000 priceless artifacts in this building. You don't think there will be a repeat—"

"No, the artifacts here are safe," Peterson said. "But we should hurry. I think it best no other people were around." He climbed the steps to the heavy glass doors. Uncertain if this was the door he was supposed to open with his heart, he paused. There was no way to enter but with his hands.

He pushed the door open.

Suddenly he felt foolish, and glanced over his shoulder. His companions waited at the foot of the steps, no doubt their hesitation due to their experience in the field at Liddington.

Peterson's hand on the massive brass door handle itched with maddening intensity. The siren call danced down his nerves in a rush of flowing chemicals, producing the orgasmic harmony, drawing him forward. A sense of invincibility blossomed from his heart, and he looked down at his feet, expecting to see he was elevated on a skin of energy.

"Ha!" He laughed, surprised to see he walked as any mortal. He motioned his friends to follow him.

As soon as he stepped through the door, the siren call sweetened, drawing him along as sure as a tether. From the corner of his vision he saw Solomon purchase tickets. He walked on toward the huge exhibition room where the sphinx waited.

Carter had told him there were storage rooms and high-tech security directly below the statue. He recalled his vision of what he must do from last night, and could not understand how such would happen.

Solomon stepped beside him and extended his hand as if offering the world, saying, "Here you are, my friend."

Peterson led the crowd for he needed no guide; the tether was inescapable. As soon as he rounded the corner, his eyes were drawn immediately to the statue. He heard Nefertiti's voice in soft, haunting bursts, as clearly as if she spoke right next to him. He walked down the marble steps and straight to the sphinx display, torn between the expectation of what he knew would happen, and the "not possible" reality existing before him.

The statue was stunning. The sphinx was a lion's body with the face of a beautiful woman. She sat upright with one paw raised, as in greeting, or as if to strike. The sapphire eyes sparkled with an animate light that gave rise to goose flesh down Peterson's arms. He swore the jeweled eyes followed him.

He didn't know what to do. There was no door to open with his heart, no clue to follow.

His mother's voice, always so clear in his memory, reminded him, "Always go by your heart." He closed his eyes and crossed his hands across his chest. He let his head drop and forced all external sounds and thoughts from his mind, seeking the perfect harmonic frequency within.

The hum fired in his head and shot down his limbs. The sensation of power rushed in to electrify his spine. He moaned with the sweet thrill. He continued to focus on how he loved and trusted those who brought him to this point, and let his amazement at the events of the last twenty-four hours coalesce into white-hot faith. The awareness of power and its thread of entanglement soared into his heart. He felt as though something in his chest expanded exponentially.

The strange voices he had heard from the past whistled through his memory, bringing the vision from last night vivid into his mind: a passage cut out of stone in broad steps, blazing torches spewing smoke and throwing wiggling shadows across the walls.

"Eli," came a whisper from below.

Peterson's spine went rigid and his eyes shot open. The passage he saw in his mind was now in the floor before the statue. The stairs curved down to his right; the smell of smoke was acrid in his nostrils. He shot a stiff glance at his companions, who stood twenty feet back near a pair of huge statues. None seemed alarmed, so he didn't think they could see what he was experiencing.

A sound from the hall near the front door roared

into Peterson's awareness—footsteps, someone in a hurry, a man of about one hundred, eighty-five pounds by the soft echo of his stride. Peterson detected the man's smell long before the tip of his shadow cleared the corner.

Someone from Hanlon.

Peterson tensed when the footsteps stopped. The stairs before him were a yawning abyss beckoning with the force of the universe, yet his friends were exposed, oblivious to the threat approaching from behind. He lifted one foot to go back and help them, when the figure from the hallway stepped out.

Butler!

Peterson froze.

Butler shrank back against the wall, but they had made eye contact. Peterson knew Butler, knew he wouldn't make a threatening move with the armed guards posted by the front door.

Peterson turned and walked down the stone steps.

As soon as his foot touched the first step, a tingling buzz rose in his hearing. Smoke from a near-by torch wafted into his face and he coughed. His leather shoes grated harshly against the grit on each step taking him down, deep below the paw of the sphinx. The sweet, harmonic frequency tickled his bones and thrummed in his fingers. His right forearm burned so he rolled his sleeve up to look at his birthmark.

"Eli," came the whisper again.

He stopped, arm and birthmark forgotten. Part of him wanted to run back up the stairs, but a larger part wanted to know—

Who calls me?

Excitement was pure hot electricity firing up his

spine, making his belly tighten. He stepped faster, moving down, going around again and again. Deeper and deeper, the stairs seemed to have no bottom.

Suddenly, the torchlight faded, eclipsed by a bright golden light that dispersed all shadow. The final step met the sandy floor of a stone chamber. The air instantly felt heavy, ancient, and mysterious.

The sphinx waited for him.

Peterson came to a stop when he saw the creature. She was a living, breathing, life-size golden duplicate of the statue above. Sapphire eyes watched him, sending a chill down his arms. He remembered the words from his instructions:

Come before the Keeper of Balance bearing the wings and anchor.

He stepped before her.

"You are the one called Eli," she said. The tip of her tail slowly moved back and forth, creating a pattern in the sand on the floor.

Peterson licked his lips. Nothing in his field training covered ancient mythological creatures with paranormal abilities. Stuttering and unable to stop, he asked the obvious. "You, you know my name?"

Her eyes drilled deep, cutting as sharp as real sapphires. He felt tiny and insignificant before one so strange. He threw his shoulders back, resisting the urge to cringe.

"Show me the mark," she commanded. She lifted her left paw.

Peterson extended his arm to show his anchor and wings. The birthmark burned and itched and tingled, screaming at him with a sensory riot.

The sphinx stared at his mark with a fixed gaze, her eyes at last lighting with recognition. She took his arm in one golden paw, and he tensed until she snorted in a burst of confirmation.

"You are truly the one." She smiled with gold lips suddenly warm with welcome. She released him.

He gasped in relief to have his arm returned intact. "And you are Nefertiti?" he asked.

"That is one name out of many," she answered. She arched her neck, preening. Tissue-thin gold eyelids dropped coyly over her jeweled eyes. Her tail slapped the sand with insistence, stirring a small cloud into the air. Her paws clenched, exposing razor sharp claws.

"Your journey began far from here, Eli," she said.

Peterson looked about the room, suddenly feeling lost. He didn't know what was expected of him.

She nodded, at once sympathetic. "You have found me, the Keeper of Balance. You bear the mark declaring you come from another time, a man not of this world. As such, you may enter. Let none other precede or follow."

Peterson absorbed her words and shook his head. His instructions ended here, leaving him with a great rush of questions. He wanted to scream, "Enter what, where? Why am I here? What am I supposed to do next?"

Desperate, he looked up and cocked his head. She was purring. He could see the golden hairs on her chest thrum, filling the air with a frequency. He extended his hand to her, barely touching the golden hairs. The frequency invaded his flesh. His heart fired up in response, accelerating, entraining to her higher vibration. An instant sense of calm spread through him.

"Fear not," Nefertiti said. "The Goddess accompanies you. She will guide your return."

Peterson was not surprised by what Nefertiti knew. Still, his heart raced with a conflicting mix of anticipation and dread.

Nefertiti nodded, her faceted eyes understanding. "You must pass, Eli, to discover where the Hall is hidden."

At last Peterson understand. From here on, the answers would not be found in this dimension.

She smiled, and a large emerald in the center of her collar lit up, sending a new vibration into the air. "Yes," she said. "It is yours to take. Consider it ... a key."

He held out his hand and the emerald twisted free of its home imbedded in the gold breast collar. When the emerald hit his flesh, he felt the thrum of Nefertiti's purr tickling his palm. He slipped the jewel into his pants pocket and walked across the sand to the stairs. The emerald's siren song joined with his body, adding a note to the symphony, as solid in his chest as if he, too, purred.

"Bless you, Eli," she whispered. "You will remember."

Her last words caused a raft of chills to skitter across Peterson's buttocks. He glanced up. She had returned to her pose, duplicating the statue up above. Her ancient voice echoed through his bones.

You will remember ...

The animation seeped from her eyes. He knew there were no more answers from Nefertiti. He bowed deeply, his hands at his heart.

He walked up the stairs. Behind him, the golden light went out. As he passed the stuttering torches, they extinguished. A wild urge to turn around and look screamed at him, but his heart said, "Do not." It took every fiber of will he had not to shoot up out of the stairwell like a cannon ball.

The room appeared just as it did the instant he took to the stairs. Solomon, Henri, Mady and Carter hung back by the giant statues as if he had been gone no more than a blink. Only Butler had moved. He stood on the top entry hall step with a clear line of sight to the sphinx.

Peterson glanced back at the smooth marble floor—where seconds ago gritty stone steps had been. The emerald sang from his pocket, drawing his eyes to the emerald collar on the statue under the glass display. The statue was missing a jewel.

Butler stood between them and the exit. With four civilians in tow, a stolen emerald in his pocket, and armed guards posted at the entrance, running was not an option. Peterson walked straight toward Butler. Solomon, Henri, Mady and Carter, with perplexed expressions, fell into step behind him.

Peterson didn't stop until he was in Butler's face. "Just walk away, Richard," he said. Butler didn't answer. Peterson could see the wheels turning in a thousand different directions.

"I can't, and you know it," Butler said. He leaned closer. "What's going on here?" he spit under his breath. "I saw you disappear into the floor."

"What's going on here," Peterson answered tersely, "has nothing to do with the Illuminati, and does not concern Hanlon."

Butler abandoned the discussion and looked over Peterson's shoulder at the small group watching. He sucked his teeth in disapproval. "I see you have baggage."

Peterson noted the threat and let confidence curl his lip. "I'd worry about my own health if I were you," he said.

Butler moved to whisper in Peterson's ear. "No. You need to worry about my health until I make my report to Hanlon."

Peterson pulled back to see the cold certainty in Butler's eyes. Obviously, Butler felt he was protected by the Illuminati. "You wouldn't do anything in here," Peterson challenged. He casually looked over Butler's shoulder toward the front door and the armed guards.

"I have a get-out-of-jail-free card," Butler said. "Do you?" His eyes echoed the cold of his smile.

Peterson knew he had a great deal more than that, but he didn't trust Butler not to shoot someone, like Mady. He had to keep the Goddess safe.

"What happened?" Butler nodded to the sphinx display. "Where did you go? What did you ... see?"

Mady moved toward them. Butler gestured at her, showing he held a weapon in his pocket and he aimed it at Carter. "You're not needed, Miss," he said. He held her in a steady gaze until she backed up to stand with the others.

"What do you want?" Peterson growled.

"All we have to do is talk—outside. Your vehicle will do."

"After you," Peterson said. He nodded, giving Butler the lead. Butler stepped back, ignoring the offer.

Peterson shrugged and motioned to his friends. "We're leaving." He stood to the side with Butler while they slowly filed past. Henri took the lead, followed by

Solomon and Carter. Mady inserted herself between the others and Peterson and Butler. She flicked a questioning eyebrow at Peterson when she passed, but he did not respond.

Henri led the way calmly out the front door. The sunlight was glaring after the cool interior, and everyone reached for sunglasses. Henri coughed in the stiff silence and pulled out his car keys.

"Take the main highway west, toward the desert," Butler said.

As soon as he heard desert, Peterson knew his time of reckoning with the Illuminati was at hand. He could imagine Hanlon pouring over the Cambridge test results, tapping the desk with agitation. After the drone was destroyed, Hanlon's eye twitch must have gone rabid. A grim smile faltered. He nodded to Henri to do as Butler said.

They rode in silence. Henri, Peterson and Butler filled the front, with Solomon, Mady and Carter in the back. Butler sat with his back turned to the door and produced the weapon, a .45. While his aim shifted from Peterson to those in the back seat, his eye never left Peterson.

The highway was a straight shot past lush watered fields that abruptly gave way to sand. A small but exclusive suburb flashed by, the blue of an occasional backyard swimming pool sparkling in the sun. Henri kept driving, and the bleak desert landscape drew them on like quicksand.

"Pull off the road," Butler said, indicating a track veering off into the dunes. He gave no other directions, so Henri drove on. The track curved around a dune and within one hundred yards, the last signs of civilization were suddenly obscured from sight.

"Stop," Butler commanded.

Henri brought the car to a halt. All faces turned toward the man with the gun.

"Roll down the windows," he said. With this done, he snatched the keys from the ignition and got out of the car. "Everyone stay right here—except you," he said to Peterson.

Mady touched Peterson's arm. "Are you sure?"

Peterson placed his hand on her fingers. At contact, the energy fired through his bones, sending the harmonic bliss sizzling down his spine. He curled his toes as the power burst down his legs. "I'll be fine," he said. "But you need to stay here, safe, with the others." He winked and added, "This won't take long. I'll be ... right back."

He stepped out and followed Butler. They walked about twenty yards. Peterson figured this to be a helicopter extraction, and knew he had no more than fifteen minutes.

Glancing around the horizon, he said, "I'm not going with you, Richard. You'll have to shoot me." He said this with a startling matter-of-fact calm.

Butler squinted at Peterson with a mix of horror and speculation. "What's going on with you, man?" he hissed, shooting a glance over the eastern sand dunes, "Hanlon has you at the center of some secret hush-hush operation." He pressed closer, glaring into Peterson's face, the gun relaxed in his hand. "Where did you go back there? Tell me what happened. It's me, man, your old buddy, Richard."

Butler was too absorbed, too close ... and in perfect position. Peterson grabbed the gun with his left hand

and pulled the weapon into his right side. He brought his right arm up for an elbow strike and delivered a ramming blow to the junction of Butler's jaw. Butler was knocked out instantly with his jaw dislocated and likely broken. As a spasm of reaction whipped through his body, he pulled the trigger before collapsing to the ground.

The bullet tore through Peterson's right rib cage and exited his back.

·

Mady never took her eyes from Peterson and Butler, sensing something awful was coming. Peterson went too willingly. In spite of his gallant wink, she didn't like the casual way he walked in front of the gun. She pulled Carter close, grateful he was safe in the car with her.

A hand touched her shoulder and she jumped.

"You must know he is protected," Solomon said.

Mady nodded lamely. There was more happening than she could explain. Her right palm tingled and throbbed, the energy seeking a crescendo. Her nerves felt like piano wire dipped in adrenaline, and her muscles were bunched for flight, even though Carter blocked her exist from the car.

They watched the two men walk away, stop, and talk. Mady reached across Carter for the door handle. A hum was filling her head and the confinement of the car was claustrophobic. Her ears throbbed and she thought she might explode.

The gun fired and both men collapsed to the ground.

Mady screamed, her voice echoing within the vehicle like the screech of a great bird. Solomon and Henri were out of the car and running toward Peterson. Mady got the door open and she and Carter scrambled over each other getting out.

Peterson lay bleeding profusely from his entry and exit wounds. Henri pulled an unconscious Butler to the side and pocketed the handgun. He dug into Butler's pockets and retrieved the car keys.

Solomon fell to Peterson's right side, pulling off his jacket and putting it against the entry wound. Mady fell to her knees on Peterson's left.

"No," she cried, "not like this." She checked for a pulse at his neck.

Carter dropped next to her and stuffed his jacket against the wound at Peterson's back. The sand beneath Peterson was black and sticky.

Mady was frantic. Peterson had no pulse. His eyes went flat.

"No," she shouted. The power in her hand was expanding ominously. She didn't know what was about to happen, but there had to be a release ... soon. She thought of the powerful explosion they witnessed in the field below Liddington and shivered. A singing tone rose in her ears, vibrating through her skull to spread through her bones, merging with the rising power from her palm. A faint smell of incense teased Mady's nose, and she heard—

Singing. I hear a woman singing.

Mady frowned, but the source of the song was unmistakable. She fumbled with Peterson's pants pocket and pulled out an emerald. It was the size of a small apple, shaped like a fat heart with a slight indentation at the top.

The song was coming from the strange jewel. Embedded with the sweet frequency was an otherworldly female voice in an ancient language even Mady didn't know. She gasped. The emerald began moving in her palm.

Solomon had ceased his ministrations and sat back on his heels, staring. Henri crouched at the edges of Mady's vision, and Carter kneeled by her side, watching.

The emerald vibrated, oscillating in a tiny movement. A half-inch wave of rippling distortion emanated from the jewel, spreading out in an apple shape. In tune with every oscillation, the wave of distortion expanded, creating a field that enveloped Mady and Peterson, even touching Carter, Solomon and Henri.

Mady felt her heart expanding, as if growing beyond the boundaries of her ribcage. She looked down—a second wave of rippling distortion was coming from her body, pulsing in sync with the emerald. A peculiar, weightless sensation filled her. She felt as though her mind expanded with a new awareness: supreme power, invincible, infinite ... eternal.

Tears of comprehension squirted white-hot from her eyelids.

One, two, three, the glistening drops fell and landed on Peterson's face. A brilliant expansion of light burst from the emerald with a crescendo of vibration, producing an intense, perfect harmonic frequency.

The field of distortion snapped out.

Mady collapsed, caught by Carter before she fell across Peterson. He held her body, calling, "Mady, Mady, are you all right?"

She blinked and slowly came conscious. "What, what happened?" she stuttered. She opened her fist. The emerald was bleached out, clear as a brilliant diamond.

"Oooh hunh ah," came a slow wheezing gasp, as if air

suddenly seeped into dry lungs. Peterson's chest moved and his eyelids fluttered.

Solomon lifted Peterson up, supporting him. Mady fell back against Carter, a great smile lighting her face. "Look," she cried. Tears of joy coursed down her cheeks in a flood. Carter stared, stunned and mesmerized.

"*Non*," Henri whispered. "It is not possible."

Peterson's eyes opened and he slowly looked around the circle. He coughed and gasped and wheezed, holding his chest. With a struggling lurch, he sat upright and pulled out his shirt from his pants, exposing smooth perfect flesh where the bullet had entered. He reached for his back, and found more perfectly smooth flesh.

A shaky smile split his face. He glanced at Butler's inert form, then to the horizon. "If you'll help me up, we have to go."

CHAPTER SIX

Hanlon's Office
11:30 AM

Hanlon scrubbed his cheeks and ground his palms into his eyes, but the facts remained. At the helicopter extraction point in the desert, Butler was found incapacitated with a concussion and a broken jaw. Peterson and company had escaped.

He shook his head sadly.

Covering this expanding affair is getting dangerous—I have to find them.

In the doorway Fischer stared at the carpet, a sure sign the news was not good. "Butler is unable to make a report until he comes out of surgery."

Hanlon massaged his cheek, feeling his facial nerves tingle, gearing up for an assault. The first spasms came, escalating in tempo to match his rising alarm. He snapped at Fischer, "Leave me. And tell those fools upstairs I will arrive when they see me walk through the door." He spun his chair around and stared out the window.

The last thing he needed right now was a dog-and-pony show with his superiors over some budgetary problem when he had a walking weapon of mass destruction on the loose. His facial muscles jerked with distress.

Where is Peterson? And Solomon? What have they found?

Peterson's little manifestation of power was exactly what the Illuminati feared most. There was no place in their plan for individuals possessing the power of mass destruction and miracles. Which is why the Illuminati wanted the Ark.

For the same reason, they would confiscate Solomon's research.

The Illuminati long ago understood humanity capable of accessing an inherent power. Any artifact or research that lent potential to such an event was confiscated. Ancient writings relating to this potential power were long ago wiped from the face of the earth, with only odd fragments surfacing at random.

But all the Illuminati's efforts to foster ignorance by suppressing knowledge would be for naught if the power evolved on its own. If Peterson's manifestation was this power, the Illuminati will want him alive … maybe.

Hanlon pressed his hands against his eyes, causing crazy patterns of dark and light to sparkle against his eyelids. A moan of dread worked its way up his throat, until he shook his head in weak denial—

Utter dismay enveloped him. He felt as if his participation in these events were somehow pre-ordained, that he was hurtling down a path on stones laid into the earth for his feet only. A horizon event loomed, and he saw, just as sure as a prophet, where all this was headed—and what he would do.

He stood and straightened his jacket, suddenly ready for the meeting upstairs. He had to get his superiors out of the way, for he had other, more important matters to pursue.

•

Cairo International Airport
12:15 PM

The Gulfstream 450 engines were running long before Solomon and his party cleared customs. Peterson climbed the boarding ramp and collapsed into his seat in the rear of the plane. The others followed and toppled where they could in like fashion, scrambling for their seatbelts when the plane moved. The Gulfstream engines revved. Cairo soon shrank behind them. Less than an hour after leaving Butler in the sand, they were in the air.

Peterson's body screamed for rest, but his mind was in overdrive. What he experienced in the desert tumbled through his head, defying words, defying all the rules ... defying this universe.

"Ba-hahahu," he blurted. The sound was a madman's laugher, emerging again from those ancient vocal chords, drawing everyone's attention.

Mady released her seatbelt with a snap. Carter was two seconds behind her. They rose and descended on the rear of the plane. Mady reached Peterson first.

"What happened," she said as she sat next to him. Carter fell into the seat across the aisle, and Peterson could see a firestorm of questions dancing in his eyes.

Solomon was across from Peterson. "My friend, are

you all right?" Beside Solomon, Henri sat, an expletive barely contained on the tip of his tongue.

Peterson was at a loss how to begin answering all their questions. He held out his hand. A thin shimmer of distortion echoed off his fingertips. He raised the hand for Carter to see. "You can do this," he pressed, insistent.

Carter's expression reflected astonishment—but not denial.

Peterson turned his attention to Mady, needing to tell her now while everything was still fresh in his mind. He grasped her hand and felt the harmonics ignite with their contact. He closed his eyes, and recalled how he stayed alive after dying.

She gasped and tugged against his grip, but he wouldn't let go. "All you have to do is hang on," he said, squeezing her fingers. "Hang on, focus on maintaining a connection to your infinite self. Don't let go. Understand?"

He released her and she sat back with a whoosh. He felt the harmonic buzz go with her, and knew she got his vision from the way her eyes bulged. Peterson looked around. The men's faces reflected concern, shock, and surprise.

Carter ventured, "How did Mady ... resurrect you?" He reached for Mady's hand across the aisle.

"She is special—blessed with the power of the Goddess," Peterson said. "You recognized this when you two first met, am I right?"

Carter gave no answer, just smiled and kissed the back of Mady's hand before releasing her.

"That doesn't mean I have some—" Mady waved at the air, trying to slow all the woo-woo talk. "I need an explanation for what happened."

Peterson could see her questions, but he didn't have an answer for her. "I don't know—" He remembered his mother's words, and how he opened the passage to the Sphinx. "Your heart showed you the way?"

"The emerald!" Mady blurted. "I heard her singing and I pulled it from your pocket. A power wave emanated from it and touched us all."

"Nefertiti said the Goddess would guide me back, and that the emerald was a key. A key to what, she didn't say. A key to another dimension?" Peterson offered. "The emerald opened the doorway, combined with the Goddess power—"

"Mady was crying," Carter said.

"This Goddess talk is silly, and tears are proteins, that's all," Mady stammered. "What could they possibly—"

Peterson shrugged. "Complex chemicals carrying information from your heart, powered by the Goddess and the emerald, or maybe—"

He stopped abruptly, letting his sentence wither into oblivion. Suspicion, closely followed by comprehension, flitted lightning quick through his mind.

Cambridge!

At the time he touched Mady in the car at Liddington, he thought the power came from the jasper. But maybe it came from—

"When I participated in your protocols at Cambridge I experienced … an awakening, an awareness … a remembrance of power. At that time I wasn't sure if this power was connected to my quest, but now—"

The power isn't about my destiny—my destiny is about the power!

He stopped and let the wheels spinning in his head choose a direction. "Tell me about these protocols," Peterson continued. "Where are they from, what is their goal?"

"What you ask about," Solomon said, "comes from very ancient documents we recovered from an extraterrestrial artifact. This artifact was left by a race we call the Masters, or the Ancients. They claim to be relatives of humanity."

Abrupt silence descended heavily.

Peterson felt himself blink, too stunned to react.

That ... was the last thing I expected.

His first thought was to look for the candid camera, thinking he had finally been made the recipient of a grand prank. He was reminded of a Michael Douglas movie about an extremely elaborate game—

Comprehension struggled for footing, and he sighed with resignation. Regular logic did not support the reality of his experience in uniting with a piece of jasper and conversing with a gold statue. He realized he had no room to shout, "Extraterrestrials? Is this a joke?" He swallowed his initial shock. "Go on," he told Solomon.

"The key to the protocols is the symbol for Divinity and its accompanying sound, a frequency that amplifies a particular wave form produced in the brain. This amplification strengthens the bridge between our mind and the quantum field. The focus of the Cambridge research was the sound of Divinity."

"The sound," Peterson said. He remembered the sound clearly. Of perfect pitch, tone and harmony, the sound of Divinity brought a sweet vibration into his body. The surge of passionate emotion and electrifying power had touched him indelibly, leaving him marked with the sound and its memory.

He closed his eyes and listened for that sound, knowing it was within reach, for he and the sound of Divinity were entangled. He drew the sound closer with desire, and the sweet, perfect harmony came humming into his body, making his bones sing with the vibration. The perfect pitch rattled his molecules.

Peterson heard Mady gasp and he opened his eyes. His companions were drawn back. "What ... what happened," he stuttered.

"What were you doing?" Mady asked.

Peterson felt Mady's excitement roll out and settle a blanket of charged energy across his shoulders. The men's faces, however, turned the excitement into anxiety.

"I was calling up the sound of Divinity, the way I felt when it first came into my body at Cambridge. Why? What happened? What did I do?" he asked.

Henri clamped his lips shut, his forehead creased with concern. Mady's eyes were glazed, lost in a dervish of thoughts. Solomon had rocked back and covered his mouth with his hand. Only Carter was able to speak.

"You ... you just ... lit up, rather brightly, I might add," Carter said.

Peterson sat back, seeing the truth by their stunned faces.

Did I light up at Cambridge? The sound and the sensation he just experienced came like an echo from what happened in that cubicle. He was willing to bet—

Hanlon knows.

He grabbed Solomon's arm and shook him. "Call Cambridge now and tell them to run," he pleaded. "Tell them to run before the Illuminati arrive."

Solomon stared at Peterson intently for long moments. Abruptly he rose, saying, "Excuse me." He retrieved a cell phone from his briefcase and stepped forward to the galley.

Peterson slumped, awash in too many changes, feeling like he had been pitched from the plane. He curled his toes and grabbed the leather armrests.

"Are you all right?" Mady asked. She and Carter watched him with concern etched in their faces. Henri stared with a worry so intense, he made Peterson's heart jump. He wanted to ask what bothered the Frenchman, but backed away from the inquiry.

He was afraid of what Henri might tell him.

"The power of the ancients," Mady murmured. She sat back and reached for Carter.

"Tell us what happened in the museum?" Henri asked. "Where did you go?"

Peterson smiled. "I went beneath the paw. What did you see?"

They looked at each other, hesitant until Carter said, "You disappeared into the floor, as though you walked into a pit."

"*Oui*," Henri murmured in agreement.

Breathless with excitement, Mady agreed. "Exactly."

Peterson nodded. "I walked down a passage cut into stone. There were torches—"

Mady grabbed Carter's arm. "Didn't I tell you I smelled smoke? I kept waiting for the fire alarm to go off."

"I went beneath the paw," Peterson continued. He glanced at Carter, who clearly waited to hear what came next. "I spoke with the statue, Nefertiti, the Keeper of Balance. She was beautiful, and very much alive. She gave me the jewel and explained why I had to die."

A gasp of expectation skipped around the cabin.

Peterson directed his look to Henri as he announced, "I had to die and enter another dimension to learn the location of the Egyptian Hall of Records."

He watched Henri's play of expression, hoping he would now learn what the Sphinx left out. "It's time to tell me what you know."

Solomon rejoined them. "Yes, it is time you knew." He sat, and the crowd turned to him. "I called an associate in charge of the research at Cambridge and told them the funding was cancelled. They are packing up and vacating as we speak." All eyes settled on him. He gave one quick look at Henri before continuing.

"In the family archives, we have documents alleging the Ark of the Covenant is in the Hall of Records, placed there for safekeeping, not to be seen—" He pointed to Peterson's birthmark before finishing. "Until anchors fly."

Peterson closed his eyes, breathing carefully, letting this information settle into his already over-filled mind. He was so surprised he had no time to think. One question surfaced.

What am I supposed to do ... with the Ark?

He had more questions than answers, and wished his mother's specific points on his destiny had been more elaborate.

"Who allegedly put the Ark in the Hall?" Mady asked. Her face was lined with fierce concentration and surprise.

"According to the thirteenth-century writings of a St. Germain family member, the Egyptian Hall of Records was accessed using documents that survived the Library of Alexandria."

Peterson barely followed the conversation. He struggled with his evolving identity. All his speculation on where his quest might go did not include the Ark and a Hall of Records. He placed a hand to his ear. A tune was rising in his head, distracting him. "Are we going back to England?" he asked.

"*Oui*," Henri answered.

Peterson closed his eyes. So much was happening. What had been yesterday's priority was today's history. With each new priority, more questions arose. Without all the answers, all he could do was hurtle forward, a blind man.

The tune filled his head and he strained to remember the words. "It's an old war song," he said, humming. He spun his finger in a circle as though turning the crank of his memory, until he heard the words of death and destruction. He called out, lost in the memory, feeling the sands of time slip again from under his feet.

"No one they hit ever needed a road to walk again," he sang softly. He hummed. The tune was becoming clearer, brighter.

A fine vibration started up, and Peterson braced himself. The power shot down his spine and rocketed through his bones. He heard the words clearly. "There they kept Pentecost, Easter and Ascension, and half the cold bitter winter … God knew," he sang. He weaved within the moment, head cocked, listening for more.

Abruptly he shouted, "Termes has fallen."

The vision wherein he existed obliterated reality. He stared up at two rocky promontories, like a woman's breasts, protecting a heart underneath. Wrapped in this vision and with eyes closed, he pointed, calling out, "Go deep, into the bosom of Bezu."

Reality was gone and time flowed outside his understanding. Panic clotted the vision, so thick he could taste it. All around him people were running and their panting breath roared loud in his ears. He heard a foreign voice call out, "Bring the parchment!"

The cries and the shouts and the panic ceased. A terrible, crackling energy erupted, and he is alone, in the bosom of Bezu. A thunderclap explosion reverberates throughout the cave. He staggers as the enormous sound ripples across his eardrums, depositing in his mind the unutterable name of God. The crackling energy responded and opened to a mad vortex of wind.

"We leave you here, in the bosom of Bezu," he shouted, "until anchors fly." The vortex closed and the crackling energy winked out.

Peterson collapsed into his seat. His last words ricocheted around the airplane cabin.

Henri swore. He sat back clutching his chest. "He speaks of Bezu."

Solomon covered his eyes and squeezed the bridge of his nose.

"What is the bosom of Bezu?" Carter asked.

"Bezu is the ruins of an old Cathar stronghold in southern France," Henri answered, his voice sharp. He glanced at his cousin, but Solomon still covered his eyes.

Henri stood. "I will tell the pilot," he said.

Solomon nodded in blind and silent agreement. He exhaled with obvious grief as Henri walked to the cockpit.

Peterson sat up, alarmed at Solomon's reaction. The

pieces came together and comprehension snapped, bringing a harsh and bitter taste to his mouth. "Hanlon."

"Yes," Solomon said. When he looked up, his forehead shouted his worry, and his eyes were old with fatigue. "We are leading Hanlon right to the Ark."

•

Hanlon's Office
1:00 PM

Hanlon paced back and forth, needing action to match the turmoil in his thoughts. After his meeting with his superiors upstairs, he had intercepted Butler's report. The communiqué, while brief, said enough.

Peterson had disappeared into a solid marble floor. He was badly injured, shot by Butler, it seems, for his weapon had been discharged and someone left a good amount of blood behind. *Yet there is no sign of him in any of Cairo's hospitals or clinics.* Their plane was in the air. All Hanlon could do was wait for them to land in London.

Was Peterson dead? If so, that would save Hanlon from further jeopardizing his career and his life. He shook his head, knowing this would not be so easy. Peterson had survived a ground zero explosion that destroyed a satellite in space.

I bet Peterson is alive.

Hanlon stopped and leaned over his desk. Peterson's new profile was accumulating an ominous stack of evidence pointing toward paranormal powers at a frightening level. The stunning possibility that Peterson had even eclipsed death would not leave Hanlon's mind.

If his superiors knew all this, they would order Peterson terminated.

"Ha!" he roared with gusto, enjoying the dilemma.

If Peterson is indeed a resurrected man, could he even be terminated?

His pacing renewed with vigor.

Please, he begged, *let me not be out of my mind.* A knock on his door interrupted, and he called, "Come in."

Fischer entered. "I—"

"Close the door," Hanlon said softly.

Fischer gave a puzzled look, but let the heavy door ease shut behind him. "I have the—" he said in a subdued tone. He gave a questioning look, but left his sentence unfinished. He held out a page.

Hanlon took the paper and waved off Fischer's confusion. He walked past Fischer and frowned as he read, then suddenly smiled. He folded the paper and tucked it in his jacket breast pocket.

"We are going to France," he said. "Just the two of us."

•

Toulouse, France

The Gulfstream with Solomon and party landed at Blagnac Airport in Toulouse, France. A brief taxi ride brought them to the Gare Matabiau train station, where Solomon purchased their tickets. He gazed over his intrepid group, seeing the fatigue in their faces. He could not help but wonder—

Would there be any more deaths?

"There is no one here I can afford to lose," he said

absently.

Silently, Mady appeared by his side. "We aren't going to lose anyone," she said. They watched Peterson walk off to sit on a bench in the sun.

"He doesn't look like a man who died before lunch," she said.

"And you, *cherie*, do not look like a woman who resurrected a man before lunch," he responded. He smiled and peered into her face, looking for changes.

What metamorphosis had occurred in both her and Peterson because of this power they shared? He tightened his fist and a faint tingling reverberated deep in his palm. The sensation had been with him since she resurrected Peterson "before lunch" as she so casually put it.

"How do you feel?" he asked.

Mady pulled her eyes from Peterson, seeming reluctant to let him out of her sight. The clear gaze she gave Solomon was reassuring. "I feel quite well, considering." She turned back to watch Peterson. "I know you can feel it, Solomon."

Her statement startled him. He flexed his fist in response. The vibration in his palm danced up his arm with tantalizing pleasure.

"The wave form from the emerald touched you," she said quietly.

Solomon followed her gaze toward Peterson. "What do you think is happening to … him?"

Mady smiled and brought her right hand in a fist to her heart. "Have you met your infinite self yet?"

Solomon looked at her and saw she was ready to burst into giggles. Her infectious glee spread, inciting him to grin in spite of the erratic jump in his pulse brought on by her curious question.

"Nooo," he answered with reluctance. "I don't believe I have … met my infinite self." Her nod of confirmation told him the event offered much to appreciate. He felt his smile grow, making him feel quite silly. "What is this infinite self?" he asked.

"You'll see," she answered. She walked down the boarding platform to where Carter stood in the sun. When she took his hand, Solomon saw a wave of distortion whistle around them in a field of shimmering energy. He blinked and squinted, but the energy field disappeared, merging with the ambient light.

The tingling in his arm climbed to his shoulder, seeming ready to spill over into his chest. Something within clamored for him to accept more, but he turned away from the intoxicating pull of the harmonic vibration.

He watched Peterson. A bird landed on the walk next to where Peterson basked in the sun. Peterson held his hand out, and the bird trotted straight for him as though they knew each other. Another bird landed, and another. Soon he had collected at least a dozen.

"Solomon," Henri said in warning.

"I see," Solomon answered. Other passengers were noticing Peterson and his birds. "I believe that's our train coming now. Time for us to collect him and go."

Henri joined Mady and Carter while Solomon went for Peterson. He approached quietly, not wanting to disturb the birds surrounding Peterson. "Our train—"

"I know," Peterson answered. He waved his hand gently, and the birds rose into the sky in a soft whir of feathers.

Solomon watched the birds—mourning doves—disappear, and gulped when a wave of unease prickled his scalp. They walked back to where the others waited and he fought the urge to turn suddenly to watch his back. Before boarding, he glanced to where the birds had clustered around Peterson, his unease solidified around a disturbing thought.

Mourning doves aren't found in Europe.

A shiver skittered across his neck. He looked around. A few people remaining on the platform stared, frowning and whispering.

Solomon boarded, grateful to hear the doors close behind him. As the train quickly gathered speed, whisking them to Rennes-le-Chateau and what waited beyond, his foreboding settled around his shoulders. While the others followed the conductor, Solomon peered out the windows at the sky, looking for carrion birds.

•

The train noise was hypnotic. Peterson watched Languedoc go by with déjà vu. The English and Egyptian countryside had passed in the same fashion, and each ride into the country brought him one step closer, and yet two steps farther from understanding his destiny.

I am going into the Hall of Records, and I don't know why.

He had expected his understanding to grow and deepen with each completed task, but the opposite had proved to be the case.

Instead of being awash in comprehension, he was left to tread carefully through a growing expanse of questions laced with apprehension.

Chagrined at his thoughts, he held out his hand to

see what his heart knew already—the power shimmered like a thin shield of light around his fingers. His numerous questions evaporated in the awareness of this force. He didn't know what was happening to him, didn't know what waited for him in the Hall of Records, didn't know what the ultimate purpose was for his quest.

What he did understand was that something infinite and powerful now resided within him. So thorough was the connection he could not recall how he had felt before the awareness came to him at Cambridge. The harmonic bliss and the miracles he participated in were an integral part of him. Even with his questions expanding, there remained no other life, no other choices, no other path for him. Whatever destiny had carved for him, he could not run.

"May we talk," Carter said.

Peterson nodded and Carter eased into the next seat. Peterson sensed the power rising in Carter, just as he noticed it in the others. He didn't know how this was happening. Perhaps the power passed from him by entrainment, like one tuning fork picking up vibration from another. Perhaps the power was transferred with physical contact, as when he touched Mady in the limo out at Liddington.

Carter fidgeted for a few moments, taking his time before speaking. At last he asked, "What did it feel like, when she saved you."

"I was hanging on," Peterson said. "Hanging on to a part of me I sensed knew no boundaries, a part of me that could go or do or be anywhere, anything, anyone, anytime."

The sense of power within Peterson stirred to life at the mere mention, sweeping effervescent through his molecules. The presence of this eternal energy in motion made his bones tingle.

He explained to Carter, "I had been told earlier that the Goddess power would return me to this dimension, so I suppose I supplied some degree of expectation to prime the event.

"Plus we have the power of Nefertiti's emerald. Ultimately, Mady's need and desire to have me return must have been transmitted through the chemicals in her tears." He wanted to help Carter for he knew what the man was destined to face. The memory of being resurrected sent a thrill of invincibility through Peterson.

If contact were the means, or one of the means of spreading, this was his chance to give Carter a boost. He grasped Carter's hand and sent the memory of his resurrection racing into Carter along with the energy and information.

Carter choked, eyes bulging, and pushed back in his seat, but Peterson held onto him. Peterson knew by Carter's physical response the memory and ability he was sending had found its mark. After a brief time, Peterson let go. "It's all about heart intelligence," he said.

Carter's face paled and he sucked up several deep breaths. He gripped the armrests like a man pitched off a cliff.

Peterson smiled. "I know the feeling." He paused to let Carter regain his bearings.

When Carter seemed relaxed and able to converse, Peterson told him, "To use this power you have to understand information and energy. Your thoughts supply the focus and the information, and the energy—the emotion, necessary for delivery—comes from your heart."

He rapped Carter firmly on his chest. "What's in your heart, Carter? Is your love strong enough to entangle her?"

Carter looked instantly at Mady. She sat resting on a banquet seat, her body rocking in time with the train.

Peterson watched a wave of energy surge across the train car between the couple. "Put your hand out," he instructed.

Carter frowned, but extended his fingers. A shimmer of distortion radiated out an inch from his hand.

"Remember this," Peterson said. He took Carter's hand again, and the field of distortion flared out several feet around them. "Know and remember your power," Peterson commanded.

Carter stiffened, electrified for long seconds before he sagged. He gently peeled his hand free.

Peterson saw Carter's eyes were clouded with doubt. Before he could speak, the field surrounding them flickered out. Carter clamped his lips together and shook his head. His expression said he felt no relief.

"Remember," Peterson said.

Carter blinked, his sole acknowledgment of Peterson's words, and stuck his hand into his pants pocket. He walked off without a word, a quiet man with troubling thoughts.

Changes in the countryside alerted Peterson to the approaching town of Rennes-le-Chateau. He rose with excitement and moved to join Henri and Solomon across from Mady and Carter.

"Henri will drive," Solomon said.

Peterson nodded. The combined energy from his companions was ringing through his body, joining with a strengthening song from the Hall of Records. He looked out the window to the high peaks at the south-east end of the valley.

Le Bezu! Would his questions be answered here?

He hummed with the sweet harmony vibrating through his molecules when a vision came to his mind. He saw the white stone peaks covering the bosom of Bezu, and knew that the harmonic perfection deep within was waiting for him. He closed his eyes and the cleft in the stone was as clear as if it were right before him. There was a door even the blind could find. Once again the enormous sound of the unutterable name of God boomed through Peterson's memory and he gasped, pressing his hands to his ears.

The scene went dark and all was gone. He sensed he was alone, more alone than he had ever been in his life. More alone than when he was dead.

The vision left him.

He sat rigid in his seat. Sweat popped up along his hairline, collected at his cheekbone and ran down his jaw. More moisture gathered and trickled down his backside, chilling him. His heart beat too fast, making his stomach feel queasy. He breathed in shallow puffs and panting exhalations.

"You will remember." Nefertiti's words came roaring into his ears, suddenly as ominous and frightening as green clouds.

The train slowed to a stop with a great shrieking of metal, bringing the Rennes-le-Chateau train sta-tion streaming past the windows. Suddenly, Peterson comprehended the inescapable double-edged price of knowledge. Weakness and fear rippled down his spine and out through his entire body.

He no longer wanted to go to Bezu.

CHAPTER SEVEN

Le Bezu

The air in Bezu was spring warm, yet crisp, and ancient. Peterson felt the power's vibration pick up in tempo as they came closer. He responded in kind, humming with the anticipation of old friends coming together. Accompanying this was a sensory assault of familiarity.

The déjà vu was so acute the memories overwhelmed reality. He futilely wished he could put on blinders to block out some part of the upheaval he was receiving.

It was a bloody day.

He shook off a heavy sense of doom and walked the path up from the designated parking area followed by Solomon, Henri, Mady and Carter.

The siren call from the Hall of Records rang deep in his bones, drawing him along. *This*, he thought, *is the place of my destiny.*

Energy, old and faded, wafted through the ruins, making his skin tingle. He could hear the shouts of battle from another time echoing beneath the cries of birds flitting above him. If he looked sideways sharply from the corner of his eye, he could see the chaotic energy patterns marked indelibly upon this place.

He came to a fork in the path. He had been here before and went to the right without hesitation.

All along the path were crumbling mortared walls, scant remains of a once glorious castle. He skirted the barren gardens and climbed up the hill to the stables, now deserted. No trace remained of the great arched, stone entryway. Wild thyme and lavender grew in abundance where troubadours once sang in a brightly lit hall.

Peterson stopped, eyes closed, and put his hands over his ears against the consuming roar of the past—the keening lament of loss, nervous horses jostling the crowd, frightened children crying from behind their mother's skirts, the reek of men rushing about with fear in their bellies.

"Hurry," he called, even though he knew the sense of imminent danger was eight hundred years past. He picked up the pace, glancing over his shoulder to see if his companions still followed.

They were faithful, his friends. Peterson saw Solomon's concern, for it was poorly concealed. Henri looked ready to slay a dragon. Mady glowed with the shimmering field. Carter was at her heels, excitement outweighing his fear for a change. Carter rubbed his palm.

Peterson smiled.

He turned back to the path. The harmonic pull from the waiting Hall was incredible, the frequency drawing him forward. He pushed on in spite of the heavy breathing coming from behind him. They passed a last outcrop of ruins, what had once been servant's quarters, and his heart ran ahead, excited as a kid.

Towering above and casting shadows across their

approach was the bosom of Bezu. One peak perfectly supported the sun, the jagged rock fracturing the sun's rays to send an eight-pointed star searing into the eyes.

A powerful vibration came from beneath the great bosom, and this frequency joined Peterson's internal symphony with a pulsing wave of energy, seeking entrainment. His heart stuttered as it struggled to match the massive and ancient beat of energy coming from deep within the earth.

"This way," he called, motioning them to follow across the grassy clearing, drawing his intrepid group on. The new grass of spring cushioned each step, releasing a fresh scent at their passing.

Peterson looked up—the ancient door was wide open.

He laughed.

Even the blind could find it.

He walked through the door.

•

Close behind them, Hanlon stared at the lone rental car parked in the late afternoon shadows. "Le Bezu," he said. "The place is a ruin. What brings them here?"

Fischer glanced at the sky. "Dusk comes soon. We'd best hurry." He looked around and finally pointed. "I believe they passed this way."

Hanlon hesitated. If any of what he suspected was true, it was possible he might not walk away from this place alive.

Or worse—

If I do survive, I may wish I hadn't.

Fischer flicked the flashlight on and off. Hanlon pushed his misgivings aside and motioned for him to proceed.

•

Carter was standing with Mady when Peterson laughed and disappeared. Carter rubbed his eyes and glanced at her. She blinked and stared with ferocious focus, mystified.

Henri muttered. "He has disappeared again."

Solomon came to a full stop and stared with his head cocked to one side. His eyes drifted as he listened—

Henri brought a cupped hand to his ear. "Do you hear—"?

"Music—" Mady whispered. She stepped to the front, taking the lead. Solomon and Henri fell into step behind her.

Carter watched them walk off in Peterson's footprints, stepping in his tracks where the grass was still flat.

Sudden unease peppered his scalp, halting his steps. He didn't want to go with them. Peterson's words, *Whatever happens at Bezu* were repeating in his mind with frightening and nauseating prophetic redundancy.

He shivered, standing in the cool shadow of the great stone. He didn't know what frightened him more: going into the heart of Bezu, or being left behind. Suddenly a bird cawed and he looked up at a pair of black birds circling overhead. A raw chill, not from the late afternoon shadows, skittered down his back.

Beware when carrion birds fly.

Quickly he ran to catch up with the others.

Mady, Solomon and Henri stood three feet from where Peterson disappeared. The rock was a solid wall of stone.

Mady said, "I can hear—"

"*Oui,*" Henri added. "The—"

"Harmonic frequency," Solomon finished.

Carter massaged the tingling in his palm and faintly detected a teasing sensation … in his bones. "Yes, he's close," he said.

Mady closed her eyes and held her hands out. She turned her head, listening, and took one step forward, and a second step—straight into the stone face.

"Ooph," she grunted when she hit the rock. She held her banged head with one hand, and threw her other hand out against the rock wall for support … and fell forward. "What?" she cried as she lurched into an opening.

Carter, Solomon and Henri crowded around her.

"Ah, an optical illusion," Henri said.

"Clever," Solomon muttered, nodding.

"How did they do that?" Carter asked.

What appeared to be solid stone face was actually a narrow opening sheltered behind a lip in the rock. The pattern on the stone lip perfectly matched the opposing wall, making the opening invisible until you reached out and touched it, like a blind man groping.

"Do we have a light?" Mady asked.

Solomon fished a small LED light from his pocket and handed it to her with a shrug of remorse. "Better than nothing, I hope."

Mady took the tiny light and stepped into the blind opening, closely followed by Carter, Solomon and Henri. As they slipped silently into the rock of Bezu, an afternoon breeze rifled the grasses, stirring their footsteps into oblivion.

•

Fischer stopped abruptly at the crest of the hill, causing Hanlon to run into him.

"What?" Hanlon asked. He stepped around Fischer and stared at a circular, grassy clearing surrounded by a rocky outcrop. Two large white mounds of stone closed off the circle.

"Now what?" Fischer asked.

Hanlon stared at the pristine grass. Unless they had sprouted wings and flown away, they were here. He and Fischer had tracked Solomon and company from the airport as though they had left a trail of crumbs. Four men and a beautiful woman asking directions to Le Bezu were easy to follow. The witnesses at the train station in Toulouse eagerly spoke about a strange man and birds.

Hanlon looked at the sky. Twilight was upon them, that moment when vision was the weakest. Soon it would be dark, and there would be no help.

"Take the flashlight," he said. "We'll go on our hands and knees if we have to. There must be a trace of their passing somewhere in this perimeter."

He dropped to his knees and carefully searched the ground and the grass and the stone. Fischer followed suit in the opposite direction. After going several yards, Hanlon paused, feeling panic rise in his throat. He stopped and sat back on his heels, panting.

Let the field training take over.

It had been a long time since he was active in the field, but such rigorous training came to the fore in times of need. His breath slowed and he focused on finding a sign of the group's passing, going inch by inch.

As he groped across the ground in the fading light, he gouged his knee on a rock and stopped long enough to wonder if he had lost his mind.

He sat back on his heels, a rip in his pants and dirt

under his fingernails. What shook him most was the contents of his heart and mind.

A hotly contested inner battle raged over whether he was sane or not. The words "madman" and "lunatic" arose with nauseating repetition, bearing down on his heart. Logic jumped into the fray delivering the condemning truth.

Here's the great and powerful John Hanlon, crawling along the geological backbone of Europe in search of a miracle.

His only rebuttal to such damning rhetoric was the even greater truth he knew in his heart.

Man was born a free spirit.

Hanlon knew this, because he, too, wanted to be free.

He bent over and continued along on his hands and knees, certain a miracle was within reach.

•

Deep in the heart of Bezu, Peterson breathed a sigh of relief when the narrow tunnel released into what felt like a much larger opening.

He sniffed.

The air was mountain dry and crisp; ancient odors from that night long past had faded away. He fired up a pocket lighter. The miniscule flame cast a glow that eerily extended to the walls of the enormous cavern.

He dropped the lighter. The song of the Hall was rising in his heart, sweeping through him. He and the Hall were entangled, and it was time for him to answer his destiny. At this acknowledgement, a response fired in his heart, sending a new frequency into the symphony.

Light exploded in a blinding flash. Peterson staggered back as a dark cloud formed and charged upon him with ominous intent. The cloud swirled and erupted with crackling energy, followed by the roar of thunder. A flurry of lightning spewed forth in a cataclysm that evaporated the cloud, leaving behind a swirling vortex of wind and energy.

Peterson faced the maelstrom, arms spread, heart emanating a singing vibration. There was no room for fear when his heart was filled with such exaltation. From his memory came the sound of the unutterable name of God, reproduced now by those strange, reoccurring ancient vocal chords.

The name of God was a boom reverberating throughout the cave. The mountain was rattled, throwing loose boulders about like gravel. Peterson covered his ears and crouched down, ready to run. But the mad vortex of wind winked out with staggering abruptness. A beautiful, shimmering curtain of lights and energy remained.

Beyond the curtain lay the wealth of many nations. Mountains of gold glittered as statues, coins, and bars. Exotic furniture and jewelry extended out of sight. Jewels piled in a haphazard manor dazzled with eye-catching color. A great stack of scrolls and documents were stacked next to peculiar devices.

When Peterson heard Mady whisper, "Oh my—" he glanced over his shoulder. His companions' faces wore identical "O" expressions. Solomon's lips were pursed in soundless awe. Henri's eyes were huge, his face intense with wonder. Carter shook his head and rubbed his palm. "Is this ... the Hall of Records?" he asked.

"The Egyptian Hall of Records," Peterson said. "Guarded by Nefertiti, the Keeper of Balance. What you are witnessing is made possible by a highly orchestrated synchronization of time, dimension and my DNA."

Carter nodded as though he perfectly understood the concepts of time, alternate dimensions, and complex genetics.

Henri nudged Solomon. "Do you see it?"

"The Ark," Solomon answered in reverent whisper.

They collected around Peterson. Mady stared at the untold wealth beyond the curtain and reached her hand out. Peterson quickly pulled her back, saying, "No one else may enter, either before or after me."

"What happens next?" she asked.

"I go in," he answered. He shrugged, hiding his trepidation. There certainly was no choice for him at this point, and he pushed Nefertiti's troublesome words from his mind. "I go in. That's all I know."

But there were other tasks to complete, and time was getting short. He took Solomon's arm in the grasp of camaraderie familiar to ancient man. "We have been friends across many lives. I am fortunate to know you, privileged to call you friend."

The memory of when he last knew Solomon, then called Thoth, swept through Peterson's mind. His love and respect for Solomon flowed from his heart in a rush of energy, fueling the vision.

A burst of light encased them.

Peterson steadied Solomon while the vision of information and energy held him locked in stiff rigor. Solomon's eyes bulged. At last the light around them went out. Solomon blinked, and gasped.

Peterson placed his finger to his lips and winked.

Solomon staggered to Henri's side.

"Mady," Peterson called.

She stepped in front of him, her eyes eager and her

lips twitching with anticipation.

"Do you trust me?" he asked.

In her clear blue eyes, he saw a flicker of doubt rise, but it dissipated in the same instant. She smiled. "I'm not afraid."

"What's in your heart? What's most important to you?" he asked.

They turned together and looked at Carter. Peterson could see the love she felt for Carter well up and flow out from her in a heart wave.

"Is it time for his miracle?" she asked.

Peterson nodded to the Hall behind the shimmering curtain. "I don't know what's going to happen in there." His words faded for a breathless span. He jerked back to the moment. "So yes, the time is now. Are you sure you're ready?"

She brought her right fist to her heart and nodded. "What's going to hap—" she began.

"Don't think about it," he said, passing his hand over her eyes. "Just hang on, like this," he said. He recalled the feeling of being resurrected. A surge of power shot through him and flowed into her.

Carter pulled his eyes from the display of wealth when an overwhelming sense of dread filled his heart. "No. Wait, stop," he cried when he saw Mady and Peterson together, for he suddenly feared what was happening.

"Stop what you're doing—" He took two steps, but Mady was already collapsing. He caught her as she tumbled from beneath Peterson's hand.

"What have you done?" he shouted. He fell with her to the ground. She was lifeless in his arms.

"Earlier, I asked you what's in your heart, Carter.

Show us, show us what you can do," Peterson commanded.

Fully hysteric, Carter screamed, "Are you insane? What have you done?" He clutched Mady in his arms, her inert head resting against his shoulder. Tears sprouted from his eyelids, splashing her with his grief. "Mady, Mady," he sobbed. He glared up at Peterson. "What have you done?"

"What I have done is not important," Peterson said. "What's important is you have the power to change what I have done. You have the power within your heart to bring her back."

"You're insane," Carter screamed, his tears falling into Mady's hair. "Why are you doing this?" he wailed.

"Show her your love," Peterson commanded. "You have the power. Remember—"

"Mady, Mady, come back," Carter sobbed, frantic. "My love, you know I need yo—"

Peterson crouched down next to Carter. "She can't hear your words. Only the power of your love can reach her now. You do love her, don't you?"

Carter sobbed. "Of course I love her. I can't imagine life without—"

"Then imagine your life with her. Put the emotion in your heart with the visions of your life with her. Information and emotion, Carter. Remember."

"Arrgghh," Carter howled, throwing his head back, screaming until the sound echoed around the cavern.

But he held on to Mady.

He held on and he rocked, back and forth, holding her tight. He hummed and the rigor of pain on his face morphed into a smile of rapture. His head rolled from side to side and the tears continued to flow down his cheeks.

"I love you," he whispered, squeezing Mady's body tight. He continued to rock with his eyes closed. A field of energy grew from his chest, surrounding the two of them in a great apple shape—the heart wave.

"Ahh ha," he laughed. He smiled softly and rocked, eyes squeezed tight. The tears surged from his compressed eyes in a glittering rainfall of emotion. A new rigor contorted his face, this one of euphoric bliss. The tears came faster and the field around him and Mady expanded. A soft brilliance emanated from him, filling the heart wave with gold light.

Mady's fingers twitched. She gasped and choked, hauling air into her lungs in hitches. "Huhn, huhn, huhn," she coughed.

Carter opened his eyes just as hers fluttered open, cognizant with life.

"Nicky, oh, Nicky, I saw you, you made the heart wave." She babbled through tears and laughter, clutching him. "You made light, you made light," she squealed.

Solomon and Henri rushed forward. Peterson offered his hand to Carter, and they helped Mady stand. She laughed and cried, and hugged Solomon and Henri. Soon they were all crying and hugging and laughing.

Peterson drew away from the emotional crowd. It was time for him to go.

"Wait," Mady cried. She rushed forward to give him a hug. "Thank you," she whispered, "for the miracle."

Carter stepped up and took Peterson's hand. They stood that way for long moments, sharing comprehension.

At last Peterson responded to Mady, keeping his eye on Carter. "Carter did all the work." He clapped Carter on the shoulder, adding, "You had the answer all along. Your heart held the power and the passion to manifest your desires."

Carter shook his head, eyes sad, and smiled. "Why was it so hard for me to see?"

"Hah!" Peterson barked in laughter. "It's a wonder we realize anything at all. We're the ultimate package of contradictions—a spiritual energy in material form, an infinite being housed in a finite shell, a mind that organizes energy at the quantum level, yet feels a stubbed toe ... We are designed to create joy, and wired to think disaster. Ultimately, we are a self-referencing manifestation of the quantum field with only one requirement: to chose. Because until we make a choice, all that exists is potential."

Carter laughed. He squinted, saying, "Well, when you put it that way, don't I feel better?"

Solomon asked Peterson, "What else can we do for you?"

Peterson stared at the great, shimmering curtain. There was nothing else to say, the sum total of his life culminated in this moment. He was ready. He approached the curtain.

He had to look back one last time.

•

Hanlon crept slowly on his hands and knees. When the ground shook with a lurching tremor, he felt the reverberations echo up through his hands. He sat back on his knees and looked up for falling debris. Twenty-five feet from the cleft in the two mounts, loose stones came tumbling down the pitted stone face, bouncing like great pin balls before crashing to the ground.

He watched a rock roll and disappear into a shadow—a shadow that should have been solid stone. His hackles rose in a stiff flash of chill bumps. He clambered awkwardly from the ground.

"Fischer," he called as he struggled to walk on legs gone stiff.

In the near dark, the great, white stone mounts of Bezu were as pale as a woman's flesh. The loosed boulders gleamed, leading Hanlon to the opening. As Fischer brought the flashlight to bear, a well-camouflaged entrance in the rock was revealed.

Hanlon sucked in a breath through his teeth. He was not a fan of tight places.

Fischer entered the rock. "This way," he said, turning sideways to make the narrow passage.

Hanlon followed in spite of the wild hammering in his already tight chest. The passageway twisted and backtracked through the rock, reminding Hanlon of intestines. He gulped, uncomfortable with his analogy, and pressed on to keep up with Fischer. Even stronger than his fear of the path was his desire to see one of Peterson's miracles.

Abruptly, light filled the end of the passageway. "Turn off the flashlight," Hanlon hissed.

They quietly slipped from the narrow passage into a large cavern. Hanlon smothered a gasp and pushed Fischer into a crouch. They hunkered down among the rock debris.

"What in heaven—?" Hanlon whispered.

A towering wall of sparkling energy floated off the ground like fabric spun with diamonds. Through the shimmering curtain he could see untold wealth in the form of gold and precious jewels. What appeared to be an ancient library was stacked next to creations and machinery outside his understanding.

Hanlon sank down deeper onto his heels and pressed Fischer into the shadows. Twenty yards away, in the full glittering light of the curtain, they watched Peterson, Solomon and Henri, and the couple from the museum in London.

Peterson ran his hand over the woman's eyes, and she collapsed.

Hanlon shrank back farther. He and Fischer watched the astonishing events, witnesses hidden in the rock until Peterson looked up and gazed right at them. Hanlon knew they were discovered. He stood and brushed himself off. Behind him, Fischer was doing the same.

"Sir?" Fischer uttered.

"Shsssh," Hanlon said. "Stay here. I'm just going to talk to him."

Peterson's small crowd had collected around him in a defensive stance. Hanlon held out his empty hands.

Solomon demanded, "What are you doing here, John? This is not Illuminati—"

"I'm not here for the Illuminati," Hanlon said. "I just want to talk to him." He spread his hands in supplication.

Solomon glanced at Peterson, who nodded.

Hanlon walked slowly, careful, unable to take his eyes from the unbelievable phenomena suspended in the air. His insides turned into brick and settled somewhere above his retracted gonads. A peculiar sensation of being disconnected from the ground pervaded his bones.

The quiet beauty of the vast wealth behind the curtain was a deceptive diversion, concealing tremendous energy. Hanlon could feel it, as if he stood behind a giant, invisible jet, silently revving for take off. The vibration settled in his gut, tickling his insides.

"What is this?" he asked Peterson. He was close enough to peer into Peterson's face. He saw no change in the man's visage, a rather disconcerting fact in light of what Hanlon knew, what he desperately hoped, and what he suspected. "What's happening to you?"

"This has nothing to do with the Illum—" Peterson protested.

Hanlon waved his hand in disgust, dismissing all talk of the Illuminati. "I have risked much to keep this from the Illuminati. I am not here … for them."

Peterson gave Hanlon a hard look.

Because he so desperately wanted the answers, Hanlon waited, absorbing Peterson's intense scrutiny. But he refused to be turned away—not when he was this close.

His heart ran too fast, and sound telescoped away, making Hanlon feel like the ground had shifted. When he spoke, his voice came out all thin and hollow, like a tin cup on a cold winter morning. "Please, explain this to me," he begged.

Peterson's expression eased, a fact that disturbed Hanlon.

"John," Peterson responded. "I have … an appointment, if you will." He nodded to the twinkling curtain.

"Is this because of Solomon's research?" Hanlon asked.

Peterson smiled and flexed his hand. He ignored Hanlon's question and instead, posed one of his own. "What's in your heart, John?"

Hanlon fought the urge to step back. He had heard Peterson ask Carter the same question. Chills rained down Hanlon's back, whether from the question or the expression on Peterson's face, he couldn't say.

Peterson extended his hand in invitation. "Let's see, John, what's in your heart."

Hanlon's chills quadrupled. Did he dare? After a life dedicated to manipulating the future of an entire species, could the contents of his heart bear the light of examination?

His lips came together in a grim line of determination. The unrelenting seed of insanity he apparently harbored—this desire to see a miracle—was clamoring for that very light, however frightening the results. He licked his lips and swallowed, preparing to voice for the first time words he knew were Illuminati blasphemy.

He stepped close, needing only Peterson to hear. "I'm here because I believe something has happened to you, something that will prove ... that man cannot be oppressed. I think you are empowered, that you can show me ... a miracle."

Peterson smiled and motioned to Carter, who stood with the recently resurrected woman. "You saw what happened," Carter said. He hugged the woman close.

The woman, Mady Fox—her eyes held a light of wisdom that made Hanlon feel ... insignificant. His mind danced around what he just witnessed of her. He wanted to know what happened to her when she went ... where? What was it like in death, and how did it feel to return to life, to bridge the chasm between the two worlds, to travel back on that one-way highway?

He stuttered. "Yes, I ... I saw. But I ... I need to understand," he blurted, embarrassed to admit he needed more than to merely witness a miracle—he needed to know how such happened. A wild thought urged him on to consider other miracles.

If Peterson can do this, then perhaps, so can—

Before Hanlon could finish the thought, Peterson grasped his hand in a death grip. A blast of energy shot up Hanlon's arm in an electrifying jolt. His spine arched backward as all his muscles went rigid. Visions flooded his mind, streaming in a continuous flow. He choked and gasped, overloaded with more than he could assimilate. He felt his slim grasp of consciousness waver like a light bulb flickering on a frayed strand.

On the edge of losing consciousness, he jerked loose from Peterson and staggered back, falling to the stone floor. Fischer was suddenly at his side, but all Hanlon could do is gape, his mouth moving in soundless mime.

Fischer's eyes were possessed with a manic intent. He thrust his hands at Peterson. "Take me ... where you took him." He stepped closer. "Show me what you showed him, give me this power—" His voice rose, strident and shrill, raising the hackles along Hanlon's neck.

Peterson drew back but Fischer followed, stalking him.

"Make me powerful, do it!" he cried. He glanced over his shoulder at the stunned audience, declaring to all, "Do you think I want to live my life with someone like him—"

He motioned to Hanlon on the ground with a venom-filled sneer. "Telling me what to do, day in and day out, watching him make decisions about people like me, without a care or a passing thought?"

Hanlon cringed at Fischer's assessment. The quiet assistant had always been loyal. Hanlon had no idea what made him so vehement.

He just wants to be free.

The answer was sudden and startling. This was the truth that ate at Hanlon's core, the truth around which all the Illuminati's failures were based. He shook his head with misery.

This is why the Illuminati will ultimately fail.

"Well," Hanlon mumbled to himself. "It's not my job to make them understand." With penance sincerely filling his face, he held his hand out to Fischer.

Fischer recoiled. Instead of reaching for Hanlon, he grabbed Peterson's hand, pleading. "Show me how to do what you did to her so I will never know fear again. Give me the power of life and death!"

Peterson jerked his hand from Fischer's clutch, a frown of revulsion wrinkling his forehead. Fischer snarled, shoved Peterson aside and ran for the curtain.

Everyone was shouting at once, but it was too late. With a warrior's yell, Fischer leaped into the Hall of Records.

The curtain rippled as he went through, disturbing the lights. Hanlon could see Fischer clearly. The man's face was a study in rapture. His eyes were lit with fascination as he cautiously picked his way through the treasure. A gold vase studded with pearls and rubies sparkled with allure, drawing Fischer like a moth to flame.

He reached for it with both hands.

When his flesh was just short of touching the vase, bolts of energy jumped from the vase to his fingertips. He threw his head back and screamed, the sound fluttering through the curtain and reverberating throughout the cave.

The look of rapture was replaced by a visage wracked in pain. Fischer tore his fingers from the vase and clawed at his eyes, screaming all the while. He turned in a circle, backing up like a scalded dog—screaming, screaming, screaming.

Hanlon stood, horrified, his hand over his mouth. Fischer's screams of pain and terror filled the cave, echoing over and over, growing in intensity. Hanlon stepped toward the curtain, but Peterson blocked his path. "There is nothing you can do."

Hanlon glanced at the others. The woman cried openly, tears coursing down her cheeks. Carter shook his head with abject sympathy. Solomon's face was pinched with shock. Henri held his fingers to his ears against the horrific sound.

Suddenly the screams stopped, even though Fischer's mouth remained open in a grimace of pain. Like a rag doll, he was picked up by an invisible hand and tossed out the curtain. He landed at Hanlon's feet.

They all rushed toward him, but Hanlon held his hand out, stopping them. He bent over Fischer's limp form.

Fischer was alive.

His hair was white as snow, and the pads of his fingertips were scorched to a flat, white oval. When Hanlon gently turned the lolling head, he found Fischer's eyes were open, staring blindly, the pupils blasted white as boiled eggs.

"How could you have been so foolish?" he whispered. "Why would you take such an insane risk?"

Hanlon's heart knew the answer. *To be free ... at any cost.* He looked up, frantic with the pain of realization. "Can you help him?" he begged. He looked at them, pleading. "Solomon? Peterson?"

Mady kneeled next to Hanlon and helped lift Fischer to a sitting position. She ran her hands over him and he accepted her ministrations with complacency, as though he cared not about who touched him. He seemed to no longer be in pain.

"Can you speak?" she asked.

Fischer turned to the sound of her voice, but made no effort to respond. He was like an animated doll, alive, yet mindless, an empty shell. He blinked his white eyes, seeming unaware of his condition.

Hanlon asked Peterson. "You're still going in there?"

Peterson studied Fischer for a long time.

Hanlon saw lines of trouble cross Peterson's face, but then came evidence of a resolute strength and faith that made Hanlon feel like a pauper. Even with the miracles Hanlon had witnessed, the knowledge he had received, the visions he experienced, he could only wonder how Peterson was brave enough to pass through that curtain.

Solomon caught Peterson's eye. "Are you sure?" He glanced from the wealth behind the curtain to the simple face of Fischer at Hanlon's feet.

Peterson put his hand over his heart and closed his eyes. A visible field of energy radiated out from him several feet. "There is nowhere else for me to go," he said quietly.

He and Solomon clasped arms in friendship.

"Again we part—" Solomon said.

"Again we will meet," Peterson added.

Peterson moved to Carter and Mady. "Do you have any questions before I go?" he asked Carter.

Carter extended a formal gentleman's handshake, but the move was softened by his expression. "We are the ultimate package of conflicts. That I will remember." He smiled and pumped Peterson's hand with affection.

Mady hugged Peterson. "Go with God," she whispered.

Next was Henri. The Frenchman's expression was a mix of awe and expectation. "May I ask what is your first name?"

Peterson looked surprised. He opened his mouth to speak, but thought better of it. Instead, he leaned over and whispered in Henri's ear. Henri's expression froze momentarily, before he extended his hand. "*Bon voyage.*"

Peterson moved in front of Hanlon.

"I would have stopped him, but I had no idea—" Hanlon moaned.

"I'm sorry about Fischer. Like you, I didn't know. Will you take care of him?" Peterson asked.

"Yes. I will see to it," Hanlon said. He pushed the white hair back from Fischer's pale eyes. "And what of you?"

"My fate lies across that boundary. Perhaps this is the end of my quest," Peterson answered.

Hanlon saw the worry flit across Peterson's eyes.

He doesn't know if he'll end up like Fischer—or not.

Hanlon asked, "What you showed me, it came so fast I'm not sure—"

"You will. And you will find a way to show the Illuminati."

Hanlon reared back, shocked, and shook his head in denial at Peterson's suggestion. When there was nothing left to say, he whispered, "God be with you."

Peterson rose and approached the curtain. As he neared, the lights brightened and moved in excitement. He threw his head back and put his hands to his chest.

A field of distortion radiated from him to the curtain.

Hanlon gasped. He felt a tingling sensation rise in his bones when the field of distortion bloomed around Peterson.

Peterson's energy field merged with the lights in the curtain. The lights danced and swirled, turning into a rainbow of light, going from diamond white to the colors of jewels. The curtain parted and Peterson jumped up. After he crossed the threshold, the curtain gently closed behind him.

Hanlon held his breath.

Like Fischer, Peterson's face took on a look of rapture. His expression was one of abject, utter euphoria as he picked his way through the treasure. He cocked his head, listening, a smile splitting his face, and brought his hand to his ear.

Hanlon exhaled, stunned. He, too, heard some sort of tune.

The small crowd gathered around Hanlon and Fischer. Hanlon glanced at their faces. Again, their expressions of power and comprehension eclipsed him. His palm tickled where Peterson had held him. The tingle in his bones merged with the growing harmonic hum that teased his eardrums, making a sweet sensation flow through his body. He smiled and rubbed his palm.

Peterson turned to face them through the curtain. He gave a salute of camaraderie.

"Till we meet again, my friend," Solomon whispered, returning the salute.

"Thank you," Carter added as he waved.

"I'll look for you," Mady said softly.

"Don't worry," Henri said calmly. "You will see him again."

Peterson brought his hands up in exaltation. In an eye-watering flash, the Hall and its contents disappeared.

The cavern rang like a bell when the energy field evaporated, leaving Hanlon's ears popping. He shutter-blinked several times and shook his head, but all evidence of Peterson and the vision was gone.

Instantly, the cavern was dark, cold and ancient. A ripple of loss waved through Hanlon, leaving him desperate to be outside in the fresh air. He looked from Fischer to the small crowd.

"Will you help me get him out?" he asked.

CHAPTER EIGHT

Several Days Later,
St. Germain Townhouse

Mady sat next to Carter in Solomon's small library. She admired the large, round-cut diamond engagement ring and wedding band on her left hand. "Forgive us for not inviting you," she told Solomon. "The moment came quietly in the middle of the night. You should have seen the sleepy-eyed clerk."

She squeezed Carter's hand and felt the heart wave expand and billow out around them. When Solomon's eyes bulged in recognition, she knew he detected the flare of energy.

So, she thought, *we are all connected by the power of Divinity. How far does the connection go? What, exactly, are we capable of?*

"Congratulations," Henri proclaimed. He stood and clapped at her announcement. Solomon rose and pumped Carter's hand in a vigorous display of approval. "Well done, old man," he chimed with glee.

"Thanks to Peterson, and the miracles we witnessed—and performed—in Bezu," Carter said.

He preened at the mention of miracles performed, doing so with a smug confidence that made Mady happy. She leaned over and kissed his cheek.

As thoughts of their experience in Bezu stirred, the air in *le petite librairie* grew somber. Henri shifted in his seat, just enough to inspire Mady to voice her suspicions. "What do you know, Henri?"

He scowled at her with false irritation. She responded with a blinding smile. He laughed. "You are too astute, madam."

Undeterred, she motioned for him to continue.

Pressed, he stalled. "I am not yet at liberty to reveal—"

She reached for him like she was going to peel off an ear and he cringed, holding his hands up in terror. Carter pulled her back. "Come on, now, give him a break."

Solomon laughed at their antics. "Relax, *cherie*, he will tell us when he has something to tell. I believe he is doing research. Now about your recent, ah, abrupt nuptials. Since you have failed to provide a party for me to attend with a fabulous gift, I must suffice with an elaborate, hmm … let's say, honeymoon trip. Please, pick a destination of your choice, on me."

"South of France," Mady said instantly.

Carter and Solomon reared back in unison to look at her with surprise.

"Had that on the tip of your tongue, did you?" Solomon stated.

Carter peered at her in silent questioning until he dropped his surprise and nodded with vigor. "You're right. Why not?"

The energy field around them pulsed.

Carter turned to Solomon. "Yes, we'd like the south

of France," he agreed. "I hear it's beautiful this time of year." The cliché rang out as false as a cracked bell. Mady snickered and looked away, on the verge of laughter.

Solomon gave them a long look. "This wouldn't have anything to do with Peterson, would it?"

"Oh, certainly not," Mady chirped a little too quickly.

"No," Carter said. He shook his head, and pulled a long, lemon-lipped face.

Seeing him, Mady gave in to her laughter. "Oohoo, darling, don't ever play poker," she chuckled at Carter. She tucked his hand in her lap.

Solomon fostered a dry, indulgent look that explained how thinly he was fooled. "How about next week? Does that suit you?"

"Wonderful," Mady exclaimed.

Solomon walked to a Louis XIV desk, rummaged through the papers on top and retrieved a passport. He handed it to Mady. "He gave me this and his wallet when we were at the train station. The wallet I gave to Hanlon. Perhaps this should go with you … on your honeymoon." He smoothly added, "Should anyone of interest happen to turn up."

"Of course," Mady answered.

"Have you heard from Hanlon?" Carter asked.

"No," Solomon replied.

The room swelled with silence after the brief answer.

"Poor Fischer," Mady began. "He—"

Carter finished her sentence, shaking his head with compassion. "He didn't understand the depth of his inherent conflicts."

Mady smiled at his calm ability to comment on the gulf between perception and reality, possibilities and choices. She said, "If Peterson does come back, do you think Hanlon will continue to pursue him for the Illuminati?"

"Ohhumph," Henri blurted. He sat back and crossed his arms, comment completed.

Mady shot a sideways glance at Henri and thought his outburst meant, "Cats don't change their spots."

She offered, "Peterson touched Hanlon and gave him something. He said Hanlon would find a way to show the Illuminati. I wonder what that was all about?"

Solomon cleared his throat. "I have moved the Divinity research to a private company. No more university exposure for the ancients' protocols." He spread his right hand wide and gazed at his palm.

Mady, too, felt her hand tingle and glanced at her husband.

Carter splayed out his fingers, a soft smile lighting his face. "This power, ultimately, is the end of the Illuminati. While I am curious about Hanlon and how he faces what Peterson showed him, I am more excited to learn what we can do—with this."

He bowed his head and closed his eyes. His long fingers closed and he placed his fist across his heart. He seemed to settle into himself, and softly whispered, "Mady."

His voice was so low Mady barely heard him. When she realized he spoke her name with such deep reverence and love, a sense of warmth spread across her shoulders. She watched a sphere of the heart wave energy emerge from Carter and wrap around them. Internally, the wave rang sweet as an orgasm. Externally, a sheen of light erupted around Carter.

Mady could not see the source for this light. Did her husband actually create the light, or was the light attracted to him—entangled?

Solomon coughed and cleared his throat.

Carter opened his eyes. He smiled like he had a secret of incomparable value, like he had touched a power beyond belief, like he was invincible.

Mady felt the power surge from him, saw the wave of energy ripple out to touch Henri and Solomon, and circle back around. Solomon and Henri spread their hands and gazed at their palms. A quick look between them broadcast the message, "We, too, feel the power, the connection."

"Yes," Henri said in confirmation. "This energy is amazing. But I wouldn't do that in public if I were you."

"Exactly," Solomon said. He slipped his hand into his pant pocket, tucking it safely away. "Lest you find yourself a person of interest to the Illuminati, or worse."

•

Hanlon's Office

Hanlon sat at his desk with Peterson's wallet in his hand.

On that night when Hanlon coaxed Fischer from the bosom of Bezu with the help of Solomon and friends, Solomon approached Hanlon afterward with the wallet. "He asked me to give this to you."

Hanlon accepted the wallet. "What do I do with this?"

"He said you would figure out something."

And so Hanlon did figure out what to do.

A humming little tune he couldn't place had filled his head since he returned from France, and he pressed his right palm to his ear for a moment. The hum skipped from his ear to tickle his palm so he jerked his hand away. He rubbed his palm against his leg not daring to think about what was happening with his hand.

He turned to his laptop and opened two files in a split screen. On one side was Fischer, M. A. On the other side was Peterson, E. J. He switched the names in the two files.

Fischer was now Peterson.

And Peterson was Fischer, now deceased, his body unrecoverable.

Hanlon smiled and rubbed his palm. At first he thought this persistent physical sensation was an artifact of the power of the Hall of Records. But when he realized this sensation came from Solomon's research, he immediately purged all of his Cambridge files. He called the university to check, and was relieved to learn the research funding had dried up and all records were removed from the property.

Good, Hanlon thought. His superiors knew nothing of the research, and he had managed to hide Butler and the entire Egyptian incident completely. Since no one upstairs cared enough about Fischer to challenge Hanlon's tale, letting Fischer's strange demise slip into obscurity was easy. His superiors' interest quickly wandered on to other pressing matters. The case was closed and forgotten.

Hanlon put aside the laptop and brought out a file from a locked drawer. Inside was a photograph of Fischer taken the day Hanlon admitted him to an exclusive, full-service sanitarium in the quiet hills of southern France. Surrounded by vineyards and wrapped in the clean mountain air, the hospital met Fischer's—or rather, Peterson's—needs with absolute dedication.

The idea to switch them came to Hanlon when he realized Fischer and Peterson were the same height and similar build—if one didn't look too closely. With Fischer's eye and hair color gone and the fingerprints ruined, possession of the wallet in Peterson's name was all Hanlon needed to admit Fischer to the sanitarium … as Peterson.

The specter of Fischer rode heavily on Hanlon's conscience. He personally paid the bill for the sanitarium and struggled with his guilt over Fischer's condition, just as he struggled with the random flashes and visions that bubbled daily through his consciousness.

These visions were alarming and intense, filling him with information and haunting recognition that seemed to ignite some sort of awareness … inciting a familiarity that was equally as disturbing.

What did Peterson do to me?

There had been no communication from Solomon since Bezu. What had Solomon and Henri been exposed to during their time with Peterson? Had they all been touched, perhaps, like Madelyn Fox and Nicholas Carter?

Hanlon's thoughts had been filled with that scene of the woman who came back from the dead, and the man who performed the miracle. What were they experiencing in their daily lives? What did their newly expanded understanding encompass? What was happening to them?

And what about Peterson? Where did he go? Hanlon couldn't begin to comprehend what happened to Peterson—that he was out of this world rendered new meaning to the phrase.

The one thing Hanlon did know was that the Hall must be protected from the Illuminati. The immense treasure, the mysterious artifacts and the ancient records must not fall into the hands of his superiors. He paused as a shiver raced across his back and he looked around reflexively as though someone might read his thoughts.

No one must discover my secrets, or the path I have chosen.

He had managed during his long career to establish a neutral position between the two Illuminati factions. One arm of the Illuminati favored a ruthless means to planetary rule; the other urged a softer approach. Any change in Hanlon's attitude would attract attention.

I can't afford any scrutiny.

Daily, Hanlon had much to hide as a result of Peterson's electrifying touch. The latest manifestation was this itch that bordered on tickling in the palm of his hand.

But there was more.

He carefully touched the eye that had plagued him with debilitating spasms since he began his career with the Illuminati. Oddly, he had not suffered a single spasm since he made the decision to go to Bezu in search of Peterson, since the day he acknowledged his heart believed in miracles, since the day such a miracle was witnessed with his own eyes … since the day his heart acknowledged he wanted to be free.

That troubled eye was experiencing an unexplained state of peace, in spite of all he was hiding. It was ironic, for any other time, the eye would proclaim to the world his duplicity.

Was this healing in my eye from Peterson?

He squinted to imitate what he knew was his trademark. If his distinctive behavior pattern stopped suddenly, someone would want to know why, and he didn't want anyone's suspicions aroused. He pinched the eye like a stuttering shutter, and released it in perfect imitation of his affliction.

No one would know he was changed. He smiled.

The intercom buzzed. His new assistant, Lorraine, was in her late fifties and content with a life approaching retirement. He had handpicked her for Fischer's replacement, a replacement that would not ask too many questions. "Yes?" he answered.

"You have someone to see you, sir."

Hanlon reprimanded himself for hiring an animated, walking plug of tofu and lamented the loss of Fischer. This was closely followed by the image of Fischer's permanent, bland visage, and a wince of contrite shame. He coughed. "Who is it?"

"Mr. Amunson, sir."

Hanlon sat up, alarms on full.

Amunson, while not an Illuminati member, was nonetheless, very powerful. His family's expertise was in the ancient practices and esoteric knowledge of the past. His lineage extended as far back as Solomon St. Germain's. Amunson's presence in Hanlon's office was bizarre and unprecedented.

"Send him in," Hanlon said. He slipped the photo of Fischer in his pocket and dropped the rest of the file in a desk drawer. His office door opened and the immaculate Raffe Amunson entered.

Hanlon held his face in an open look, even though a wave of revulsion swept over him. Amunson was handsome and powerful, but he was too smooth, too quiet in the eye. The thought of what arcane knowledge Amunson's family harbored and practiced gave Hanlon the shivers. Raffe's cold, accessing manner reminded Hanlon of a rat's speculation of a buffet table.

"Come in, Raffe," Hanlon said. He stood and motioned with his right hand, dodging the moment for a handshake, guiding Amunson toward informal seating by the gas fireplace.

Amunson wore a black suit and dark blue tie, perfect with his sculpted, sharp, good looks. In the morning light he looked to be in his twenties, although Hanlon knew Amunson to be in his late forties.

"Thank you for making time for me without notice," Amunson said.

"What can I do for you?" Hanlon smiled, feigning congeniality until he knew more. "Without notice, as you put it?" he added.

Amunson took the seat with the window at his back, putting his face in shadow. Hanlon countered by pulling his chair at an angle, causing Amunson to have to turn, casting half his face in the glow from the fireplace.

"I was hoping you could clarify something for me," Amunson said.

Hanlon straightened his jacket cuffs with a subtle, precise snap. "And what would that be?"

Raffe leaned forward, his face looking like a Mardi Gras mask. One half of his visage was lighted, clearly human, the other half dark and … not so human. "Can you explain to me how a satellite valued at two-hundred million Euros was destroyed?"

Hanlon was shocked.

How did Amunson know about the satellite?

Knowing better than to waste time claiming ignorance, he replied smoothly. "No, I cannot tell you exactly what destroyed the satellite. We believe a device of unknown origin was employed, and that device was subsequently destroyed along with the satellite."

He gazed at Amunson with a calm face, controlling his breath, thankful his tick was silent. He could feel Amunson's eyes on him, and Hanlon had the unsettling sensation that Amunson's one shadowed eye was drilling through him all the way to his marrow.

"There were witnesses—" Amunson said.

More shock. This continuing revelation of information that Amunson shouldn't know caused the breath to stop mid-track in Hanlon's throat.

He knows more, Hanlon thought, *than I gave my superiors.* He managed his breath in an easy exhale to control his rising heartbeat.

"A man and woman," Amunson finished. "What about this couple? What is their involvement?"

Hanlon fought the urge to gulp. Without knowing how Amunson had such information, anything Hanlon said from here on could be fatal. He felt time stop and marked the moment in his mind, for his next lie, he knew, was the beginning of the end for all he had concealed since Cambridge.

"Those two were insignificant," he said. Unfazed and fully committed, he gazed at Amunson long enough to show his sincerity, his timing carefully calculated.

"Sounds sanitized," Amunson stated bluntly.

With a snort of disgust, Hanlon thought, *and so the party is over.* It was time Amunson understood he had reached the end of his complimentary call. Hanlon couldn't afford any more conversation that could leave him exposed. He squinted and shuttered his eye in imitation of the tick, emphasizing his words. "The report on this incident does leave us with a mystery, but that is Illuminati business."

Ignoring the rebuff, Amunson probed. "And what of the man, Peterson?"

Hanlon smiled to cover the need to grind his teeth. In the face of this ongoing challenge on information he couldn't deny, he would have to deviate from the story he gave his superiors.

"Peterson is not your concern," Hanlon said. He worked his eye furiously and sat rigid in his chair, glaring at Amunson with sincere animosity.

Unphased by Hanlon's display of agitation, Amunson continued. "Oh, I disagree … where is Peterson?"

Hanlon knew he tread dangerous ground. He reached into his pocket and fingered the photo of Fischer/Peterson. Reluctant, he continued. "As you well know," he said, "there are some mysteries best left alone." He calmed his eye to give Amunson a hard look before placing the disturbing photo on the table between them.

Amunson's eyes narrowed and a faint whistle flowed from his inhalation. He picked up the photo and examined it. "This is Peterson?"

"He's in private care," Hanlon answered, gliding over the white lie of identification. He left the unstated details of Peterson's whereabouts obvious.

Amunson peered at Hanlon over the photograph. The look was long and full of assessment. "Tell me, what is Solomon's involvement in this?" he asked. Wanting his statement to appear as a trump card, Amunson's lips formed a smooth smile that did not reach his eyes.

But here, Hanlon knew Amunson was fishing—if he

knew anything about Solomon, he wouldn't have to ask Hanlon. And Raffe certainly couldn't ask Solomon personally, for he and Solomon held vastly opposing views.

He reached for the photograph, forcing Amunson to return it. "All leads in this matter," he evaded, "have been satisfactorily investigated, nullified, or terminated. The case is closed." Feeling brave, he added, "If you have questions for Solomon, you must ask him yourself."

Hanlon settled the photograph into his pocket with Amunson's eyes following his every move. For a wild second, Hanlon thought Amunson was going to demand the photo again. Hanlon stood, cutting off his opportunity.

Amunson rose. Before he spoke, his eyes showed his discontent as he declared, "Well, thank you, John, for all your cooperation." In further contradiction to his words, he extended his hand.

Pressing flesh with Amunson was the last thing Hanlon wanted to do, but he couldn't find a way out of it. His right palm rippled with sensation and he dreaded the moment of contact, wondering if Amunson would detect anything. With that thought, the sensation in his palm blinked out just before their hands met.

For a moment Amunson held onto Hanlon a little too tight, peering too closely with eyes too cold. "I have a … special interest in these events, John. Please, will you call me should anything new turn up?" He deepened the handshake, bringing his other hand to Hanlon's forearm.

Showing Amunson how to lie professionally, Hanlon returned the gesture, placing his free hand on Amunson's shoulder. "Of course," he said.

Amunson's face reflected a deep level of distrust,

and yet he nodded and left.

Gratefully, the door closed and Hanlon was alone.

Bitterness soiled his tongue. He walked over to his desk and sank into his chair. The battle line had been drawn. Amunson would not let his interest in this die, because he had the drop on Hanlon. And he knew it.

As soon as Amunson left, the tingle had returned to Hanlon's right hand. He swiveled in his chair, seeking solace and answers in the busy city scene outside his window. His palm demanded attention, and he massaged gently, gazing out the window.

Abruptly, one of Peterson's cursed visions rippled through his mind, the force of the image sending a shudder all the way to his bones.

He closed his hand and rested the fist on his heart.

How long before Raffe discovers my lies?

"So," he sighed, little more than a whisper. "It will be a race to the end."

CHAPTER NINE

Outside Brussels, Belgium

"Hanlon's definitely hiding something," Raffe Amunson said.

He scooped up the black Sturgeon caviar and downed the expensive treat with practiced ease. "And although he tried to cover, he was disturbed about how much I knew. I believe he hides far more than he tells.

"Details were scarce about the destroyed satellite. He mentioned an unknown device that was subsequently destroyed, but I think he's lying. I'd like to find this man named Peterson." Raffe paused to watch his uncle, needing his support.

The old man picked up a spoon and carefully ladled a precise amount of caviar onto his crostini. The old fingers were still straight and firm, unmarred by their long sojourn in this lifetime.

The perfectly loaded tidbit was consumed and savored with elegance before Raffe's uncle deigned to speak. Raffe relaxed. Time meant nothing to the Amunsons, especially when it came to the accumulation of power.

"You were right to pursue this," Uncle finally answered. "The power to destroy such a satellite is considerable and must be investigated, particularly now.

"Like you, I, too, believe the moment of the next power transition is upon us. The great constellations are aligning themselves, placing the wheels of power in motion. For this monumental transition, the miscalculations made in Egypt at the time of Aten cannot happen again."

Much had been stolen from the Amun-ra Brotherhood during the time of Akhenaten, and placed out of their reach into the Hall of Records: vast wealth, knowledge and technology, even their ancient machines from their time in Atlantis. Raffe nodded with the ancient memory—but he could feel there was something his uncle was not telling.

"A battle of Armageddon is most certainly coming," Uncle said. "Because of our power losses in the last transition, we cannot afford to lose again. For us, there are no options this time. We must take back that which has been slipping from us for several millennia. If there is a power, you must locate the source. Use the Illuminati as you will. We have no allegiance to them."

Uncle dabbed his napkin to his lips, signaling their appointment was over. Raffe gave a subtle nod of understanding and stood. "What about Solomon St. Germain?"

The old man froze and his eyes clouded with something Raffe shockingly recognized as fear. Amazingly, the old man said, "St. Germain holds all the cards at this time. I would not engage him."

Raffe watched his uncle look cautiously side-to-side, the action absurd considering the high-tech equipment that protected their every word. That his uncle should make such a gesture stunned Raffe. He stifled the compulsion to look over his shoulder.

Uncle continued in a whisper. "Maelstrom's network and hold over the Illuminati has disintegrated; it seems someone finally skinned that old cat. That makes one less player on the field—now is our chance.

"Solomon was, and is, your nemesis, Raffe," Uncle stated. He grabbed Raffe's wrist with the strength of a young athlete, not a man over one hundred and fifty.

"Investigate this power, pursue what you want, but steer clear of Solomon St. Germain. You are the last pure blood male from the line of Amun-ra. We cannot lose you!"

Raffe peeled Uncle's fingers from his wrist. The words, "You are the last pure blood—" were a laughless joke. He was immortal—almost. But he was sterile. He gave a silent curse at the futility of it. Nothing in modern technology could reverse the facts.

But the ancient technology could.

His expression must have displayed his thoughts, for Uncle said, "You cannot access the Hall—"

"A way to save us exists," Raffe countered.

His uncle scoffed aloud, the sound thin and brittle. "And that knowledge is secreted away where no one can enter—"

"Save the marked one, the Eschaton. You believe the time of transition is upon us, which means the Eschaton could be here now. Let me find him—without the ancient technology, our bloodline will inevitably pass and it won't matter what happens in the coming transition. We need the Eschaton!"

Uncle sat back. Raffe watched the old man evaluate

options he apparently had not considered. "The Eschaton will be very powerful," Uncle mused at last.

"Yes, and we have something he needs."

"Something he can take from us—" Uncle objected.

"Until he figures that out, we have a chance."

Uncle nodded with a slow concession. The suggested scenario gradually gathered strength as he realized this measure of last resort was exactly that—their only chance.

"Yes, we want the Eschaton. Find the one marked with the winged anchor."

•

Southern France, the Languedoc Coast

Madelyn Fox Carter settled back into the beach chair and adjusted her wide brimmed hat. From their well-chosen position, she and Carter could see the length of the beach, the bar, a restaurant, and the bathrooms. If Peterson were here, they would see him.

"Madam, you have that look on your face."

Mady laughed and extended her bare right foot to stroke her husband's tanned, muscular calf. "What look is that?"

"The look of a woman on a mission," Carter answered. "I've come to know the expression well." He reached out to twine his fingers with those of her left hand. "You realize this plan has a one-in-a-million chance."

At Carter's touch, Mady felt the tickling hum in her hand flare. The sensation raced through her heart and sang into her bones. A field of heart wave energy blossomed around them, rippling out in waves of distortion before settling into invisibility.

She lifted the brim of her hat to gaze at the people near by. No one had noticed.

I love you, came her husband's thought clearly into her mind. *And we'll find him, don't worry.*

Mady squeezed Carter's fingers. This mental aspect of their new paradigm—communicating with thoughts—made a giddy sensation swoop through her belly. "Everything about Peterson seems so … unfinished. I don't believe he's completed his task," she said. "There has to be more. Since we're entangled with Peterson until his destiny is fulfilled, I'm certain we will find him if we follow the power."

Carter sat up, opened the sun block and liberally spread the coconut-scented lotion down Mady's long legs. "We've been to Saintes Maries-de-la-Mar, Sete, Agde, and every small coastal village in between. Tomorrow we go inland to Beziers—"

Mady stretched like a contented cat under the ministrations of her husband's strong hands. "Before we leave for Beziers, I want to go down the coast a ways. There's a small town—"

Carter chuckled. "You'll leave no stone unturned."

"Exactly."

He stopped with the lotion and scooted in next to her, squeezing into the lounge chair. He bent down and lifted the brim of her floppy hat and whispered, nibbling lightly at her ear. "Speaking of stones—"

•

Outside Brussels, the Amun-ra Vault

Raffe descended the two hundred steps down to access the famed vault of the Amun-ra Brotherhood. Flame torches had long ago been replaced with LED lights, but the smell of smoke permeated the rock walls.

The stairs were roughly cut, many centuries old, so he stepped carefully, avoiding the over worn and slick center of the steps.

He went deeper and deeper, into what many would call the border of hell. But the Brotherhood called this unique vault sanctuary, for it held the memories of times past and glory lost.

At the bottom of the stairs was a cavern over seventy-five feet wide and one hundred feet deep. The walls were covered with mysterious symbols and writing from the ancient, lost technology. In the middle of the room were clustered dozens of bookshelves overflowing with books, scrolls, and loose sheets.

Raffe picked up an LED lantern sitting by the entrance and went to the book stacks. Here was all that remained of the lore of the Amun-ra Brotherhood, from before their time in Atlantis, through the travails of Aten and on to Nefertiti's curse.

The Brotherhood maintained three copies of every document, dispersed through private libraries around the world to prevent any further loss of knowledge. What existed in this vault were the original pieces, available to only a handful. As the last pure blood male of the Amun-ra, Raffe was allowed full access.

Many of the ancient documents were of a material unknown to modern man, supple yet indestructible. He walked among the stacks, his blood flaming with the desire to reclaim what the Brotherhood had lost. He wanted once again the power to move mountains, the ability to venture into alternate dimensions, the knowledge to manipulate the hermetic code.

All this they had known and lost.

"Nefertiti, you dog," he cursed. He went to the Egyptian era and located the documents of Akhenaten, the pharaoh who had laid low the Amun-ra.

He scanned the titles, reading the ancient language. His family's unique DNA gave Raffe two traits: an inherent knowledge of the ancient languages, and a greatly extended lifespan. Such genetic alteration was a lingering reminder of what the Amun-ra once could do, a reminder of who they were, a damning testimony to what they had lost.

"I will see that glory return," he said vehemently. "Or die trying."

Time was a tool of the Amun-ra, or at least had been in the ancient days. Raffe let his mind disconnect from the earth dimension of time and wander through the ancient words, immersing himself in the wildness of that long-ago day, absorbing the emotions of the people—hearing their thoughts, knowing their fears.

Such memories were painful for the Amun-ra, for the days of Nefertiti and Akhenaten were a time of betrayal and defeat. Nefertiti's power and beauty had held sway over King Tut, even after he changed his name from Tutankhaten to Tutankhamun. While he may have taken the Amun name, a love remained in the young boy's heart for the great Nefertiti and his father, Akhenaten.

"What power she held," Raffe whispered. Drawing energy from the ancient documents, his hands fed him the life of Egypt at that tumultuous time.

All of the events—the Hall created by Nefertiti, King Tut's betrayal of the Amun-ra priesthood, the theft of their wealth—all came pouring into him as he experienced it.

He cried out in pain.

The shame and anger, the horror of falling from grace rushed through him, until the end of power came and there was no longer a place for the Amun-ra as rulers.

Sweat formed on Raffe's face and scalp, running from his temples. This moisture he wiped clear. The tears he let flow unhindered.

Many great pools of arcane knowledge and power have been collected since the beginning of time. Besides the Amun-ra were the Sumerians, the Phoenicians and the Greeks. Even the Celtics knew a science modern man had yet to discover. More ancient science and technology had been lost than saved over the eons.

Raffe moved on to another book.

"The Wheel of Transitions," he read. Here was a ponderous tome, one of the most ancient of all, a treatise on the lost science of time and dimensions.

Raffe took the book to a table and sat. He ran his hands over the worn cover, absorbing instructions on how to open the knowledge. Images and sensations traveled up his arms and into his mind, images of a world gone by, a world of elements existing long before man appeared on the scene.

"Wind, water, fire, earth, time," he intoned.

The words were a simple introduction, a calling of the elements spoken in a language from the past. His voice commanded notes and tones most humans couldn't even hear. Within the vault, a dimension shifted. At Raffe's wrist, the second hand of his Rolex stopped mid-beat.

He opened the book.

Across the pages were mathematical equations in a language no man knew outside the Amun-ra. Raffe ran his fingers across the scribbled pages and down the long columns, absorbing the science. He threw his head back, soaring with the electric tingle of information and comprehension sent sizzling through his neurons.

Next came the astrologic charts, star maps from long before man's presence on earth. He flipped through the pages, drawing his fingers lightly across each page until he absorbed all.

The sweat now soaked his head and ran down his back. His fingers trembled, as they had touched massive amounts of energy. His head rang with the sound of a thousand doors thrown open.

Barely was he able to push the book away before he slumped in his seat. His sweat ran and formed puddles on the floor while he absorbed what he could of the complex science. At last, the heat from concentration coming off his body began to cool down. His hair dried, the intense humming in his head grew distant.

He lifted his head and let his breath whistle through his teeth with a hiss.

Even Uncle didn't fully understand the implications of this coming change. The next power transition would be the final one; it was the end game in the battle between light and dark for the planet and humanity.

Which meant his suspicion about the Eschaton was most likely accurate. But who was this person?

Who bore the mark of the winged anchor?

•

Southern France

"He's a strange one, all right," Ramon whispered.

"*Oui*," Celine answered. "But he is harmless." She had worked at La Paillotte Bambou long enough to see a lot stranger. She wiped the table and passed a surreptitious glance at the man sitting alone in the shade. "There is something so sad about him."

"How old do you think he is?" Ramon asked. "He won't look up long enough to get a good look at him. As long as he's been here, he still gives me the creeps," he protested. He dumped the bucket of ice into the bartender well and peered at the man in question. "And, in the last ten days he has yet to leave a tip."

"He runs a tab—" Celine defended.

"I always get screwed on a tab," Ramon complained.

The elderly man looked up at them, as if able to hear them. Celine scolded Ramon. "Hush your talk. He has heard you."

"Aiiyee," Ramon hissed. "He is the devil himself. There is no way the old coot could hear—"

"Don't look at him," Celine cautioned.

Contradicting her own words, she peered aslant at their mysterious guest as he attempted to rise. Movement was obviously difficult for him; he leaned heavily on his walking stick.

Celine left Ramon and went to assist. "*Monsieur*, let me help you," she said. She extended her forearm for him to grasp as he slowly took a step.

"Good afternoon," he said, almost breathless from his exertions.

They walked slowly, side by side. After a few steps,

he paused and looked at her. She had the briefest moment to see the clear gray of his eyes, eyes that seemed to have witnessed things they would rather not have seen. Those eyes were somehow lost.

"Do you—" he started, then faltered. "Do you know—"

"No, *Monsieur*—" she answered, knowing what he would ask, for he had asked this same question each day.

"—anything about me?" he finished.

"I'm afraid I don't."

Celine's heart went out to him. He asked her this every day as though he didn't remember asking her the day prior. She wasn't sure what bothered her more, that he didn't know who he was, or that he didn't remember discussing this with her each day.

His step faltered on the uneven brick path and he stumbled. Celine reached to grab him as he went down, but all she got was his shirt. Her grasp caused the sleeve to ride up his arm, revealing a curious mark. Celine stared at the mark. When she glanced away, she met his grey eyes.

"I don't remember—" he said.

"It's okay," she encouraged. "You'll remember—just give yourself time."

•

Brussels, the Amun-ra Vault

Time, Raffe thought, *had always been their ally, but that was when they ruled the dimensions.*

"How do I use time for my purposes without the old

power to control the dimension?" he mused aloud. He stared about the vast repository of knowledge, feeling his quest hopeless.

"There must be a tool, a technique, a loophole ... something left from before the last great change I can use."

Was time even the answer?

"Or is knowledge the key?" he challenged.

He returned the Wheel of Transitions to its place and looked for a different text. If power wasn't going to be his strong suite, then cunning would have to rule the day. He must be careful—very careful, to out maneuver his prey.

Especially one as powerful as the Eschaton.

The Eschaton would be a dimensional being, born of this earth, grounded in this dimension, but genetically engineered to access energy and dimensions for the purpose of ... anything he desired. He would be the ultimate power source, capable of opening doors humanity didn't dare dream existed.

Raffe closed his eyes and clenched his fists to keep from screaming his rage. The sense of being cheated riffled through him, stirring a nuclear tide of anger. He slammed his fist onto the wood table, causing a crack to split down the middle of one board. Energy trapped in the wood rattled through the table legs, beating against the stone floor.

He opened his hand, releasing the energy.

Control returned slowly.

Raffe's breath rasped through his lips and his hand throbbed. He rubbed his sore flesh that had pounded the table and felt the tissues already healing the impact bruise in a wash of blood cells and enzymes.

This genetic trait of instant healing came from a thousand generations past. Healing was so effective and constant it was erasing the signs of time from his body. He would survive and recover from all but the most catastrophic injuries.

Knowledge is what I need, or catastrophe is what will come.

"The Eschaton will be in the prophecy," Raffe said with certainty. He went to a desk and peered into a cubbyhole, finding a leather-bound text in the back. He retrieved the slim volume and read the title, translating the ancient language.

"On the Last Day."

The pages were filled with tiny handwritten scribbles so small Raffe couldn't read them. He laid his hands on the pages and let his chin drop forward while the information streamed into his mind.

Pictures ran through him like a rapier, so real he felt he was bleeding out onto the cold stone floor. He writhed with pain, but held the volume tight, riding the tsunami of visions.

Images ripped along like an out of control roller coaster. But one picture froze in his mind's eye.

He shrank back from the horror with a shudder, his heart crying in a primeval scream, "No!"

The picture dissolved and Raffe collapsed forward, crashing to the floor. Before darkness swamped his mind, his last thought reverberated.

The Eschaton. I will find you—I must stop you!

•

The London Museum

Raffe settled into the seat across from the museum Director. "Sir John, thank you for seeing me on such short notice."

"What can I do for you?" Sir John asked.

Raffe pulled out an enlarged photocopy of a sketch he made from the last page of the book, *On the Last Day.* "Can you tell me about this symbol?"

Sir John took the photocopy and peered over the top of his spectacles. "Ah," he said. "Kheti's jasper. An intriguing piece, made all the more so by your inquiry today. What would you like to know?"

Raffe frowned at Sir John's words, confused. "So you're familiar with this image?"

"Oh, most certainly, and I'm not the only one. I was just showing this piece about two weeks ago. This is from the Tut collection."

Nefertiti, Raffe thought, *for once, your conniving manipulations have backfired.* "Yes, from Tut. So you have the jasper here?"

"Would you like to see it?" Sir John asked.

Raffe knew the jasper's secrets were meant only for the Eschaton. "No, but I am interested in who else has been here inquiring."

"Nick Carter came asking about the jasper with a group," Sir John said.

Raffe recognized Carter as one of the names from the couple Hanlon claimed was insignificant. Were they insignificant to the Illuminati, or was this the lie Raffe had heard in Hanlon's voice as he misdirected Raffe. "Can you tell me who was with Carter?"

"Mady Fox, an anthropologist. Of course her family is quite prominent," Sir John said.

Raffe nodded. She was the other half of the insignificant couple. "Who else?"

"Two gentlemen, one quite wealthy from his appearance, and handsome in a dark, commanding way. Rather reminded me of the old Aegean kings. The other man was not introduced."

Raffe's heart picked up pace. The first description sounded like St. Germain, the one person he was warned to avoid. But the unknown man could be the Eschaton. He needed this man's name, his face. He should ask for security tapes from the museum and see whom—

"Mr. Amunson, I venture to guess you haven't seen this, have you?" Sir John said.

Raffe bolted from his wild thoughts with a snap. He wondered if Sir John had read his mind and had the tape on file, ready to view—

Sir John held up a tabloid paper.

Raffe's jaw dropped, for his brain refused to process what his eyes saw. "A crop circle?" he asked. He took the folded paper. On the front page was a photo of a crop circle in the shape of a winged anchor.

"They went there," Sir John said.

Raffe struggled to catch up. "Who went there? Are you saying Carter made this circle?"

Sir John smiled, obviously enjoying his little game. "Well, I rather doubt that. However, after viewing the jasper, the one man asked about Liddington Castle, and I believe they went there straight away."

Raffe shook his head, the information finding no roots. "What does this have to do with—" He paused and looked at the caption under the crop circle photo. "In the shadow of Liddington Castle—" he read.

If they saw the jasper and went to Liddington, and now the circle appears, this could be a manifestation of energy. Likely left behind after the event that took out the satellite. Which meant—

The man with Carter and Solomon could be the Eschaton.

"May I see your security tapes from that day?" Raffe asked. He grasped the tabloid paper in a death grip, making the fanned corners flutter.

Sir John's smile faded. "I'm sorry, but the tapes are recycled. We have nothing for you to see, I'm afraid."

Raffe refused to feel any disappointment. He knew he was close. He would find this man, the Eschaton, if it were the last thing he did. He rose with tabloid in hand.

"Liddington Castle. That's due west, right?" he asked, staring at the tabloid photo. He looked up from the paper, his pulse quickening. "May I keep this?"

•

Liddington Castle

Raffe stared at the newly green crop field, instantly feeling the emanations of power rippling like waves in a pond. Whatever had happened here had been powerful enough to literally shake the earth and the heavens. The GPS coordinates he had from the Ministry of Defense on the origin of power in the satellite event matched this location.

Even though Raffe was barren of any of the old powers, the memory in his DNA detected the remnants of this huge power release. Since all his inquiries at top level revealed that no government claimed this power event, he felt certain only the Eschaton could have done this.

The Eschaton was here.

"Can I help you?"

Raffe turned.

A man climbed out of a farm truck and approached. He wore faded denims and a shirt open at the throat, exposing a dark farmer's tan over his face and forearms. "I'd appreciate you not traipsing into the crop," he said. "Pringle's people have already been here and left. The photos are all over the place." He held a copy of the tabloid.

"Do you know what happened here?" Raffe asked.

"No more than is known about any crop circle. There were some folks from the Ministry out here with instruments, but that was a couple weeks ago. This appeared night before last."

Raffe had no desire to traipse through the man's crop. The power echo told him what he needed to know. He walked to his car.

Unwilling to let him go so easily, the man called out. "It's the damnedest thing, you know."

Raffe's ears picked up. "What's that?"

"I didn't plant this," the farmer said. He bent down and pulled up a plant that was eighteen inches high.

Chills flooded Raffe's scalp. His heart cried out for an answer that his mind already recognized—this answer would encompass Raffe's dream—and his nightmare.

The farmer insisted. "This crop came up by itself."

Raffe stopped and sucked air through his teeth.

Rapid generation.

This was one of the old powers, well-documented

in the Brotherhood vault, and once practiced by the Amun-ra priesthood. Once the seed was laid, the priests would come to the field and by that afternoon, the field would be green.

Raffe's certainty that he was on the trail of the Eschaton solidified. But he stopped short when the farmer's next words sent more chills skipping down his back.

"What I'm trying to say is, I never planted this crop in this field before," the farmer protested. This statement came laced with wonder at an unknown mystery. Incomprehension whistled through his steady brown eyes. He dropped the plant and rubbed his right hand against his pant leg.

"But I was going to."

CHAPTER TEN

Hanlon's Office

Raffe was short on patience with Hanlon after what he learned out in Liddington. He pushed his building anger aside and pressed as politely as he could.

"I'm curious, John, about the events we discussed last. It seems there are ... oddities ... about the satellite event that bother me." He watched Hanlon's answer carefully, for he knew how skilled the old man was at subterfuge.

"Well, the satellite was Illuminati, and we have closed the case," Hanlon replied. "What questions do you have otherwise that are relevant to the Illuminati and your family?"

The ball had been tossed neatly back into Raffe's lap. He did not feel like playing. "I believe events are unfolding that would mean the end of the Illuminati."

Hanlon leaned forward in his seat with interest. "And how are these events you speak of connected to the loss of an Illuminati satellite?"

The old man was smooth, Raffe noted, forcing Raffe to show his cards. Raffe might not want to play, but neither did he intend to be easy. "I believe the power that destroyed the satellite came from an individual."

There, Raffe thought, *clean that up if you can.*

Hanlon sat back, undisturbed. "No. This was not an individual. There was a device—"

Raffe noticed Hanlon move his right hand to his lap. Raffe turned an inner ear, sensing a faint resonance of energy—something of an unfamiliar vibration. He strained to get closer, but the power was gone.

Something was seriously out of place with Hanlon. Raffe wanted to knock him to the floor, to set aright whatever had gone awry with the old buzzard. "What if I told you a series of events is prophesied, heralding a change for all life on earth," Raffe offered.

Interest sparked in the corners of Hanlon's eyes.

Raffe went on. "I speak of a change that will not serve either my family or the Illuminati—a nightmare, the utter destruction of all we have worked to achieve. Imagine a world free of fear and oppression, a world alive with an empowerment humanity has never experienced."

He paused to measure his words, and leaned forward to deliver them with deadly intent. "I have seen this catastrophe. It will come on the heels of a special individual, a man of incredible power, a man who will take from both of us all that we have conspired to build. He will be our nightmare."

Hanlon's eyes bulged.

Raffe rushed to deliver the coup de grâce. "Should this individual manage to succeed, our old model of manipulation through crisis and chaos will cease to be effective. We will no longer be able to control society, John."

He dropped his voice, preparing to speak blasphemy. "Man will rule himself."

Hanlon's face took on a shocked look and he rocked back in his seat. He sat stunned for long moments, then gasped.

Raffe smiled.

Good. I have set Hanlon's priorities back in place.

•

Southern France, the Languedoc Coast

Carter turned to his wife, feeling her anxiety rattle his molecules with a ragged vibration.

"We're running out of time," Mady said. "I thought the power would draw us to him by now."

They sat in the shade of a huge umbrella. Behind them was a small fishing village, the perfect prey of tourists who preferred to travel off the beaten path. The strip of beach was graced with small white plastered bungalows, and the glittering sea was blinding on a cloudless day.

Carter stroked Mady's shoulders, watching the goose bumps flash down her arms. "What if we canvass?" he suggested.

"I do have his passport," she replied half-heartedly.

Carter gazed past her shoulders. At the small beachside bar, the bartender and a pretty girl sat talking. "And there's his mark," he ventured. "We could ask if anyone has seen—"

His words faded as he watched the two by the bar. The young woman was staring at a newspaper front page with an intensity that drew Carter's attention. His palm began to sizzle and tingle.

Mady gave him a tweak in the ribs. "Come on now, let's keep a focus—" She stopped suddenly and rubbed her hand on her thigh, whipping her head around. "My hand—I felt that. What? Do you see him?"

"Look," Carter said. "Over there, at the bar."

His hand was alive and the hum fired up in his head; his heart sang with the vibration, drawing him to his feet. He had to see—

The newspaper. I must see the newspaper.

He grabbed Mady's hand. "Let's go."

They walked to the bar and sat on the high stools. Mady was looking at everyone within twenty feet. Carter had eyes only for the paper.

The bartender smiled. "What would you—

"May I?" Carter asked.

The waitress looked up, startled. "*Oui, Monsieur?*" When she realized Carter wanted the paper, she passed it to him.

Carter took the paper and unfolded the front page, poking Mady in the ribs. "Look."

She turned around. The moment she saw the photograph, she blurted, "Good Lord!"

At Mady's exclamation, the waitress said, "It is very strange, *non*?"

Mady clapped her mouth shut.

Carter laughed. Rare was the moment his wife had nothing to say. "Why do you think this is strange?" he asked. "Do you know this symbol?" He saw the girl's hesitation, and added, "This is my wife, Mady, and I'm Nick."

"*Madam, Monsieur*, I am Celine and … this is Ramon," she said.

Ramon interjected. "Perhaps they can cover—"

"Hush," Celine spit. She turned to Mady with a hesitant smile. "I should not say anything—"

"Go ahead," Ramon prompted. "Maybe they know."

Celine silenced him with a sharp look. He shrugged and turned away, reaching for a glass to polish.

"We are looking for our friend—" Carter began.

"He has a mark—" Mady added.

Celine nodded. "It is here, *non*?" she asked. She pointed to her forearm.

Carter felt Mady's rise in excitement from the flood of energy she emanated. "Easy, now," he said. He grabbed her hand and the power flowed through them in one clean shot.

They asked in unison, "Who, Celine?"

"First, I must tell you, he is not well," Celine warned.

Mady and Carter reacted as one, standing.

"Please, you must show us," Carter said.

Celine nodded to a bundled figure out on the beach beneath an umbrella. Mady and Carter stepped from the bar. Celine stopped them. "You are his friends, *oui*?" she asked, protective. "You know who he is, where he is from?"

Carter passed Mady a troubled look at the girl's strange questions. "Yes," Mady answered quickly. "We've been looking for him. You say he is not well?"

The concern in Mady's voice seemed to set Celine at ease. "Your friend, he is very special." She passed the paper to Carter. "He has not seen this yet. Take it. Perhaps it will help."

Carter frowned, but took the paper. "Help with what?"

Celine shaded her eyes to stare out at the beach and

the solitary figure bundled in the sun. "You'll see."

•

Hanlon's Office

When Amunson said, "Man will rule himself," the power in Hanlon's hand exploded, sending a shot of energy up his arm to his heart, rocking him back in his seat.

A vision flew through his mind of this ultimate renaissance where humanity blossomed to its full creativity and potential expression. The vision was beautiful: a world of wonders like he saw in Bezu. He quivered, knowing something within his comprehension had burst free and realized—

What Raffe describes as a nightmare is the incredible vision Peterson gave me.

Hanlon would give his life to see such a vision fulfilled. He wanted to be a part of bringing this vision to fruition. He wanted to see this utopia of peace and enlightenment. His first reaction was to jump on the desktop and shout for joy.

They must never know how I feel.

"We can't have that, can we?" he responded, letting angst rattle his voice. He loosed a rampage of spasms across his right cheek, savaging his eye.

Raffe's smile faltered, but Hanlon rushed on. "What else do you know about this ... prophecy? We have to prevent this from happening!" Amunson nodded in agreement, but Hanlon knew he was holding something back.

"What can I do to help?" Hanlon said. "The Brotherhood and the Illuminati have co-existing goals and similar paths to the same end." He placed his right hand over his imitation eye tick. "Excuse me, as you can see, this topic disturbs me greatly. Please, continue—" He waved his free hand, encouraging Amunson to tell more.

"I refer to the legend of Elijah. The One who will return to this plane with many powers and a quest is Elijah, known as the Eschaton." Amunson leaned forward and drilled Hanlon with a cold, hard look. "The Eschaton's presence heralds the impending discovery of an ancient cache of knowledge—knowledge that will free mankind forever. He must be stopped."

At the mention of Elijah, Hanlon covered his reaction, buying time for his heart to slow down. He rubbed his face and willed the power in his hand to be quiet, sensing he tread upon very dangerous ground. "What connects this legend to our satellite?"

"Your satellite was killed by the Eschaton."

"And your proof?" Hanlon asked.

Amunson drew out a newspaper and placed it in front of Hanlon.

"Is this some sort of joke?" Hanlon protested. He allowed his eye to dance in agitation.

Amunson hissed. "The Eschaton bears this mark, the flying anchor. He was there, in this field, with your friends, the insignificant couple, Carter and Fox."

Hanlon wondered how Amunson had learned this, but now the lies Hanlon told in their last conversation had come around to bite him in the ass. He squinted and said, "I don't know who is this ... this Eschaton. And my information on the couple eliminated them."

He stopped. How far would Raffe push the subject? Hanlon saw Amunson was considering his next pursuit, and stopped him the only way he knew how. "Raffe, they are under Solomon's protection."

The look from Amunson was long and calculating, making Hanlon wonder if he had somehow fumbled with that last declaration. But Amunson seemed to file it away, and took another path. "The man in the photograph you showed me—Peterson. How did he come to be that way?"

Hanlon answered with a long-practiced look of absolute innocence. "The power that took out the satellite rendered him so."

Amunson sat back abruptly in his chair, his expression shuttered in a fashion that said Hanlon had finally screwed up.

What does Amunson know?

In a rapid shift, Amunson asked, "Have you ever seen this mark before?" He pushed the tabloid paper toward Hanlon.

"No," Hanlon answered. Surprising, the easy truth didn't seem to calm Amunson's ire. With curiosity, Hanlon probed. "What is the significance of this symbol?" Amunson's expression relaxed, warning Hanlon his lie had been revealed, and it was too late to change his story.

Raffe explained, his anger heating up, beginning to scale dangerous heights. "This is the mark of the Eschaton. The symbol's appearance in this field ... in conjunction with the energy blast that destroyed the satellite, is a marker indicating the Eschaton was there," Amunson spit.

He rose to stand over Hanlon from across the desk. "The power that destroyed the satellite would come through the Eschaton without harming him."

Placing his hands down on the desk, he dared to accuse Hanlon. "You lie about the man in the photograph."

Hanlon let his eye spasm go wild in a display of outrage. He stood slowly, as Amunson had, placing both hands down and leaning across the desk in as threatening a manner as he could muster. In a quiet tone that made most men question their mortality, Hanlon said, "You forget yourself."

Amunson snapped back. He continued to glare, but the accusation was gone from his eyes. Hanlon could see anger shooting out of Amunson's ears like a cartoon character.

With a show of considerable effort, Amunson said, "I see you do not take this threat I speak of seriously." He skewered Hanlon with a lengthy pause before declaring, "I wonder why?"

Amunson walked out without another word.

Hanlon stood rigid at his desk until Amunson was out of sight. When his office door was secure, he sagged and dropped into his chair. He dragged his hands across the sparse flesh of his face, scrubbing. At last he whispered in frustration.

"Eli J. Peterson, what are you? Where are you?"

After considering his options, Hanlon opened a drawer and drew out a throwaway cell phone with a temporary, unregistered number. From another drawer came a small Phillips screwdriver and tweezers. He removed the back plate from the cell phone and picked off the GPS chip.

He held the chip with the tweezers and torched it in an ashtray. The plastic curled at the edges with a flare and Hanlon swore he heard the chip cry. When it was a black, hardened glob, he put the phone back together, booted it, and dialed a number.

"Imperative we speak, your house, tomorrow, 8:00 PM."

He hung up in less than ten seconds, disassembled the phone and dropped it piece by piece into the chute going down to the basement incinerator.

•

Southern France

Mady approached the umbrellas with Carter close behind her. She knew something was wrong, but refused to let her imagination run wild. They came around to the front and she stopped in her tracks, causing Carter to bump into her.

Feeling her mouth sag open, she stared at the man beneath the umbrella.

Carter came to her side and gasped.

It's him, Mady thought.

Yes, came Carter's response in her mind—but hesitant.

While Mady could not reconcile what her eyes were telling her, the ecstatic tingle in her palm confirmed that this was Peterson. She knelt beside the covered figure. Carter stood at her back. "Hello ... " she said softly.

The covers stirred, releasing first a wizened hand, then a head sparsely covered with hair, followed by gray eyes in a heavily lined face. The man had to be at least ninety.

Mady watched as he slowly came to focus on her face. She smiled, for this was Peterson, she recognized his eyes. Also, the power was singing with joy, rocketing through her bones.

We found him!

She reached for Peterson's hand and felt the power twitter with excitement before they made contact. He accepted her hand with a weak grasp and looked from her to Carter, eyes slowly filling with tears.

On his lips, a tremulous smile fought for life. His voice was thin as he asked, "Do you know me?"

•

London

Raffe stormed from Hanlon's office building. His car and driver waited with the engine running in a No Parking zone.

"Damn you, Hanlon," he cursed.

Why was Hanlon lying? What did he know about the Eschaton? In the old days, Raffe would have had the power to open a portal to hell, or at least that dimension commonly referred to as hell, right beneath Hanlon's feet.

He needed to think. Unable to sit still, he walked.

The visions from the vault teased and tormented him, springing from his memory to dance across his mind's eye with horror. Disjointed facts charged him, attacking like dogs, spurring his thoughts.

"The Eschaton is here, I know it!" he ground out between rigid jaws. The double-edged irony of the Eschaton's arrival was not lost on him.

"The one individual who could save me, who could get me into the Hall to access the ancient knowledge, is here to destroy me."

Needing an outlet, he stopped to let the energy rise and overflow. The anger erupted in a flash, pouring out from his deep well of fear. "Aaaughhhh!" he roared.

He slowed his breath and opened his eyes.

He stood on the edge of a children's park. Among the carefully landscaped wonderland, a circle of mothers held their offspring close, lips trembling, staring at him with huge fearful eyes.

Raffe let his gaze drift past the crowd of frightened women and children. Even though he didn't have the Eschaton within his grasp at this moment, discovering he was here on this plane did create an option for Raffe.

"The Eschaton and I are destined to meet." He spoke the words, testing their threat level on his existence, for in truth, the threat was extreme.

The display of power Raffe had seen in the field in Liddington was testimony to what he faced. The contrast of his own limited powers up against what he saw told Raffe he better discover the Eschaton's weakness before that fateful meeting occurred.

A lone concern remained to nag Raffe's thoughts, insisting with a budding new terror.

The crop circle.

The Amun-ra priests could make a farmer's field spontaneously produce without seeding, regenerating the crop that was last harvested. But to have a field spontaneously generate an immaculate crop was astounding, beyond anything he knew.

What is the source of this power?

He abandoned his thoughts, bringing his attention back to the present. Mothers still held their children in the park. His car engine was running at the curb.

And somewhere, the Eschaton walked the earth.

I must go back to the vault.

Everyone had a weakness, and somewhere in that vast repository he would find a way to destroy the Eschaton.

He knew the Eschaton would have to come to him for the Key to the Babylon. At that point, Raffe must destroy the Eschaton. Otherwise, the Amun-ra's last resort would be to find a way to destroy the Key before the Eschaton came for it.

Raffe looked up at the children. With all his considerable malevolence striking from his eyes and mouth, he snarled, "Boo!"

The little girls squealed and their mothers cringed.

Raffe laughed. All was not lost … yet.

•

Southern France

Mady pulled her cell phone out while Carter helped Peterson rise and collect his belongings. She dialed Solomon's townhouse number. Henri answered. She cut him off before he could finish, "Halloo."

"Henri. We have him."

Silence was absolute, and brief, followed by a quick rush of relief. "That is so good to hear," Henri blurted.

Mady watched Carter help Peterson, who walked with a limp. She measured her words to Henri carefully. "He's changed."

"You must—" Henri said.

"We're on our way."

"Wait, here is Solomon."

Mady heard Henri spew a short explanation in French to Solomon. St. Germain's voice sounded strained. "*Cherie*, can you make it back to England tomorrow?"

"We'll try … he's … not quite himself."

"How? Is he—?"

Carter had Peterson ready. They moved one baby step at a time, with Peterson leaning heavily on a walking stick. While Peterson looked terribly frail, the power had responded with vigor, giving her hope he would respond in like fashion. They would help him find his memory somehow.

"Solomon, he has aged, and he has amnesia. He doesn't know anything about himself, or us, or—"

A silence stretched painfully before Solomon answered.

"Bring him tomorrow night, by eight if you can."

CHAPTER ELEVEN

Perpignan Airport, Southern France

Carter pushed Peterson's wheelchair through the busy airport while Mady ran in front of them, clearing a path.

Peterson sat quietly, his walking stick across his knees.

He had not said a word since yesterday, other than to ask several times, "Do you know me?" as though his memory of events evaporated immediately. Carter grimaced.

"We can fix him if we can just get him home," he mumbled with insistence.

"Here's the check-in," Mady called. She stepped up to the counter and laid their tickets down.

"*Bonjour*," the baggage counter attendant murmured without looking up. She accepted the first of their bags, then glanced at Peterson. "You can't take that on board," she said, pointing to Peterson's walking stick.

Mady looked up with a startled expression.

Peterson peered up at the woman behind the counter and tightened his grip on the stick.

Carter cleared his throat. "Ah, as you can see, our

friend is quite helpless—"

"Perhaps, but the stick isn't allowed. You can't take it on board. You'll have to pack it," she said. "Or leave it behind."

Carter leveled a measuring gaze from the one large suitcase he traveled with to Peterson's walking stick. The stick was not going to fit. He looked for a luggage shop to buy a new bag when his hand suddenly warmed and the tingling began.

What's happening? came Mady's quick thought. He saw her flutter the fingers of her right hand.

Carter knelt down to speak with Peterson. The aged hands maintained an insistent grip on the walking stick, proclaiming his opinion on the matter.

"May I pack it within my bag?" Carter asked softly.

Won't fit, Mady thought.

Watch, Carter returned.

Peterson cautiously let go of the stick, obviously not convinced. He followed Carter's movements carefully.

The walking stick was plain wood devoid of decoration or markings of any kind. At first contact, Carter was startled. A tingling surge of power flowed through his arm, down into his hand and into the stick, quickly followed by an image of him placing the stick into the bag and then zipping up that bag.

Carter didn't know if the event originated with him or with the stick. He gave the plain, smooth wood a quick glance of surprise and assessment before proceeding as "instructed."

He knelt and unzipped his bag under the highly skeptical and scrutinizing eye of the attendant and a security guard. Mady stood to the side, just in the edge of Carter's peripheral vision. Fear of manifesting a power event in front of all these people prevented him from looking full at her.

His hand was alive with sensation and his heart a beacon of desire; the stick and his suitcase were singing a sweet duet of common purpose so loud in his mind he glanced at the crowd to see who else could hear.

No one was aware. Except Mady, of course. In his side vision she glowed as if dusted in gold powder.

Peterson whispered, "It's okay," talking to the stick.

Carter eyed his suitcase, estimating it to be several inches short of accommodating the walking stick. *I don't know how this is going to happen,* he thought. He shot Mady a look aslant. She was a pyramid of glowing light.

Again he looked across the crowd. No one noticed her; they were all staring at him. He laid the stick corner to corner across the bag. He could not say how it happened, for he detected no change in the staff. But with utter surprise, the too long staff fit inside the bag.

Carter felt his heart wave radiate with a song of completion. He sensed the stick and the bag were both satisfied, and he closed the zipper without any sign of complaint from either.

A sigh rustled from the crowd. Carter rose and hefted the bag onto the scale.

The baggage attendant stared with lips tightly pursed. Carter thought she wanted to say something, but he imagined it would take a crowbar to pry those lips apart.

"Hmm," he murmured. "Must have been an optical illusion that it wouldn't fit. Well, it's all put away now. Happy?"

He glanced down at Peterson, who stared at the attendant with innocent eyes. Mady stepped up beside Carter, and he felt the energy release that came with her blinding smile.

The combined display was too much for the attendant. She glared at the security guard, waiting for him to make an assessment.

He shifted his weapon and eyed Peterson with speculation before studying the suitcase. Seeing no real identifiable threat of a terrorist, he grunted and walked off.

"How did you do that?" the woman asked, pointing with her pen. She glared at Carter, the bag, and Peterson until agitation bloomed around her like the stink of a carnivorous flower.

She stared fiercely, fluttering her pen back and forth, beating a *ratt-a-tatt-tatt* against the counter. Exasperation drove her fingers so fast, the pen flew from her grasp, shooting over the counter and landing in Peterson's lap.

Peterson passed the pen back to her. Their fingers touched in the hand-off.

Carter felt the power flare when Peterson picked up the pen. He glanced at Mady. She massaged her right palm and her smile radiated. They looked in unison at the attendant.

She was holding the pen in her right hand, frowning. She abruptly tossed the pen across the counter, but the pen seemed to roll of its own accord back toward her.

No one saw, save Carter and Mady.

The attendant's eyes bulged and she looked askance at the oddly behaving pen. She opened a drawer. The pen compliantly rolled off the counter and into the drawer. She slammed the drawer shut, ticketed Carter's bag, and stapled the receipts to his ticket without a word. She waved to the next person in line.

Carter grasped the wheelchair handles, and they moved out into the flow of travelers. "Sssss," Mady whistled her relief and moved back to her point position. "Don't look back, just keep walking."

They went about twenty feet when Peterson looked up at Carter. "Do you know where my walking stick is? I can't lose that, you know."

Carter gave Peterson's shoulder a squeeze. "Not to worry—your stick is safe."

Their next challenge was customs. All was well until the agent opened Peterson's passport. "When was this photo taken?"

He stared from Peterson to the passport, a dark look gathering.

Mady said, "He has dyskeratosis congenita. You know, premature aging."

"With sudden onset of symptoms and rapid deterioration," Carter added.

The agent ran his fingers over the passport, looking for a frayed edge or some evidence of tampering, but the passport was in pristine condition. He came out from his station to look at Peterson, searching for evidence of tampering in the old man. He bent down just inches from Peterson and held the passport next to his face.

Carter knew Peterson was incapable of guile. With nothing to remember, he had nothing to hide. As the agent got close to Peterson, Carter felt the power quicken. He held his breath.

When the agent was closest to Peterson, a tiny flicker of light jumped from Peterson's chest to the agent's hand holding the passport. The agent didn't notice. But he cocked his head to one side as if a conversation down the hall suddenly caught his interest.

Carter looked away to hide his grin.

The agent brought his attention back to Peterson. A look of disorientation clouded the agent's eyes and he shook his head like a wet puppy. With a goofy smile, he stamped Peterson's passport. "Come back to France, *Monsieur.*"

Carter nodded to Mady. She took the front again, and he pushed the wheelchair. Before they turned the corner exiting the customs area, Carter looked back at the agent.

He was rubbing his right palm with his left thumb.

•

St. Germain Townhouse

Mady followed Carter into the lift up to Solomon's. Poor Peterson was exhausted, sleeping with his chin on his chest. She pulled the blanket up over his shoulder and tucked it in. The elevator stopped at the penthouse, and she sighed with relief.

Solomon would know what to do.

The door opened, and Henri was there. "*Mes a—*" he began, his eyes sweeping over them. When he came to the wheelchair, the tail of his greeting withered into a question. "*—miiee?*"

"We would have been here earlier," Mady whispered, "but we had to stop and eat."

Carter pushed the chair into the foyer as Henri backed up, stunned. Abruptly, he turned and hurried.

They followed. At *le petite librairie*, he paused in the door while Carter and Mady caught up.

"Solomon, they are here." He stepped aside as Solomon stood up from a small sofa.

Mady stood at Carter's side behind the wheelchair and saw Solomon when he turned to look at them. Shock plastered his face.

Carter put his hand on Peterson's thin shoulder. "He's worn out. Can we put him—"

"Of course," Henri said. He led the way. Mady nodded for Carter to take Peterson. "You go with him."

She joined Solomon. He stood with mouth open, the concern riffling his brow. They sat before he was able to speak. "How? Where?"

"He was found wandering a back road by Madam St. Etienne, who owned a small rooming establishment and restaurant on the shore. Madam thought Peterson was touched by God, and gave him shelter."

"How generous of Madam," Solomon said. "We must see to compensate—"

"She would be insulted—" Mady insisted.

Solomon's eyebrows drifted up in inquiry.

"There was a young daughter in the St. Etienne household, only seven years old—she had Down's syndrome. Apparently Peterson and the daughter developed a rapport. By the time we communicated with Madam St. Etienne, her daughter was reading *Pride and Prejudice*."

Carter and Henri entered the room.

"He's sleeping," Carter said. He sat next to Mady. She opened her bag and withdrew a leather pouch. "He was carrying this—"

Solomon and Henri gasped. She knew they were

thinking about Fischer's repercussions for touching treasures in the Hall of Records. "It's okay, you can touch this."

A gold piece like a domino tumbled from the bag into her hand. She turned the gold piece over and put it to the light.

Henri leaned over her to peer into her hand. "What's this?"

"What do you have, *cherie*?" Solomon asked.

On one side of the gold piece a pyramid was engraved. The tiny Capstone was crowned with rays of light and filled with what appeared to be a doorway. On the reverse of the rectangle was a line of vertical text in Babylonian Aramaic. She read, "Bring the Key of Seven."

She flipped the gold back to the pyramid side. "If you look close, you'll see Bab-el above the doorway. It means Gateway to God."

"*Mon Dieu,*" Henri gasped. "It is the Capstone."

•

Outside Solomon St. Germain's townhouse address, Hanlon paid and was out the taxi door before the driver could mutter thank you. He sprinted across the walk to Solomon's building. When the doorman approached, Hanlon said, "St. Germain, penthouse."

The doorman said, "Yes, sir."

Hanlon entered the foyer and waited while the doorman called upstairs. Another quick "yes, sir," and the doorman motioned Hanlon to proceed.

The ride up was both interminable and all too brief. Hanlon's thoughts swung wildly from his memory of Peterson's vision, to the imminent betrayal of Hanlon's own former values.

Because of the sweeping changes to his life brought by the visions Peterson passed to him, including and not limited to subsequent unknown memories coming alive, unexplained physical manifestations, and the ethereal tune that lived within him—in the face of such internal chaos, the Amun-ra and the Illuminati simply had ceased to be important.

Hanlon stood at Solomon's door and his hand was a riot of tickle and itch, compelling him in a fashion he could not decipher. The door opened and Solomon greeted him. "Come in, John. We're waiting for you."

Hanlon followed, unsure what manner of gathering he was joining. When Solomon revealed who was waiting, Hanlon arched his brows.

"Your message sounded dire," Solomon said. "So I called everyone in."

Hanlon smiled with relief. "Yes, dire is correct." Now that he was inside Solomon's home, his hand had calmed down. He resisted the urge to whisper his thanks. "I need to speak with you about Peterson." At the mention of Peterson's name, his sensory-rich palm became excited.

"Have a seat," Solomon said.

Carter motioned for Hanlon to sit next to him.

Hanlon's hand was a distracting riot. He shoved it in his pocket and sat. "I had a disturbing visitor yesterday. I thought something I learned could help you find Peterson." He saw the quick glances that flew around the room.

Before he could speak, Solomon nodded. "Please, continue. You are among friends here, John."

Hanlon didn't know where to start. There was so much, he didn't know if he could put it all into words.

Carter touched him on the shoulder, and said, "Just start at the beginning."

Only his lips didn't move.

Hanlon drew back. Solomon smiled like a crazy man. Henri was opening and flexing his right hand. Hanlon could feel their glee. He shot to his feet.

"What the hell's going on?" he cried. His panic exploded. First Peterson's vision, this madness in his hand, Amunson's suspicions—

Carter smiled and motioned for Hanlon to sit. "Peterson has touched you, as he did all of us … and now we are entangled, at least as far as our common goal extends."

Mady said at Carter, "Are you getting anything from the baggage person or the customs agent from the airport?"

"No, thank heavens," he answered quickly. He turned back to Hanlon. "I believe we all have a part to play in Peterson's quest, which we believe remains unfulfilled."

Carter flexed his right hand and waved his fingers. Hanlon felt a fluttering power surge flow through his hand and up his arm. He watched Carter, amazed.

"We're all here for the same reason," Carter said. "So why don't you tell us why you're here."

Hanlon couldn't deny the strange sensations in his hand, the odd little miracles that had sprouted in his daily routine, and the paranormal door that had opened in his life. If he was receiving thoughts from these people … well, better them than most he knew. He blurted out his concerns. "Raffe Amunson is asking about Peterson."

Solomon went rigid. Henri looked shocked.

Mady asked, "Who is Raffe Amunson? Is he Illuminati?"

Solomon answered. "Raffe is not Illuminati, he is worse than Illuminati." His expression, more so than his words, spoke his opinion of Amunson. "His family and the Illuminati have similar goals, only Raffe has more personal interests in the outcome." He shuttered his eyes, clearly unwilling to say more.

"I agree," Hanlon said. "The Amunson family goes back millennia, and are reputed to have access to certain arcane information—"

"They are the Amun-ra Brotherhood," Solomon stated bluntly. "They are direct descendants of the Amun-ra priesthood."

Hanlon watched the incredulous look dart around the group. He added, "Yes, *the* Amun-ra. Such is their reputation that even the Illuminati prefer to give them a wide berth."

Mady sucked in a breath of surprise. "The Amun-ra was very powerful. It was written that they could manipulate time, matter and energy." Skepticism of her words lined her face, but this faded as she massaged her hand. "I used to think such talk was born in mythology."

"What did Raffe want?" Solomon asked.

"His initial interest was in the power event that destroyed the satellite," Hanlon said. He glanced to Mady. "He knew facts that I hadn't revealed to my superiors; he asked about you and Carter. I tried to steer him off course, but he came back."

Hanlon scooted to the edge of his seat, feeling silly, and yet the hesitancy to speak of these topics was primeval—some things were best not spoken out loud. He waited for them to lean closer.

"Amunson spoke of the legend of Elijah. He called

this person the Eschaton and claimed this individual would mean the end of a subjugated world as designed by the Amun-ra and the Illuminati."

Solomon grabbed the arm of his seat and his face slowly eased into shock, as though pieces took their time before coming together.

Henri's lips closed up like a pharaoh's tomb.

What do those two know? Hanlon wondered. He watched Mady shift in her seat and shake her hand. Her action sent the energy sizzling down Hanlon's spine. Did this power that connected them originate with Peterson?

Hanlon recalled the electric vision that came from Peterson and knew it was the same vision Amunson spoke of, only from a different perspective. Amunson classified the event as a nightmare of utter devastation.

Hanlon saw something else. And why did the Eschaton's presence terrify Amunson so?

A movement at the door caught Hanlon's eye. He stopped as a little old man shuffled in the room. He appeared ancient, and although Hanlon was shocked, he wasn't fooled. The energy in his hand fired up and he was drawn to his feet.

He went to Peterson. Solomon and the others rose to follow as Hanlon approached. When Hanlon got close, he could only wonder what Peterson had experienced to render him in such a condition.

Confused gray eyes skirted the room and locked onto Hanlon. Hanlon couldn't miss the small fire of hope that ignited in the tired visage.

"Hello," Peterson said. He took Hanlon's arm and looked up. "Do you know me?"

Suddenly, Hanlon understood what his role was in

Peterson's quest. Tears filled his eyes and he dashed them away with his free hand, the hand that had somehow become empowered with a vibration he didn't understand. That and his eye, after so many years of distress, was calm, were blessings he couldn't explain.

All of these swirling emotions pushed and pulled at Hanlon at once, making his chest fill with a sense of expectation he had never known. These unexplained events, miracles and emotions had come to him through Peterson, and while Hanlon did not understand what was happening to him, he would not lose this new feeling.

No, I will never go back. Fischer may be gone, but perhaps I can save Peterson. If the vision Peterson left with me is his destiny, I will do anything to bring him back— to make this vision come true.

As Hanlon guided Peterson and eased him onto the sofa, Hanlon swore Peterson's eyes perked up. The vibration in his hand accelerated and became a little sweeter.

Hanlon spoke softly. "Yes, I know you. I have known you all your life." Behind him, he felt the crowd gathering around. He cleared his throat, for he wanted them all to hear.

"Your name is Peterson. Eli J. Peterson."

CHAPTER TWELVE

St. Germain Townhouse

Solomon followed the events and was shocked over the changes in Peterson's appearance. This was eclipsed only by his shock over the changes he was witnessing in John Hanlon.

Closer to home, he struggled with his own metamorphosis. Since Peterson electrified him in the cave at Bezu, doors had been flung open in his mind to expose him to startling impressions.

What he glimpsed was sometimes ... familiar.

The vibration sang loudly through his bones, sending a near-orgasmic tickle skipping along his spine and all through his nerves. When Hanlon said, "Amunson spoke of the legend of Elijah—" the vibration in Solomon responded with a keening internal pitch that set his world on edge.

The bottom dropped out of his stomach and he grasped the arm of the sofa. He looked down. Instead of black dress shoes, he saw tanned bare feet sporting brown leather sandals he'd never seen before. The hem of a green silk robe rippled with a richness that made him sigh with contentment—

Someone called his name, but they did not call Solomon. A deep voice said, "Thoth, dear friend," and the ringing in Solomon's ears rose to a frightening crescendo. He put his right hand up to cup his ear, afraid the energy was going to make his head explode. Certain the others were participating in the vision and likely staring at him, he looked up.

Hanlon was still speaking, as if time in this room had not changed, while he, Solomon … or was he Thoth? … left this dimension.

Hanlon said, "—called the Eschaton, claimed this individual would mean the end of the world designed by the Amun-ra and the Illuminati."

Solomon's vision, from the ringing in his ears to the sandals and robe—all disappeared. He felt the room shift from that other dimension back to reality, leaving him with a peculiar sensation, as if a wrinkle remained in his energy.

Hanlon was finished speaking. Henri's lips were clamped shut, a clear sign he knew something. Mady and Carter still sat on the edges of their seats.

Solomon's stomach settled and he relaxed his grip on the sofa. Hanlon rose, and Solomon stood, knowing Peterson was near from the way the energy pulsed. He glanced at Mady, saw her flick her fingers. Oddly, her hand gesture seemed to smooth out the residual wrinkle he felt in the power from his skip through time.

Peterson appeared in the doorway.

Hanlon rose, rubbing his palm with his thumb, wearing an expression of abject devotion. He approached Peterson, who responded with a curious and anxious face that proclaimed more than words could as Hanlon approached.

"Hello," Peterson said. "Do you know me?"

Hanlon gently guided Peterson to the sofa, took one wrinkled old hand and sat next to him. "Yes, I know you. I have known you all your life."

The group crowded around to hear.

"Your name is Eli," Hanlon proclaimed. "Eli J. Peterson."

Solomon's ears picked up at the mention of Eli, but half of his mind lingered in another dimension, with another name.

I was called Thoth.

•

The Amun-ra Vault

Raffe descended the two hundred steps a little faster this time. With all his many visits to the vault, the irregular steps were getting familiar. Also, his work in the vault was proving productive. He felt he was closing in on the Eschaton.

"I'm coming for you," he declared.

The arrival of the Eschaton and the final battle known as Armageddon were prophesied in the very oldest Amun-ra documents. At the time of earth's first occupation by intelligent life, those who came to be known as the light and the dark chose separate paths. In that one moment, the eventuality of Armageddon was created. When two opposite forces strive to dominate, only one can succeed. At some predestined point, one must be annihilated.

The original tactics of the Amun-ra were simple.

They quickly captured control of time and several other dimensions. The priesthood excelled, expanding their strength with an aggressive confiscation of physical wealth and political power. They overtook the ruling class using tools that had proved to work well in all societies: greed, war, chaos and crisis.

The arrival of the Eschaton meant all such mayhem and manipulation would come to a stop; never again would mankind be subject to the whims of a ruling class. Raffe pushed such an awful possibility from his mind.

No matter, he thought with a smile. *Darkness will prevail. It always has ... so far.*

And it had to, again, for darkness was all he knew. Darkness infiltrated his DNA. Darkness was the energy that drove his heart. Darkness employed against humanity was what his mind understood.

He whistled and picked up the lantern. Today was a very special day. Today he would do more than rummage through old texts and plow through the ancient languages. He announced to the vault with pride, "Today, I will steal the Eschaton."

His plan was daring, but Raffe, fortified by all he had learned in the vault, felt his odds of success were good. He went to the back of the library, to the oldest documents. When he saw an ancient desk, a relic from Atlantis, occupying a section of the back wall, he turned out his lantern.

The document he sought could not be exposed to light. He shuffled back in the dark, banging his shins before stubbing his foot on what felt like a bag of bricks.

When he reached the desk from Atlantis, he sighed in commiseration. The desk, made of a material no longer known to mankind, called literally to Raffe's mind with its energy signature.

"I know," he whispered in consolation to the desk. "It's not fair you are made to wait back here. But I promise, a new day of darkness will come, and I will bring you back to your days of glory."

A large drawer in the center opened with a creak. Raffe reached in. He found the document he desired, knowing it by touch immediately. "Sss," he hissed as his fingertips turned red and bubbled with contact.

In the absolute darkness he ran his fingers down the ancient text; a thin wail came from the page as his flesh and blood passed over the writing. A stinking vapor of scorched tissue wafted up to water his eyes. If he hadn't possessed the ability to self heal, he could never have read this text.

He pressed on, willing to suffer any discomfort to see this transition go in the Amun-ra's favor. If he failed and the Babylon was opened, death would not be an option—it would be mandatory.

"Not yet," Raffe swore. "Death is not yet upon the Amun-ra."

The document transferred its knowledge directly into Raffe's blood, giving him what he desired: the Eschaton's weakness. For a very brief period, before time returns the Eschaton his power, he will be weak and vulnerable.

"Ripe for the picking," Raffe hummed. "Ah," he smiled, coming to a special passage. "Here it is. My key to a dimensional door."

His scorched and rapidly healing fingers held the page carefully. These particular symbols drew upon the sciences of power and forces that existed beyond the human ken, symbols that spoke not of words, but of energy. Here were the symbols to attract and amplify energy.

No human voice could produce the sound of these symbols. But as a pure blood Amun-ra, Raffe had two extra strands of vocal tissue. He could produce the sounds, his DNA knew the ancient language, and his heart was a natural magnet for dark energy. Such were the very effective tools of the ancient Amun-ra.

He placed the document on the Atlantean desk, bowed his head, and prepared his mind before taking the Eschaton.

•

St. Germain Townhouse

Solomon let go of the past with its hypnotic draw and focused on the present. His palm was ringing with a new tone, a vibration that set his nerves on edge.

"Your father worked for my organization," Hanlon recited to Peterson.

Solomon noticed that Peterson sat a little straighter, and his eyes seemed a bit more alert. Excitement for Peterson's recovery stirred the energy within Solomon. Along with that excitement came a rapidly building sense of dread.

"My father," Peterson said.

His voice was so … little. And yet, he did sound stronger than he did earlier.

Solomon could not ignore his hand any longer—he was ready to scream. He looked at Mady and Carter, and saw with relief that they, too, were distressed.

Solomon rose. Carter stood up, too.

"What is it?" Mady asked. She was on her feet, and flexing her hand. Solomon could feel the energy bunch in time with her movements.

"I feel something, too," Hanlon said. He stood and covered his right ear with his hand, wincing.

Solomon edged closer to Peterson. He had heard from Carter about the miraculous staff and its impossible fit at the airport. The staff was propped on the sofa arm within Peterson's reach. Solomon's hand screamed for him to take the staff.

The power's frequency ripping through Solomon's body was now anything but pleasant. Pressure was building to ominous levels, scraping along Solomon's nerves like ground glass. He turned to the fireplace that was filled with a huge display of summer flowers. The agitation harpooning his nerves erupted to a full-fledged wave of panic.

He reached for the walking stick.

•

The Amun-ra Vault

Raffe was ready.

He opened his mouth and uttered the sounds for the strange and ancient symbols that had never seen light.

Air moved in and out of his odd vocal chords, creating sound from another place and time. An old force, older than ancient, stirred, reaching through the darkness of night in answer to Raffe's call to power.

The dark energy came, responding to the primal song in Raffe's forty-thousand-year-old, multi-strand

DNA. The energy crowded eagerly around him, flocking to the call of his mind, his body, and the symbols. He felt the energy accumulating, speeding from hidden energy pockets across the many dimensions of time and space.

The energy soared into his mind and scooped up his thoughts. In a few blistering seconds Raffe's conscious mind skipped through several dimensions. That part of his psyche that maintained the connection to his body registered the hair lifting all across him to stand at attention.

His travel through dimensions slowed, coming to a standstill where the darkness beckoned to him with invitation. He opened his mind and peered through a dimension portal held open by the dark energy.

I smell the blood of the Eschaton.

•

St. Germain Townhouse

"The fireplace," Solomon whispered, dropping the stick.

Like sentient darkness, a black malevolence crept from behind the flowers in the fireplace, reaching toward Peterson with long, thick tendrils.

Mady cried, "Hiee-ah," and stomped on the darkness closest to Peterson. The tendril moved like fog, evading her, reforming and continuing toward Peterson.

Carter shoved Peterson back into the corner of the sofa and planted himself in front of him.

Hanlon fell to the floor and swatted at the malevolence. "No," he shouted. But the disturbed essence simply dissipated and re-coalesced. Mady joined him, yet the darkness advanced on Peterson.

The black tendrils slipped under the sofa and came up the back. Peterson was huddled into a ball, his face covered with his hands. The essence flowed over him like liquid fear, poking here and there to find an entry.

"Fire," Henri shouted. "Fight it with fire!" He darted around the room grabbing several large candles. "Solomon, help me," he cried. They lit the candles and placed them around the fireplace. Where the flame touched the malevolence, the darkness withered and drew back.

"More?" Mady shouted at Solomon. He pointed to the door. "Dining room, left." She bounded out of the room.

The tendrils found purchase around Peterson's neck. When he raised his arms to bat at the creeping attachments, they slipped around his arms, tightened—and pulled. He was jerked across the sofa toward the floor.

Carter wrapped his arms around Peterson and planted his legs against the brick on the floor before the fireplace. He cried, "I can't hold him."

Hanlon wedged himself between Peterson and the fireplace.

In a sudden move, one tendril of the blackness grabbed Hanlon and tossed him aside like he was nothing.

Mady came running into the room with an armload of candles. She and Henri lit them with frantic fingers. Hanlon joined them, stabbing at the essence with the candle flames.

Carter's face was red with the strain of holding onto Peterson against the darkness.

Peterson mewled with fright.

Solomon's fingers cried out for Peterson's forgotten staff. He grabbed it and beat at the tendrils.

At the first strike the essence pulled back and Solomon swore he detected a beastly scream. The darkness released Peterson and swelled to a large mass in front of Solomon. He lifted the stick to smash the darkness back to hell when he saw deep within the malevolent energy the wavering image of a face glaring at him with hatred.

"Amunseraf," Solomon hissed with vengeance. He lifted the stick. The malevolent essence drew back and puffed up like a giant hooded cobra preparing to strike.

"Solomon, your feet," Mady cried.

Before Solomon could move, black tendrils wrapped around his feet and jerked him straight up before dropping him flat on his back. He lost his grip on the staff and it flew into the air.

The dark energy wrapped around the stick. In a smothering burst of black, the menacing essence disappeared back through the fireplace with Peterson's miraculous walking stick.

•

The Amun-ra Vault

Raffe's scream of agony reverberated through the vault, rattling the bookshelves and blasting loose sheets of paper into the air. There was a sonic boom and a great crack split one wall. Dust and crumbled masonry rained down.

"Aaargh," Raffe cried, as he fell to the floor. He lay in the dark shaking, not daring to look at his injuries until they had healed. He gasped as the bare bone of his hands touched the stone floor of the vault. The stink of his blackened flesh made him retch.

"He called me Amunseraf," Raffe gasped.

Solomon was and is your nemesis.

Raffe rolled across the floor in pain while new ligaments and tissue formed. The ability to heal did not include having no pain. He felt every single bite of agony.

He bit back the cries, until finally the stink was gone. He struggled to the table and flicked the switch on the lantern, eager to see what he had stolen from the Eschaton.

The light came up slowly, as if hesitant to enter such a dark and angry place.

The Eschaton's staff lay on the floor against the cracked wall. Raffe eyed the venomous thing with distaste and sniffed. He recognized the wooden staff as an artifact from the Hall, could smell Nefertiti's energy. The damned thing stank of incense and Egyptian sand.

He turned on the full lights and approached the staff with caution, eyeing the vault's structural damage. When he returned through the portal and released the staff, it must have hit the wall. The crack was substantial, indicating incredible power.

Raffe pulled a hanging from the wall and threw it on the floor by the staff. He used the lantern to push the staff onto the linen, rolling it around and around. When the staff was fully wrapped and out of view, Raffe whistled with relief.

"Well, I didn't get the Eschaton," he said. He looked at his hands. The scars that pulled his fingers into claws told him the flesh had been eaten to the bone where he hung on to the staff as he came through the portal. He snarled with the memory.

The adhesions in his hands healed and disappeared. His fingers straightened, eliciting a keening moan from his throat. The flesh sped through the metamorphosis, advancing to a healthy pink, as strong and vigorous as an eighteen year-old.

He flexed his reformed fingers. Fully healed, he turned his attention to the staff. While he had not been successful, neither had he failed. He eyed the linen wrapped staff, knowing instinctively it was incredibly powerful. With plan A not entirely successful, he would need a power source for plan B.

"I'll find a way to use you."

•

St. Germain Townhouse

With his feet jerked out from under him by the malevolence, Solomon hit the floor unprepared. His breath burst loose with a great *oomph*. His stunned lungs silenced him.

Henri appeared over him. "Are you all right?"

Solomon nodded, still unable to speak. Henri gave him a hand and pulled him to a sitting position.

Mady was putting out the candles. Hanlon and Carter were assisting Peterson back onto the sofa.

"Holy mac, what was that?" Mady said.

Solomon still sat on the floor. Henri looked askance at him until he finally drew a breath. With a nod, Henri helped Solomon to his feet.

"Is everyone else all right?" Solomon's ears still rang from the massive boom he heard when the stick disappeared. "Did you hear it?" he asked, cupping a hand to one ear.

Carter said, "I heard a scream and a boom. Whatever that was, it didn't enjoy its visit."

"*Oui*," Henri said. "I heard the same."

Mady and Hanlon nodded.

Solomon shook his head. A great deal was moving very fast in his mind. Thoth, Amunseraf, Peterson's electrifying visions, images and sensations, glimpses from the past ... or are they from the future? All cascaded through his mind, looking for level.

Every eye was upon him.

Mady asked, "Who is Amunseraf?"

"Raffe is Amunseraf," Solomon said. He rubbed his forehead. An image popped into his mind of his skull releasing a genie like the proverbial lamp. He stopped rubbing when a burst of mad laughter seemed ready to erupt from his throat.

Carter gasped.

Hanlon said, "Look."

They stepped aside and Solomon looked up.

Peterson's eyes were fever bright; the air around him crackled with energy. Solomon looked at Mady. She was reared back, a silent "whoa" pursing her lips. Carter stood next to her with his arm around her. Hanlon, too, pulled back, staring at Peterson with startled eyes.

Chills shot down Solomon's arms when Peterson spoke, for his voice was the ancient, foreign sound they heard the day he first appeared.

"Take me to the fountain."

CHAPTER THIRTEEN

St. Germain Townhouse

The questions came at Solomon all at once.

"What fountain?" Mady asked.

"What about the stick?" Carter added.

"Who is Amunseraf?" Hanlon repeated.

Solomon held his hands out for silence. "Please," he begged. He went to Peterson and sat next to him. The ancient energy and voice Peterson spoke with was gone. The hum in Solomon's head was pleasant once again, and his palm was at ease.

Peterson was tight-lipped now. He was huddled in the corner of the sofa, slowly shaking his head. Yet the lost and helpless look in his eye was ... not so lost. And there was a crinkle of determination at the corner of his mouth.

Solomon had to wonder, *is he back?*

He looked carefully. Peterson's skin was not so thin and the age spots were less pronounced. He picked up one hand, and Peterson squeezed back with a good deal more strength than Solomon expected.

"I think—" Solomon began, but he stopped.

The vibration within him fired and accelerated to light speed, shooting from his heart down his arm and out through his hand. The power was pouring from him into Peterson. He closed his eyes and placed his other hand on Peterson's forearm ... and opened up the gates, feeding back to Peterson what was seeded to Solomon in the cave at Bezu.

The images erupted like a fountain.

Solomon felt a vortex of power forming, swirling around him and Peterson, pushing and pulling at them. He stiffened when it felt like the floor fell away beneath them, but he dared not open his eyes to look. He just tucked his head and focused on the images.

The vortex increased in intensity with a roar. "Here and now" became "then and there." Moments were millennia, and all of space and creation existed within a single pinpoint. Solomon's internal vibration was intense, powerfully fueling the exchange of energy and information. With both hands, he held on to his friend as they traveled through ancient days and lives long forgotten.

The images stopped suddenly.

Solomon gasped as the volatile energy jumped from his hands into Peterson, blasting his hands free. Suddenly, his ears were ringing, and he realized he was on the floor again.

"Solomon," Henri was shouting.

Solomon looked up, dazed. Hanlon was pressed against the wall, his hand at his throat like he had seen— what? Mady and Carter stood side by side, producing a matching pair of open mouths.

Solomon laughed at their expressions and struggled to sit up. "What happened?"

Mady squealed and wiggled like a two-year-old. Carter grinned ear to ear. Hanlon kept shaking his head. Henri seemed ready to burst.

Solomon couldn't stop the smile. He didn't know what there was to be so happy about, and yet the feeling welled up inside him. He was halfway standing when he repeated, "What happened?"

"You lit up," Mady said.

Carter added, "Rather brilliant, old man."

Hanlon supported this with a vigorous vertical nod; his eyes were enormous.

Henri pointed to Solomon's wrist. "And your watch broke—it sounded like a woman's scream."

Solomon looked at his Rolex—the crystal was shattered. Before he could express his dismay, Carter drew his attention.

"Look what you else you did."

•

Peterson knew nothing until Solomon grasped him with both hands, opening the fountain.

And then he knew everything—instantly.

Information came with a jolt of intense energy. He felt as though he had been tossed into the sun. He was on fire without burning, ablaze without combustion, consumed, yet intact. He was filled not only with images rushing through him, but emotion—the bliss and joy, the challenges and defeats, the births and always … death.

There was no time to react, for it all came too fast. How could he weep for death when ecstasy and sadness took its place without a break? He could only take it in.

Beneath the rigor of energy and information absorption, he detected a sweet tingling hum, like a silken thread made from a rainbow … a sensation within him that he knew was key. The end of the thread came without warning like a mighty caboose, knocking Solomon's hands free and flinging him to the floor.

The energy plastered Peterson into the sofa and sent it sliding. He gasped for air and felt his body electrified as energy continued to pour through him. He was morphing; his molecules and atoms were on fire. He felt like a bell struck by God. He writhed, for there was awful pain.

Somewhere he heard glass shatter with a high-pitched scream.

•

Solomon was in a half-risen position when he looked up, but the shock of seeing a youthful Peterson made his legs waver, and he fell back on his butt.

Peterson laughed.

Solomon smiled. "You're back."

The words were unnecessary, for the power was a great swelling expansion in Solomon's chest, loudly announcing Peterson's return. Solomon looked around. A series of resonant heart wave energy patterns had blossomed, one from every person in the room, even Hanlon. The waves overlapped, creating a Fibonacci pattern centered on Peterson.

"Yes, I'm back," Peterson announced.

Carter and Mady sat next to Peterson on the sofa. Henri helped Solomon up from the floor as Hanlon stepped hesitantly into the group.

"We found you in the French countryside," Mady said, "Where did you go after the Hall?"

"You were old, and you had complete amnesia—" Carter added.

Hanlon mumbled in awe, "Who are you people?" He rubbed his right hand with his left thumb, and edged a little closer.

Solomon laughed and stepped over to grasp Peterson's hand. "Welcome back, old friend. I don't know where you've been, I only thank heaven you have returned."

Henri spoke, his voice seeping into the group although he stood apart. When Solomon looked up, his cousin's expression made the hairs on the back of Solomon's neck stand up.

"You went forward in time," Henri rushed to say. "And now you are back, you have laid time upon itself."

Solomon caught Henri's eye, knowing something was about to happen by the change in the power; the hum was sweet, guiding him along with subtle pressure. He was recalling the hem of a green silk robe, when a vision of ancient text bolted through his mind. It was an announcement. He looked to Henri, who seemed ready to speak. "Henri, say it, please," Solomon said.

The others stopped their chatter.

Henri stepped within their midst and all eyes turned his way. He gazed at Peterson as he spoke. "You are the Herald, the Eschaton. He who satisfies the legend of Elijah, who prepares earth for the end days, who brings enlightenment to humanity."

•

I am the Eschaton.

Peterson felt the energy shift as his circle of friends looked at him with new reverence. The enormity of what his quest had become dared him to question his sanity. Only one element kept him on track—that he had not chosen this quest. The quest had chosen him.

As the Eschaton, he would change the world.

What happens if I fail?

He never gave that idea traction, for failure was not an option. From what he understood, the die was cast and humanity's future was … settled. He didn't know what "settled" meant. But not knowing the final outcome was not a deterrent to him, for the stage he occupied had been designed by forces beyond his understanding.

What he wondered more often was—

What happens when I succeed?

They all watched him for the next step. The power, too, waited. He felt the energy singing in his bones, alive and well with encouragement, not for him, but for his companions. "Tell them, Henri, what you know," Peterson said.

Henri was breathless before he began. Peterson felt Henri's excitement, his awe, and his desire to help. The same desire rang through the room, echoing his companions' common goal to assist him.

"I believe you are a reincarnation of Elijah the Biblical prophet. Your quest as the Herald is to prepare the earth and mankind for the Song of Creation, last seen during the genesis of the cosmos."

No one moved or spoke.

Peterson nodded for Henri to continue.

"Your tasks are many. Secure the Ark, the manna, the anointing oil, return memory to an ancient soul who will assist you in locating the Capstone of the great Pyramid, and open the Babylon gate."

The silence was impenetrable. Outside, no car honked, no passerby spoke, no bird flew by the window.

Inside, not a breath found release.

Peterson gave them time to mull over this new information; he knew comprehension of such a task was daunting. It had taken all of the fifty years he aged and the fifty-year return trip through folded time for him to assimilate the full picture of what his quest had become.

He stood.

Carter pulled the sofa back into place, where he and Mady sat. Henri pulled another chair over and eased into it. Solomon took the remaining chair. Hanlon was collapsed where he sat.

Peterson felt the power bumping along in fits and starts as they mentally assimilated what they just heard.

Solomon and Henri traded looks, inspiring Henri to leave the room and return with glasses and a decanter. He placed them on the table. "Please, help yourselves," he murmured. He retreated to a desk in a corner and opened a laptop.

Mady spied the decanter. "Yes, I'll take some of that," she said when Carter offered. She took her glass of premium whiskey and downed a shot.

Carter gave her the eye.

"It's that Yankee blood," she said, wiping a stray drop from her lip with her thumb. "A bit of the old west and all that, you know."

She aimed her glass at him, her pointer finger sticking out like a gun. "And you don't want to get into a spitting contest with me, either."

Her assurances on the outcome of that event were delivered with such utter aplomb, Carter choked on his whiskey. He dabbed at his chin with a handkerchief and gave her a look that made her laugh.

Hanlon was quiet, having said little since Peterson returned. He pulled his chair toward the sofa, and nudged Carter. "Please, can you help me understand what is going on?"

"Whiskey helps," Mady quipped with a smile. Carter gave her an elbow in the ribs and she chuckled. "All right, just kidding. Solomon's research opened the door to entanglement," she said, setting her empty glass down. "I think all matter possesses a sentient awareness of entanglement—only human consciousness is shielded from this awareness.

"The sound of Divinity from the protocols pierces that shield and ignites the awareness of entanglement. The awareness first came to Peterson, and now spreads from him."

She turned to Carter and asked, "Are you picking up anything up from the people that were touched in France?"

"No," Carter answered.

"Me either. So maybe active entanglement only comes with common goal?"

"I certainly hope so," Carter proclaimed. "Otherwise, it could get really busy." He rolled his eyes.

Mady returned to Hanlon. "We—" She circled her hand to include everyone. "Are connected to each other and to Peterson through this power, apparently, because we have a common goal."

At Hanlon's confused look, she added, "Once awareness is established, all matter within the known and unknown universe becomes attuned to your emerging awareness, responding through quantum entanglement, I think."

She said to Solomon, "On our return from France, Peterson—shall I say ... activated a couple of people.

But we aren't picking up anything internal from them."

Hanlon still sat on the edge of his seat. "Tell me what happened out in Liddington? How were you not killed?"

Solomon chuckled. "We were protected by the power because we have a part to play—"

"—in Elijah's quest," Carter added. "And, apparently, so do you."

"Here, I have it," Henri said. He returned to the group with a stack of papers. He poured a stiff drink and sat down.

"First, something in response to Mady's discovery just before Hanlon arrived concerning the gold rectangle," he said, passing a sheet to everyone.

"From there we go to the next topic I'm sure is on everyone's mind. The Capstone. It's more than the missing top physical thirty feet of the Great Pyramid. It represents intellectually the pinnacle of achievement available to man. Those who claim the Capstone is myth insist man is incapable of such elevation."

Mady pulled the rectangle gold piece from her pocket and passed it to Hanlon.

Hanlon squinted at the gold. "Bab-el?"

Mady gave her whiskey glass to Carter for a refill. "Bab-el: the Gateway to God. Peterson was carrying it when we found him."

Hanlon looked at Peterson. "You got this from the mountain in Bezu?" At Peterson's nod, Hanlon jerked his hands back and the gold fell to the floor.

Carter picked it up. "Don't worry, you're protected." At Hanlon's quizzical look, Carter asked, "If I may, I'd guess that your hand has gone all weird, right—ever since Peterson touched you in the bosom of Bezu?"

Hanlon nodded, rubbing his palm against his

thigh.

Peterson prompted Henri, "What else do you have?"

Henri rattled the pages drawing everyone's attention. "*Oui*, there is more." He paused to give a speculative glance between Peterson and Solomon.

Mady squirmed in her seat. "What, what? You're killing me."

Henri gave her a sympathetic look. "We have a riddle." He gave them the next page.

"Great, a riddle," Mady muttered. She scanned the page. "This is Babylonian Aramaic." She read, "Bring him the key." She glanced at the back of the page, saw nothing, looked up and asked, "What's this? Who wrote it?"

Henri said, "It's from the back of the Emerald Tablet—"

"That's not possible," Mady objected. "There's no such thing. The Emerald Tablet is a myth—"

"No, it is not a myth. It's real," Peterson said. "Very real." All eyes turned to him. "Just ask Solomon."

CHAPTER FOURTEEN

Brussels

"He knew me," Raffe said. "He called me Amunseraf."

Despite his trepidation over being identified by his ancient nemesis, Raffe was nonetheless euphoric over his accomplishment.

A servant entered the dining room. While she removed the first course utensils, Uncle stared at Raffe with a closed expression that shared little. As soon as the servant passed through the door, Uncle hissed, "Of course he knew you!"

He threw his napkin down on the table and rose. Flinging his arms about in agitation, he paced. When he came to Raffe's chair, he paused and stood at Raffe's back in seething silence.

Raffe held his breath until the pacing renewed.

What does Uncle know that he isn't sharing?

Uncle sat and drew his napkin into his lap with stiff, precise, measured movements. A chill settled into Raffe's neck, for the look on his uncle's face spoke of defeat and loss.

"Solomon killed you once before, Raffe—when he

was Thoth. Will you give him the opportunity again, in this life?"

The servants returned with the next course, a perfect vichyssoise, but Raffe's appetite had wandered off, replaced by an uncontrollable rage. When the click of footsteps told him they were alone, he protested. "What are we supposed to do? Sit idly by and watch the cosmos take everything from us?"

Raffe's fear and rage was fast accelerating to a colossal eruption. He took a deep breath and folded his napkin neatly, carefully, calmly, so he would not forget himself again … as he did with Hanlon. "I cannot let go without a fight."

"And that fight will kill you, once again."

Uncle sipped his vichyssoise once and pushed it angrily aside, splashing the soup onto the tablecloth. "The priesthood made decisions long ago—they chose a path. At the time, considering the wealth they held and the power they brokered, that path seemed like a good idea."

Raffe didn't like the tone coming through the words he was hearing. He didn't want to hear what others had done before him. He didn't want to hear how decisions best made by him had been decided long ago. He didn't want to hear why everything had been stolen from him.

A nasty bitterness began to consume his tongue— the bitterness of having all your choices made for you.

They did not have the right!

Raffe felt his face go rigid as stone.

Uncle leveled a look across the table that spoke of a shared consensus. He shrugged. "Who can say where we would be today had the priesthood made different choices long ago. Considering the power they wielded, corruption is inevitable. Still, I venture to guess not one of them would have traded one cherished crumb of wealth for the welfare and safety of future generations.

"No, they opted to give themselves a huge party, and destroyed the future in the process," he finished.

Raffe nodded, although deep in his heart he couldn't blame his ancestors. From what he had read in the vault, the wealth and power the priesthood obtained must have made them nothing less than the King of gods. Under such pressure, the admittedly shallow tactic of sacrificing tomorrow to purchase today won out. He couldn't say he wouldn't do the same, given the opportunity.

Uncle pierced Raffe with a look of deep regret. "We were told we would have hell to pay for what was done in Atlantis."

He rang the bell for the course to be removed early. Before the servant arrived, he lamented in a whisper. "It has taken thousands of years, Raffe. But our hell has finally arrived."

•

The Amun-ra Vault

Raffe paced. The rancor of paying his ancestor's debts ran bitter through his heart. "I will not be sent to hell so easily."

He wheeled and approached the Eschaton's stick, giving the powerful staff plenty of space. Since he failed in Plan A—kidnapping the Eschaton and forcing him into entering Nefertiti's Hall so Raffe could access the science to save his bloodline—Plan B was to prevent the

Eschaton from entering the Babylon and completing his tasks.

While Raffe's last-ditch efforts wouldn't save the Amun-ra bloodline, perhaps some satisfaction was to be had if he could prevent the coming renaissance of humanity.

Anything was better than going straight to hell without a fight.

•

St. Germain Townhouse

With everyone's eyes on him, Solomon suddenly felt like a bug under a microscope.

I wrote the Emerald Tablet in another lifetime, when I was called Thoth.

The thought wrapped around a gurgle of hysteria and stuck in his throat. This was followed by another thought that threatened to knock him to the floor again. "Bring him the key—" Solomon said softly.

I know about this key.

The power was bouncing in his palm, tickling with insistence. He shook his hand, but the message was clear. "All right," he muttered. He closed his eyes and let go, allowing the power to work through him, giving his thoughts no boundaries, allowing a void to form in his mind.

One, two, three, he counted ... and the sweet smell of incense filled his nose.

•

The Queen's Hall, Akhenaten's Palace
1333 BCE

Kheti Kadash carefully shuffled his tired old feet along the slick tile floor—it would not do for him to fall and break a leg on such an auspicious day. He slowed and tucked his head, slanting an eye behind him. A shadow flitted in the distance, too far for his ancient eyes to identify. But he didn't have to see to know who followed him.

The evil nature of the Amun-ra priesthood would be their undoing. To catch a dark heart, he always said, bait the trap with a dark deed.

"Must hurry, must hurry," he chanted, making sure he babbled loud enough for the shadow to hear. "The Queen calls." At every doorway slaves bowed to him and stepped aside. None would slow him down, for he answered the call of Nefertiti.

Knowing the complex route well, he wound through the twisting hallways of the huge palace. He and his queen had worked many long hours in preparation for this day. At a corner, he stopped to catch his breath, and let the shadow edge a little closer.

After the final turn approaching Nefertiti's apartments, Kheti paused long enough to see his follower's shadow breach the corner. Breathless from excitement and a pounding heart, he called out, "My Queen, it is your slave, Kheti Kadash, come at your bidding."

Nefertiti answered his announcement herself, appearing at the gauzy fabric drapes that obscured her chamber opening. Her eyes asked him if all was as it should be and he nodded yes. She smiled, but he saw the sadness that lined her brow.

"Come, dear friend," she said. "You are no slave in this house." She winked and stepped aside. Kheti entered her apartments and she led him to the open veranda. They stepped outside, giving the shadow opportunity to enter within hearing range.

"I have completed the Key of Seven," Nefertiti said. She drew an object from her side.

"Ah, I see," Kheti answered. He took the object. It was a gold ankh, but the normally blunt shaft was razor sharp and honed to a dagger point. Symbols of power were etched across every surface.

"You must hide the key to the Babylon from the Amun-ra. Can you do that for me?" she asked.

The pleading that filled her eyes was unnecessary. She was so beautiful. He would do anything for her, including this small sacrifice they had planned. He inhaled deeply, praying to take the smell of her incense with him into the next life.

He nodded yes in answer to her question, then remembered the shadow. "Of course," he said, louder. "I will hide the key to the Babylon. Amunseraf will never discover the Key of Seven exists."

After this fatal announcement, he smiled, even though leaving her in this way broke his heart.

"Good," she responded loud enough to carry. "Then we shall all be safe." She placed her hands on his shoulders and leaned to whisper in his ear. "Peace be with you, my friend. I promise you will see a grand afterlife."

She drew back. Kheti saw the tears glisten in her eyes. He wrapped the gold ankh in a cloth and slipped the package into an inner pocket of his robe.

With more love in his heart than his lips could say, he spoke. "Fare well, my Queen." He gazed for the final time into her flawless face, needing the image of her beauty to last him many lifetimes. When he knew he could no longer delay the inevitable, he turned silently and left the way he came.

After Kheti departed with the evil shadow in tow, desert silence blanketed the Queen's chamber. Another guest emerged from the night.

"It is done," Nefertiti said. She bowed and held her hands out for acknowledgment.

Her visitor stepped into the light cast from a small silver brazier hanging from the wall. He was dark and handsome, with a regal face, and wore an emerald green robe of the finest quality silk.

"He will be rewarded for his sacrifice," he said.

"I wish there was another way—"

"The Amun-ra priesthood has engineered a return to power, but thanks to you, they will acquire a good deal less than they expected. You have emasculated them, Nefertiti. Kheti's sacrifice will place the Key in Amun-ra hands. There it will serve its purpose. You have Kheti's journal and the jasper?"

She nodded.

"Good. We will keep the priesthood from the Babylon until the Wheel of Transition opens the final cycle. The time of power for the Amun-ra priesthood is history; they simply fail to realize it. Perhaps one day when the dark hearts of the priesthood are a distant memory, the true Amun-ra will return to the light."

"Tut has taken their name," Nefertiti said, "For his duplicity in helping me, they will probably kill him next." She grabbed Thoth's hands and pleaded. "Please, is there no other way? We condemn so many with this plan."

He put his arm around her shoulders and drew her close, to assuage her trembling with his warmth. "Ssshh," he comforted. "This is only one life in many. Do not fret over Kheti. For his sacrifice, old Kadash will go on to his next incarnation with a vigorous new body and more virgins than he can handle."

Nefertiti laughed, but the joy was brief. She pulled Thoth's face to the light so she could see his eyes. "And you will remember?"

"Yes," he answered. "Forces beyond either of us are at play, pulling into motion a chain of cosmic events. That I will remember is written in the stars."

She nodded, seeming content to let the responsibility at last flow from her hands. "Then I have done all I can."

They waited, and sadly, not long. All too soon, the evidence of their successful plan slowly erupted. First came the sound of panic as sandaled feet ran through the palace, followed by the distant cries of horror.

"The evil deed has happened," Nefertiti said. A single tear rose in her eye and sped down her cheek.

Thoth stood behind her. "Cry, dear Nefertiti. Cast your tears for brave Kheti and feel his loss. Let your grief be real, so Amunseraf will think he has won."

•

The Amun-ra Vault

Raffe held the Key of Seven. The golden ankh was every bit as beautiful as Nefertiti.

And probably just as treacherous.

Raffe had to admit the piece was a work of incomparable beauty. Stylized after an ankh, the head was solid gold and fit neatly into the palm of his hand. Power symbols flowed all over it. The blade was razor sharp, the end viciously pointed.

He palmed the key as a dagger and felt the deadly power flow up into his arm. He lunged, stabbed, twirled, and gutted an imaginary opponent.

The key sang with power.

While he had tried to destroy it and failed, he was not surprised when that task proved impossible. The metal wouldn't melt and the blade wouldn't break. Neither cold, nor fire, water, nor air had any affect on the key. After handling the artifact for hours, Raffe decided the key was imbued with a desire to fulfill a task, and would not leave this life until the task was completed.

The key sang with death.

Was the key a part of his salvation? Or was it a treacherous assassin sent by Nefertiti?

The key's song was the siren of fate.

If the Eschaton was successful and the Babylon opened, he might as well use the beautiful ankh to slit his own throat.

"No!" he screamed to the heavens. He plunged Nefertiti's key into the table, sinking the blade two inches into the wood. When he let go, the blade hummed like a tuning fork. He raised a fist, daring fate to come and do its damnedest.

"If you want to open the Babylon, you will have to take the key from me!"

•

St. Germain Townhouse

Peterson sat still while the images of Solomon's past life as Thoth played out in the minds of everyone in the room. When the transmission was complete and Solomon appeared to have returned to this world, Peterson raised his glass. "You're back," he said, grinning.

Solomon's eyes were as large as dinner plates.

Hanlon had his hands raised to cover his face. Carter and Mady held each other as if riding a roller coaster. Henri pressed his glass to his head, muttering, "*Mon Dieu*, I knew something was up—"

Solomon licked his lips, starting slowly. "I wrote the Emerald Tablet an age before Nefertiti. The notation on the back of the Tablet was added as part of her plan."

Mady, reaching for the whiskey decanter, was the first to muster her voice. "I'll have a little more of that, thank you," she said. Her movement inspired a flurry of activity as everyone followed her lead.

Henri gulped his whiskey. He pointed at Solomon, sloshing what remained in his glass. "You are the old soul who will show him the way to the Capstone."

"What about this riddle?" Hanlon asked.

"And Peterson's staff?" Carter chimed in. "We're still down one miracle stick."

"And the mythological Capstone?" Mady added. "I guess this means … it's not a myth after all." She scrunched up her face and peered at Solomon. "You wrote the Emerald Tablet?" She shook her head and took another drink.

Hanlon asked, "The riddle says bring him the key? Do we have to get this key of Nefertiti's?"

Solomon and Peterson stared at each other, laughter tickling their lips. "First things first," Peterson said. He placed his glass on the table and rose. "I must go and retrieve the staff."

They all stood. Drinks were dusted off and pockets patted down for car keys. Mady went for her purse, and Carter helped Henri return the room to order.

Solomon didn't move.

Peterson cleared his throat, bringing all activity to a stop. "For this, I need to go alone," he said.

A rash of complaints were silenced when Solomon asked Peterson, "Where do you go?"

"I'm not sure," Peterson said with a shrug and a when-is-it-ever-easy look.

One hand in his pocket was sending a sweet vibration all along his nerves. His bones rattled with excitement and he felt the hair on his body stand on end. The sensation in his hand reminded him of Liddington when the jasper appeared.

He pulled his hand from his pocket.

"Oh!" Mady squeaked.

"It's green again!" Henri exclaimed.

Peterson held the large apple-shaped emerald from Nefertiti's breast collar. "Wherever I'm going, this should get me in."

Solomon motioned to the emerald. "She thought of the emerald as a ... chest she could refill." He smiled with amazement and memory. "She created a hyper-dimensional key with a rechargeable battery. This emerald can open portals to many dimensions."

"I'll not be long," Peterson said. "And, you might want to step back a little." He waved his hands at them, and they all took a great step backward.

"One more," he said, until there was five feet of clearance all around him.

He brought the emerald to his chest and bowed his head. A ripple of distortion slowly emanated from the jewel, at first just a few centimeters, then expanding to reach his heart. He focused on his need for the missing and powerful staff.

We share our destiny. Where are you?

His internal vibration picked up and he closed his eyes, for the energy was now fierce and demanding. He could feel the vibration climbing, increasing to an impossible pitch that threatened his physical integrity.

Suddenly, he smelled incense and heard Nefertiti singing.

He opened his eyes. Before him, a portal of energy opened, swirling in a mad vortex, pulling at his clothing.

Following the golden sound of Nefertiti's voice, he stepped into the vortex.

•

The Amun-ra Vault

Raffe looked up with alarm.

"Nefertiti's incense—" he growled.

The Eschaton is coming!

Static crackled around the vault's low ceiling, pushing aside atoms of time and space. Raffe's DNA naturally detected power by sensing the pressure exerted against the environment as the power entered the vault. Raffe sucked air through his teeth. The Eschaton was very strong. Were they not in such a life and death crisis, Raffe would avoid confrontation with such a being.

But life and death were here.

I must stop the Eschaton.

Raffe stood just as the dimensional portal opened. A wave of energy preceded the Eschaton's arrival, leaving a signature area of distortion to radiate out all around him. The Eschaton walked into the Amun-ra vault as if entering a restaurant. After a quick look around, he said, "I'm here for my staff."

Raffe walked out of the shadows. His heart was pounding a little too fast and adrenaline coursed through him, slick and heavy. "Perhaps the staff is mine now," he stated.

"I don't think so," Peterson answered. He raised his hand, and commanded, "Come!"

Raffe turned with shock as a racket came from the back of the vault. He had put the wrapped stick in a padlocked chest wedged against the wall behind a desk covered with books. At the time he figured his effort was futile, but he didn't expect the Eschaton to find the damned thing so quick.

He winced when he heard the lock explode from the steel-belted wooden chest. The heavy desk was now screeching across the masonry floor, and books were tumbling and crashing.

Raffe suddenly felt himself in the line of fire and moved.

The stick shot by, passing right through the space Raffe's head recently occupied. Sweat sprouted on Raffe's scalp, but he gritted his teeth and shrugged as if losing the staff was nothing. He said, "I can take that stick back any time I want."

The Eschaton brandished the staff. Raffe's linen wrapping had been lost in the staff's battle to be free. The bare wooden staff was now tucked safely in the Eschaton's arm like a long-lost lover. The Eschaton waved his hand, negating Raffe's threat of future theft. "We both know that's not going to happen."

Raffe strolled, working to feign an unconcerned appearance. "You will not find the key so easily," he purred with silken enmity.

Instead of reacting as Raffe expected, the Eschaton said, "You don't have to do this, you know. You can join us."

The Eschaton's words, however ridiculous at this point in time, pried their way under Raffe's skin. "Ha," he cried. To his ears, the sound was a whine of bitterness. Chagrined, he snorted his contempt. "There's no room for a dark heart in the Babylon."

The Eschaton's eyes bored into him with a sadness that irritated Raffe.

He dares to pity me.

Raffe's anger began to rise. To keep from launching a foolish suicide attack, he shouted, "Go ahead to the Babylon. I have the key, Eschaton. You can't get in." His taunting words reverberated throughout the vault. When the echo of his anger faded, the Eschaton answered. His quiet words took Raffe's breath away.

"Are you sure?"

There was no time for rebuttal from Raffe. The Eschaton left in a wave of distortion. His three damning words remained.

Raffe staggered to a chair and sat. A mass of swirling images raced in a great circle in his mind. He panted, fighting to relax and allow his mind to work.

He bent over, feeling he might retch. A wave of cold sweat plastered his back and he ground his teeth for control. His breathing steadied and the nausea passed.

He sat up and the sweat rolled down his back, clammy, but harmless.

The chaos settled, leaving a single question.

Has Nefertiti screwed us again?

Something else bothered him. He got up and paced, his long legs pumping the blood through his brain and body. An annoying thought flitted and bounced, refusing to solidify. He stopped and pressed his hand to the bridge of his nose.

The idea came at last, as soft as death in the wee hours.

Why didn't the Eschaton take the key?

CHAPTER FIFTEEN

St. Germain Townhouse

When Peterson returned from his exchange with Raffe, he found his companions gathered around a table. Mady looked up just as he arrived. Hanlon had his hand pressed to his ear, and Carter was ready with a casual salute.

"You had no difficulty?" Solomon said.

Peterson showed his walking stick.

"How did Amunson react?" Hanlon asked.

"I offered for him to join us, but he declined," Peterson replied. "Still, I don't think we've seen the last of him."

"We were just discussing a likely location for the Capstone," Henri said. "Any ideas?"

Peterson nodded to Solomon. "Ask Solomon. He built it."

Solomon made a face.

Mady laughed. "Come on, Thoth," she teased. "I mean, if you're really Thoth, you must know where the Capstone is."

She glanced around the group, explaining. "Various Arab legends have it that Thoth, whom the Greeks called Hermes, built the Pyramid before the flood to preserve knowledge of the secret sciences."

Mady saw Hanlon's face wrinkle with intense concentration as he tried to keep up. She laughed and pushed the decanter at him. He emptied the last of the whiskey into his glass.

"Thoth was also an Egyptian god of wisdom and writing, bearing a host of names with a lot of consonants," Mady continued. "In Egyptian mythology, Thoth overcame the curse of Ra, allowing Nut to give birth to her five children."

She massaged her palm and gave Solomon a serious gaze. "If I make jest, you know I am just teasing." She gave him a nod of respect. "So you have battled Ra before."

Solomon answered. "According to the legends, that battle was with Ra, the god. Amunson is of the Amun-ra priesthood, and they have … a private agenda."

Henri returned with a stack of papers. He eyed Solomon and grinned, but kept his comments private. He passed a packet of papers to everyone. "I present to you, for the sake of time, a limited review of the works of Thoth. I have selected what seem to be the pertinent parts."

No one picked up the document.

"Why would I read this when the author is here?" Carter announced.

Peterson watched Solomon and understood how difficult all this must be. He understood because he had experienced much the same feelings over the last two days.

Solomon took an uncharacteristic gulp from his

glass and wiped his chin. "All right, then." He cleared his throat and picked up the papers to read.

"Far in a past time, the children of light looked down on the world. Seeing the children of men in bondage, they knew that only through freedom would man rise from the earth to the sun.

"Before me stands a great throne of darkness, on it a seated figure of night, dark with a blackness not of the night."

He paused and a look passed around the table, a look that said each one remembered the darkness that came from the fireplace. Solomon perused the papers, picking his passages. "In a time yet born will I return, requiring an accounting of those who would enslave man."

Hanlon choked on his whiskey.

Carter smacked Hanlon on the back with a good-natured leer.

"Please, go on," Hanlon sputtered.

Solomon spoke with hesitation. "I, Thoth, Atlantean master of mysteries, sent the sons of Atlantis in many directions, that they may make their own path."

He flipped through more pages, coming toward the end. "I watched a mighty pyramid raised, and carved a circular passage within the summit, where I set the Book of Thoth for all man to receive. Know ye those who bargained with the cosmos, who usurped the Law of the Universe and strove to be gods—from beyond time I will return and cast ye down from your high estate into the darkness of the caves whence you came."

Solomon wiped his brow. "Well, I—"

Mady looked at the last page. "There's nothing here about the location—" She flicked the fingers of her right hand and gave Solomon an expectant look.

"Do you remember where you left this ... summit?" Peterson asked.

Solomon massaged his palm. Peterson felt the tingle from across the table. He glanced around: everyone was feeling the increased pressure. Something was building.

"The last time I saw the Capstone—" Solomon mumbled.

Henri groaned. His left hand held his empty glass pressed to his head again. "Ah, *mon Dieu*—"

Solomon rubbed the bridge of his nose and closed his eyes, feeling the onset of energy and information. He felt a heart wave expanding from him, filling the room as a vision occupied his mind, transporting him.

"Can you see him?" he whispered. He hummed a melody, and said, "A figure comes with hand raised, and a flame bursts forth, shining clear and bright. Bring him the key. When the heart of Ra opens you will see a new sun rise over Babylon." He slumped in his seat. "Whew. The vision—did you see—?"

"I knew you could do it," Peterson said.

"The Red Mountains," Carter offered.

"Very good, Carter. Well, how soon can we get there? We need to get going," Peterson said.

Hanlon asked, "Does your ... dimensional door ... emerald—"

Peterson smiled. John really was trying hard. "While the emerald is a key, it is not the key to the Babylon. And we'll have to reach the Babylon door by more conventional transport. And we should get started."

Solomon nodded to Henri, who rose, and said, "I'll call the airport and tell them to start the engines."

"The Red Mountains," Mady said. "We'll need clothes, water, food, transportation."

"I can expedite these arrangements with a phone call," Hanlon said. He pulled out a cell phone. "Where are we going?"

Mady stood and picked up her purse. "Hey, Thoth, do we need a map?"

Everyone stopped suddenly and stared at Solomon. A smile twitched at his lips. He asked, "Can't you hear her?"

Mady cocked her head. She flicked her fingers and pressed her hand to her ear. Her eyes brightened with delight as she said, "Oh, she's singing again."

Peterson pulled Nefertiti's emerald from his pocket. The stone was a deep dark green. The song emanated from it, as sweet as a harp.

"I hear her," Hanlon said, whispering as if his words would disturb the performance. He glanced around in wonder. "Where is she? Where are these Red Mountains?" He touched Carter's arm. "Tell me where are we going?"

"To Egypt—" Carter said.

"West shore of the Red Sea," Mady added. "Rugged terrain."

"We need to hurry," Peterson urged.

"What about the riddle?" Hanlon asked as they collected at the doorway. "And the key?"

Peterson caught Solomon's eye and winked, the gesture in stark contrast to his words. "Make your call, John. We really should go. Raffe knows where the Babylon is, and we want to get there before him—seeing as how he has the key."

•

Brussels

Raffe summoned the servant. "Tell him I need to—"

"He has retired—"

Raffe knew his anger was about to hit the danger zone. He visibly fought for his breath, to keep from killing the servant with a snap of his powerful hands. He gained a measure of control. "You tell him I'm here."

"Yes, sir," the manservant said. He backed up, his eyes telling Raffe he would not be responsible for his coming reception with Uncle. When the man was no longer within Raffe's reach, he added, "Wait in his drawing room ... if he'll see you."

Raffe clutched Nefertiti's Key of Seven and thought about plunging it into the servant's heart just for practice. He ground his teeth and took the grand staircase in leaps. "He'll see me," he shouted.

In the old man's drawing room, Raffe waited and paced. Angry energy poured off him like sweat from a laborer. His mind screamed at him a single repeating thought.

Betrayal. But by whom?

A door opened and Uncle entered. He wore a deep burgundy dressing gown and his favorite slippers, indicating the servant told the truth that he had retired. Uncle was not pleased. "Yes?" was all he said.

Raffe cocked an eyebrow. If anyone had the right to anger, it was Raffe. "Why did we never go?"

Uncle cocked an eyebrow in return, offering confusion.

Raffe barely managed to keep from screaming at his

Uncle. He took a deep breath and spoke very low. "The Eschaton walks the earth, the Babylon is in danger of being opened, and you bother to play games with me?" He carefully set the gold key on the table. "Why did we not go to Nefertiti's temple and ... and—"

"And do what, Raffe?"

Uncle glared at Raffe, his sharp eye and tight lips displaying no small amount of animosity. "What would you have us do with the Babylon?"

"Destroy the damn thing ... move the witch's lair ... hide it from the Eschaton. We could have done something to prevent this day—" He looked around, drowning in desperation.

Rage and a sense of futility for his life were consuming him. He couldn't face what his mind was thinking, couldn't face what loomed before him. "Tell me," he pleaded. "What are you hiding from me?"

Uncle eased into the chair and picked up the key. He palmed the gold as a weapon and hefted it, feeling the weight and balance. Light glinted off the razor edge. "Nefertiti's Key has always been a weapon—the ultimate weapon of final destruction for us."

Raffe didn't like the tone or the expression coming from his Uncle. A wad of ugly feelings was building in his stomach, anger being just the beginning.

"And it may very well be a key," Uncle continued. "We don't know, because she hid the Babylon from us. We have been to the temple a host of times, but never could we find the Babylon."

He shrugged and set the key down. "I never believed that story—Old Kheti and Nefertiti working together." He laughed. The sound was a bark of defeat. "And they call us devious."

Raffe used to believe the key was their line of defense against the opening of the Babylon. But not now, not after the Eschaton's parting words. With one small question, the Eschaton had neutralized everything Raffe believed.

But Raffe sensed another lie was afoot. "So we are finished," he said. He eyed Uncle, giving him the time to be forthcoming with what he was hiding. He probed, testing. "There is nothing that can help us?"

He spoke without rancor, yet the words tasted more awful than he imagined. With Uncle's continued silence, Raffe's desperation began to stir. "How?" he asked. "How did my life come to be worthless?" He eased into a chair, the sinking sensation a soothing paralysis drawing him down.

Uncle answered slowly. "You have a right to know the truth."

The words were barely more than a whisper. The hair on Raffe's nape lifted.

"The priesthood did many things in the day," Uncle continued. "They were out of control—whatever they wanted, they either created or stole. To them the trick was a grand game, until they dared trick the gods."

The knot of bad feelings in Raffe's stomach hit bottom, sinking along his nerves and his bones and into his heart. *Here it comes,* he thought, *the finale.* His gaze caught the drawing room door, and for one wild fleeting breath he thought he would run—as if that would change anything.

Uncle drew his shoulders back with resignation. "Raffe, we stole the scales and rigged them to weigh in our favor."

Raffe frowned, unprepared for what he just heard.

The genetic tampering, he expected, or the risky dimensional escapades perhaps. But what scales did Uncle refer to?

Suddenly, he saw the scene of Anubis weighing the heart of the dead against Ma'at's feather. "The scale of Ma'at, the winged Egyptian goddess?" he asked.

"Can you believe the grand audacity of the fools?" Uncle said. He shook his head and clenched his lips. When he exhaled, a thousand generations of grief spewed forth.

"The priesthood, your ancestors, the generation who made you what you are, attempted to re-write an immutable, Universal law. They thought they could step out of the line of karma, to do as they pleased without ever paying the consequences."

Raffe was stunned. He felt as though every molecule slid to a stop in time. While his mind fought to process his Uncle's words, the wind of debt came to take his future away.

"They were caught," Uncle said. "It is beyond me how they thought they could evade the final reckoning. The principle of energy return is the basis for the entire universe. To think they could run with carte blanche, racking up karmic debt without settling any ... was the height of arrogance, even for the Amun-ra."

The wind whisked through Raffe, scattering his life's ashes. He felt old and ... used.

Is there not another way? Why am I here?

He picked up the key. "There is a great deal of power here."

Uncle shook his head. "There is no bargaining. Ma'at's rage was ... unfathomable." He leaned forward, finishing the tale.

"New scales were made. When dark energy protested, Ma'at damned them by removing divine choice from the dark hearts of the priesthood, condemning us to darkness for all eternity. With the new scales, there was nowhere in time or space the priesthood could run or hide. Our path to this fated day was designed long ago."

Raffe recalled all the ugly wisps of thought, the lurking sense of doom, the feeling that something hung over his head, all ended right here. He dared to put into words the fear haunting his heart. "Leaving us to settle all debts at the final transition, which is why the Eschaton is here."

I must pay hell for the debt of ancestors long gone.

"So they sold the future, my future," Raffe said. He drew his thumb across the blade edge of the key to test its ability. His skin parted and blood welled. He stuck his thumb in his mouth and sucked.

If only I were free—

"They'll find the Babylon. Solomon is with them," Raffe said. He pulled his thumb from his mouth. The cut was already healed. Irony for the situation washed over him, and he snorted. "Since I have the key, I suppose I should be there to welcome them."

CHAPTER SIXTEEN

Suez, Egypt

Traveling in a brand new Range Rover, Peterson sat in the front seat. Henri drove and the rest were sandwiched in the remaining seats. They bumped along a dusty desert track, the Red Sea at their backs and the Red Mountains of Egypt closing around them.

Peterson glanced at the sun and gauged the solar time. He didn't know where they were going, but he knew they had an appointment with the solstice this afternoon. He was counting on the power to get them there on time.

"Remind me to travel with you more often," Mady said to Hanlon.

Carter added, "I'm quite impressed. The Illuminati really reaches this far? I mean, we're in the back end of nowhere, and all you had to do was make a phone call."

Hanlon smiled. Looking rather cheery and proud to be of service, he smoothed his new khaki pants. "Yes, we reach even here. Our preparations did not begin yesterday, you know."

Mady added, "Well, I thank whoever did the shopping. And God bless you for getting a car with good A/C."

Henri probed Hanlon. "When did Illuminati preparations begin?"

Carter joined in good-naturedly. "Come on, John, tell us what the Illuminati have planned."

Peterson turned in his seat to watch Hanlon answer.

"Money is the simple means to our end," Hanlon explained. "Money is power." He shrugged in apology for his next words. "Money is also the quickest way to corrupt a man's heart.

"With the creation of currency, a new power was born. What you see happening currently—unsustainable sovereign debt—is the prelude to dissolving all the old currencies. As the Bible says, usury is the root of all evil."

Looking out the window, he spoke in a robotic, matter-of-fact tone. "The goal is global financial governance, which will set the stage for total domination and subjugation. A small population, docile and ignorant, will be maintained for services to the elite." He turned and gave them a hollow smile. "It's just the end play in a centuries-old game."

No words came in retort. Silence rode oppressively with them. They bumped along in the nothing of the desert, winding down ravine and gully, stirring up sand and dust. Henri followed Peterson's subtle directions.

Mady turned to Solomon, who sat alone in the rear-facing last seat. He saw nothing of their passage but the tsunami of desert dust roiling in their wake.

"Does anything look familiar?" she asked.

At her comment, Solomon looked over his shoulder and pulled a dry expression. He ignored her and asked

Carter, "Did you know she had such a mean streak when you married her?"

Carter smiled and rubbed her shoulders. "She was rude from the moment we met. I think that's what attracted me the most."

Mady laughed, but she wasn't deterred. Her face remained filled with expectation for an answer from Solomon.

Solomon sighed and answered with dry levity. "It's been a while since I was here last, *cherie.*"

Peterson pulled himself from the chatter. The power was singing, leading him to their destination.

Henri slowed. They were surrounded by a Martian landscape. Ravines cut from out of nowhere and disappeared just as easily.

"Left," Peterson said, pointing. They drove along the bottom edge of a ravine. "Now right."

"This is it," Solomon said. He leaned over the seat and looked out the front.

"You recognize something?" Mady turned to Solomon, breathless and excited.

"Sorry, no," Solomon said. "But I expect that—" He pointed. "—is Raffe's car."

•

Nefertiti's Temple, The Red Mountains

Raffe parked his car and grabbed his hat, a bottle of water and the Amun-ra map to Nefertiti's Temple. He checked his watch and shaded his eyes to look at the sun. "High noon in the desert on a summer solstice," he said.

This was planned down to the second.

He picked up Nefetiti's Key, now tucked away in a leather case. "Fate," he whispered to the key, "has brought us here. Let us see what fate will be served."

His map was current, the details having changed little over the centuries as each succeeding wave of the priesthood came with the key and tried to find the Babylon in Nefertiti's Temple.

"Ha," he laughed with vigor. He once thought they were fools, and yet here he was, treading in their footsteps.

The ravine dead-ended in a sheer cliff of bedrock. Raffe's map provided instructions for a common, single-phase dimensional doorway. He let his fingers slip over the ancient writing on the map and read.

His vocal chords called up a fraction of dark energy and the symbols provided the path. The result was a spear that tapped into time, allowing him to access an alternate time-space continuum. A wave of distortion swirled and formed in front of Raffe. He stepped into the rock … and emerged in Nefertiti's Temple.

He stood within a great cavern, on a platform—one of several stone platforms that closely hugged the rock wall of the mountain and were connected by stone steps that reached the floor of the cavern. On one side the cavern was filled with a mountain of rubble, no doubt remnants from the excavation. He frowned, for the tumbled heap of stone was curiously out of place in comparison to the other side of the cavern.

Opposite the rubble, the walls curved down from the domed ceiling like the inside of an egg. The lower reaches of wall space were filled with strange pictographs and writing in symbols ancient before the time of man. Alongside these were hieroglyphs and art in the style from the time of Akhenaten and Nefertiti. Raffe descended the steps to the writing; his DNA gave the language to him.

It was a great storyboard.

His fingers sped over the wall, touching the writing, absorbing the where and the why of the events that created this cataclysm so far in the future.

At last, full understanding came and Raffe rocked back on his heels. The Eschaton was the culmination in a cycle of destiny planned for humanity eons ago. Raffe and the Amun-ra priesthood were nothing but minor players in a side story.

A wash of bitter, angry regret flooded Raffe's heart. The final insult did not escape him. Were he human, and not Amun-ra, he could have accepted the Eschaton's offer to participate in the renaissance peak ready to open for humanity.

Deflated anger sprang to life anew. Bit player or not, Raffe remembered his own ancestors had sold him out. Dark energy gathered, even in this holy place, flickering in the shadows, aroused by his presence and awaiting his call.

He pulled the Key of Seven from its leather case; the gold was alive with a sentient power and it was lit with some form of light. Raffe examined the blade and was unable to discern if the gold was merely reflecting light, or if the key actually emanated light.

Suddenly, he felt a dimensional door opening. The Eschaton was coming. Raffe darted back up the stairs as a vortex of energy hit the rock wall, spinning out a wave of distortion. The Eschaton stepped into the Temple. Others followed him in, leaving Raffe blinking in astonishment. Solomon he expected, but also came Henri and the insignificant couple.

"And Hanlon gives us seven," he added with a snort when the dimensional door finally closed. Astonished, he looked at the key and murmured, "The Key of Seven."

"Raffe," Hanlon said. Henri nodded to Raffe and walked down the stairs to Nefertiti's storyboard. The couple passed and Raffe acknowledged them as they slipped by to follow Henri and Hanlon down the steps.

He turned to Solomon. "Solomon, or should I say Thoth?" He finished with a good look at Peterson. "And the Eschaton, at last." Raffe called down to Hanlon. "So this is your man in the institution, eh?"

No answer came. As Raffe watched, Henri and the couple descended on the storyboard with fervor.

Solomon came to Raffe's side. The Eschaton stood at his other shoulder.

"Well, we're all here," Raffe said. He paused as the woman exclaimed over something she found written on the wall.

"It is a little awkward, don't you think?" Raffe said with a congenial smile. "I have the key—"

With his hands spread expansively, he motioned from the rubble to the egg-shaped temple. "But I don't see the Capstone or the Babylon, do you?"

The weak attempt at humor withered under the heat of his rising anger. His moment with congeniality over, he asked harshly, "Seems odd, don't you think, to go to the trouble to carve all of this and forget the Babylon? Please, someone feel free to let me in on the joke," he spit with venom. He looked from the Eschaton to Solomon, his anger going from simmer to boil.

Solomon recited, "Bring him the Key. When the

heart of Ra opens, an oasis will be born. See the new sun rise over Babylon."

Raffe flicked an eyebrow. He held out the razor-edged key to Solomon. "Would you like to do the honors?" He turned to the Eschaton. "And you, Peterson, how about you. Would you like to open my heart with Nefertiti's Key?"

Their lack of response was jet fuel on Raffe's anger. Everything he desired, all the dreams and expectations he hoped for in his long future were delivered to him fully disintegrated. Whatever he might have achieved— his own destiny, his own legacy—would never happen.

Everything in his life terminated right here.

He weighed the betrayal by his own blood next to the offer of compassion he received from the Eschaton. The Eschaton's compassion rankled Raffe even further. In his hands, Nefertiti's Key rang with power, another poke at him from the past.

His rage and fear were fanning the turbulence in the dark energy within the cavern. He stepped to the edge of the platform. He could see small particles of darkness dancing in the air, congregating and growing.

Raffe closed his eyes.

He knew when Solomon and Peterson stepped away from him, but soon the growing power was all he knew—the Key was drawing more and more to him. He let his head come forward and focused on his heart. The anger came churning from his center, driven by images of his ancestors having the party that cost an eternity. His sense of being cheated consumed him.

Hot breath stormed from his nostrils with a blast. Power massed around him, clamoring, feeding upon itself ... growing uncontrollable.

•

Peterson stepped away from Amunson when the hot anger started coming off him in waves. The stink of fear joined in a noxious mix, driving him and Solomon from the platform.

Halfway down the stairs, they turned for a look at Raffe. Seeing the darkness swirling around him, they picked up the pace.

At the storyboard, Peterson grabbed Mady. "We have to go—"

"Oh, no," she protested. "I've just started with this—"

Solomon grabbed Carter by the shoulders and pointed him toward Amunson. Carter's eyes bulged and he spun on Mady. "Time to go, darling," he blurted.

Something in his tone reached her. She looked where he pointed. Her lips pursed in a silent 'ohhhhh' before she bounded in front of Carter, joining Solomon and Henri in climbing up the mountain of rubble.

Hanlon had seen the ruckus and didn't need to be told; he climbed ahead of them.

Peterson felt the power rising within him in response to Raffe's anger. Energy was building pressure at a massive rate—his hand was throbbing like a crushed bell, vibration coursing through him in giant waves.

He looked up.

Mady had hold of Carter. She flicked her hand and a brilliant heart wave encircled her and Carter. More waves flared and encompassed everyone in the group.

Peterson looked back at Raffe. He stood with arms raised, the Key palmed in his right hand like a dagger. The tip of the blade spit sparks. Darkness had built into a churning mass obscuring Raffe until all that could be seen were his legs and the tip of the key.

The disturbance in the energy was palpable, bordering on rampage. Peterson shouted to those above him, "Go, go, go—" They scrambled with urgency.

The darkness enveloped Raffe with more power than he had ever felt in his life. Tears coursed down his cheeks as the pressure pounded against his DNA, building to a point he recognized would be beyond his ability to control. Dark energy was an ally only as long as he could control the power.

Once he lost control, he would be destroyed.

He opened his eyes. A massive cloud in a highly agitated state surrounded him. The Key was alive, pulsing in his hand with power.

"No," he whispered, hating his fate, his sacrifice. "I was built for a power I will never know."

His body was on fire with an energy that needed direction. The pressure was building, threatening him with apocalypse.

"Nefertiti, you witch," he cried. His tears ran faster.

The anger and rage expanded. The power was becoming discontent, seeking release, something to destroy. Raffe knew any moment the dark energy would turn and consume him—and yet he loved the thrill, for this fatal wave of infinite power was all he would ever know. The darkness begged him to direct it to any weakness.

"No!" he screamed, throwing his anger at Nefertiti's Temple. The ground shook. Raffe smiled. If he could hang on for another few seconds, he might coerce enough power forth to destroy Nefertiti's Temple and take out the Babylon.

Destroying the Babylon would be worth his death.

From half way up the hillside, Peterson felt the ground shudder and jerk beneath his feet. He looked over his shoulder and saw the stairs and platforms shift, watched as great cracks split the beautiful storyboard into fragments. The cracks burst loose, and he shouted to the others, "Run!"

The darkness fed on Raffe's rage. It needed chaos, needed all he had and more to expand. The darkness surged around the cavern, looking for weakness to exploit. Rocks covered in the cloying dark energy began exploding.

Raffe saw through the dark cloud, saw the cracks burst the walls of Nefertiti's Temple. Astonished, he watched water come flooding through the wall, slowly, then increasing with an all-consuming wave.

The base of the rock stairway supporting the series of platforms crumbled, and the water washed away the loosened rock. The stairs screeched and came sliding down, disintegrating from the bottom. Raffe was thrown to his knees on what was left of his platform.

The power was too much. He was losing control. It was turning on him, looking to exploit his weaknesses. In his heart, he held no desire for life. In his mind, he imagined no future to cling to, saw no pardon for the sins of his ancestors—he was vulnerable.

Hell had come to collect the Karmic debt of the Amun-ra.

He struggled to stand. He dashed his free hand across his eyes. There was no more time for tears, no more time for anything. He threw his arms into the air with exaltation for these last few moments of his life. The last large piece of Nefertiti's wall collapsed and a sea of water came rushing in.

"No!" he screamed a final time before the water took him.

Peterson and the others climbed for their lives. The water was rising, swallowing the rocks far below and reaching for the rocks at their feet. Peterson looked up and saw Hanlon had reached the top of the mountain of stone.

The domed roof of the cavern was breaking away in great chunks and falling into the churning water with huge splashes. The clear desert sky was exposed, with the sun at noon overhead. The ground stopped rocking, the sky stopped falling, and the waters began to recede, washing away the rubble.

Peterson checked his group. Mady and Carter clung to each other at Hanlon's feet. Solomon and Henri were firmly lodged with their backs against the rock. As the water receded further, Peterson looked down and laughed.

"It's granite," Henri called out.

"These mountains are limestone," Carter argued. "Not granite."

"This is it—the Capstone," Henri declared.

Mady, Carter, and Hanlon descended to a lower level. Mady peered at the rubble and flicked her hand. Loose rock jumped away, clearing the top stone. A perfect triangular peak was revealed.

Henri grabbed Solomon's sleeve, pointing to Peterson, who had climbed the peak with his staff.

Peterson was drawn to the top by a new song within—the Song of Creation. The harmonics were clean and sweet and sublime, until his heart expanded in bliss. This moment was the culmination of his quest, what destiny had planned for him.

Looking down he saw they stood on the top of a pyramid, about thirty feet on a side at the base. Above them, the sky was full of sun. At their feet, the ground was bare of shadow.

Energy fed the Song of Creation, causing the power to rise in Peterson's hand, dancing across his nerves, pushing him. He straddled the peak of the Capstone. The power poured through him white hot and cold, like icicles in the sun.

Above, the sun reached its solstice perigee—

—and paused. Time stopped.

Peterson placed his staff on the peak of the Capstone. The staff locked onto the granite with an energetic snap.

The hum in Peterson's ears went beyond his hearing. A beam of light shot up through the staff as a wave of light expanded horizontally, blasting him off the top of the Capstone.

He fell like a sand bag. A series of grunts came with flailing arms and legs as Solomon and the others landed near him. Protected by the power, they landed without injury.

Mady sat up and blew the hair from her eyes. "Holy mac—" she said with a groan. Her words slowly faded into a gasp. "Oh!"

Peterson followed her gaze. Above them, in the Capstone, a circular doorway pierced the triangle.

"Do you see it?" Mady asked. She stood and brushed herself off, helping Carter and Hanlon to rise. They gathered to stare in wonder at the Babylon.

"See Peterson's birthmark. The Babylon circular door within the triangle is the flying anchor, minus the exterior wings," she said.

"Where's Raffe?" Hanlon asked.

They looked around. The roof of the cavern was gone, and the Capstone rose from an expanse of water.

Peterson called, "I see him." He clambered down to the bottom of the flood debris with the others close behind. Raffe's body lay broken and face down in the water. Peterson lifted him free of the water and laid him on the wet sandbank.

Raffe's face was at peace.

The Key was broken, the oval hilt in Raffe's hand and the blade buried in his chest. Peterson pried the oval from Raffe's fingers.

Solomon knelt down by Peterson and took the gold oval. He spoke softly, as if speaking to someone not present. "I remember, my Queen. I remember."

He showed them where the hilt had snapped clean, exposing writing from the inside. A tiny swayback figure seven with a dot under the peak was impressed in the gold.

"Nefertiti knew the symbol for Divinity," Solomon said.

"I saw the Divinity writing on the story board," Mady said. "Nefertiti used the symbol. Raffe's fate and Nefertiti's Key were entangled."

Solomon pulled the key blade from Raffe's heart and closed Raffe's hands over the fatal wound.

"I believe he wanted to be free, don't you?" Peterson said softly.

Solomon answered, "Amunseraf was Nefertiti's beloved enemy. She cried for his trapped soul, knowing he was doomed to this sacrifice. She made the Key to set him free. "

"I think we're all going to be free now," Mady said.

"What was that energy, that light that came when you put the staff on the Capstone?" Hanlon asked.

"It was like at Liddington," Mady said. "Only stronger." She smiled and pulled Carter closer. "The world has now received the Song of Creation."

"And the Babylon? What will we find in this Babylon?" Hanlon probed.

Peterson smiled. His hand hummed with a different vibration, something new, a sensation exquisite beyond anything he felt before. "Mady's right," he said. "The energy was the Light and Song of Creation. What we experienced in Liddington was just a … tuning … to set the tone for the song to follow. What happened here has not been seen since the birth of the universe."

Looking at Hanlon, he answered his question. "Inside the Babylon we will find all knowledge, all wisdom, all answers, a record of all history. Inside the Babylon is all peace and harmony, for war and strife cannot exist in the shadow of the Babylon." He cupped his hand to his ear. A perfect vibration echoed though his body. "Do you hear the change?"

"I hear *le harmonie*," Henri declared. Tears brightened his eyes as he said, "This is the Song of Creation, *oui*?"

Carter grabbed Mady and pulled her close. "God, I love you," he cried. "Look what we did, sweetheart."

Mady kissed Carter and took his hand, pointing to the writing over the circular opening. She read the Divinity symbols. "Babylon, the Light and Song of Creation." Tears coursed down her cheeks. "Come on, I want to see the new paradigm."

She laughed, and turned to Solomon, pointing at Peterson. "And bring him—for he is the key."

"Peterson is the key?" Carter asked. "Ah, not bring him the key, but bring *him*—the key."

"Nefertiti's story board explained the ruse in the Divinity symbols. She was brilliant, and quite sneaky," Mady said.

Solomon joined them at the circular Babylon doorway. "She was powerful," he said. "She was compassionate, and she was dedicated to seeing this day happen." He placed his right hand over his heart and prostrated himself to one knee. "I bow to your wisdom, your beauty and grace, and your determination, dear Nefertiti. This day has been a long time in the making."

He rose and clasped Peterson's arm. "You heard the lady," he said, nodding to Mady. "You, dear friend, are the key."

Peterson stepped up to the threshold. The new vibration within him was like a beacon, drawing him forward, pulling him deep into the Babylon. His mother's face came suddenly to his mind and he heard her voice.

Know what's in your heart and follow it always.

He stepped across the threshold. A beacon of light never seen on earth erupted within the Babylon, radiating out three hundred-sixty degrees. The power burst was like a carnival in Peterson's blood. A vision of the future, the new paradigm, joined the Song of Creation within his mind, bringing completion to his heart.

His destiny and his quest were fulfilled.

He turned to his companions. "The Babylon is open. Who wants to go first?"

They looked at one another up and down the line. Henri stepped out. He shot a look at Solomon, who smiled and nodded. "I would go first," Henri said. "But, please, explain to me about the manna and the anointing oil that were part of your tasks."

"That's easy," Carter said. He held his hand out to show the skin of light that surrounded his flesh. "The manna was the Divinity symbol, and the ancients' protocols delivered the power of Creation to anoint us."

"Ah, of course," Henri said. He held his hand out and his light matched Carter's. "*Oui.* We are very blessed to receive this new paradigm."

Peterson extended his hand in welcome invitation to the Babylon. Henri stepped through the door and was out of sight for two seconds before he returned. He came out and ran to the end of the granite blocks housing the Babylon and looked around the corner. He returned, his head shaking in wonder. Before anyone could ask, he said, "The inside ... is bigger than the outside—" He shrugged. "You will see." He waved his eyebrows in surprise and stepped back into the Babylon.

Mady giggled and squeezed Carter's hand. She looked at Solomon and asked, "How does it feel to be Thoth?"

Solomon smiled, eyes sparkling with a universe of secrets. "Today, it feels good to be Solomon."

Henri shouted from within the Babylon, "Everything is written in French—"

Mady frowned and Carter laughed. "Ready?" they asked in unison, and stepped together into the Babylon.

Hanlon came to Solomon's side. He shook his head, seeming overwhelmed.

"What's the matter, John?" Solomon asked.

Hanlon looked down at his feet for a long time before answering. In his silence, Peterson and Solomon glanced at each other over his head. At last Hanlon said, "I was hoping you would go with me to see Fischer.

Maybe now that the Babylon is open—"

Peterson nodded. "Of course, we can go whenever you like."

A great weight seemed to be lifted from Hanlon's shoulders as he nodded with relief. He looked at his palm and flexed his fingers—the distortion rippled and flared out to engulf his hand.

Hanlon chuckled and abruptly turned to Solomon with an expression that boded a wealth of brotherly mischief. He put his hands in his khaki pants and rocked back on his heels, obviously quite pleased with what was on his mind. "I have a meeting next week with all my Illuminati superiors."

He wrinkled his nose, not with distaste, but with delight. Engaging Solomon with a look of devilry, he suggested, "Shall we go and shake everyone's hand?"

Solomon barked in laughter and clapped Hanlon on the back. "I'd like that, John. I'd like that a lot."

"Good," Hanlon beamed. He turned to the Babylon and brushed his hand against his thigh, suddenly hesitant.

"The door is open to you, John," Peterson said.

Hanlon stepped through and walked out of their sight.

Peterson and Solomon stood together. "What's going to happen with this new paradigm, Solomon?" Peterson asked.

Solomon took his time answering. "We will never be the same, my friend, as was predicted. Humanity has been given a rare and exquisite destiny. As a species we will experience an apotheosis no less than the caterpillar morphing into a butterfly. I would say the universe is open to us, like a heart filled with infinite compassion and power."

From within the Babylon they heard Mady and Henri arguing good-naturedly.

"I'm telling you, I don't read French," Mady proclaimed.

"But everything I see is in French—" Henri protested.

Carter joined in. "Everything I see is in English, Henri. I think she's right—whatever language you speak is the language you will see."

Solomon and Peterson laughed. Peterson held his hand out. "Shall we, dear friend?"

Together they entered the Babylon.

•••

Read the book that
started the adventure!

Dana Lyons

Dana Lyons lives in the mountains of western North Carolina with her husband, Randy, three cats and two horses. She loves to work out and live healthy, ever ready to discover new mysteries in life, explore the limitless boundaries of the mind, and find the true power of the heart. Says Lyons, "Love is not just an emotion in your heart—love is a measurable force that travels the universe like the light of a star. Learn the power of love, and you will create a world you can love."